THE IMPERFECTS

STEFANIE JOLICOEUR

THE IMPERFECTS

STEFANIE JOLICOEUR

THE IMPERFECTS

The Happy Heart Studio
22 Danielle Lane
Dover, NH 03820
www.thehappyheartstudio.net

Dedicated to my perfectly imperfect crew

Love you to pieces – just the way you are

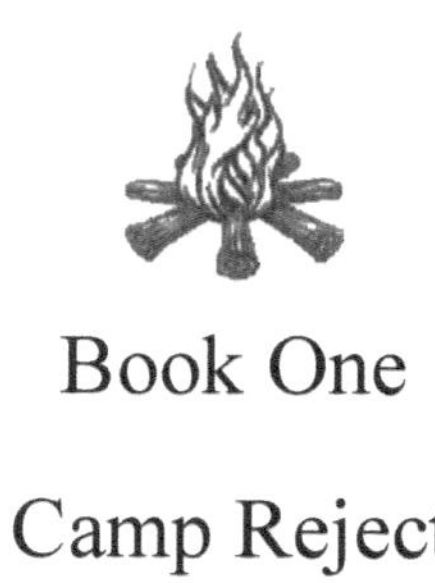

Book One

Camp Reject

1

Happy birthday to me! I'm free today. A confused mix of excitement and terror roiled inside my empty belly. Preparing for my exodus, I stuffed all of my belongings into a plastic grocery bag. Yes, everything I own fits into this small, pathetic sack. I also stuffed a small, red Swiss Army knife that had been recently confiscated from a resident into my front pants pocket. It had been stored in a drawer in the main office, only to be stolen by yours truly. It was a perfect weapon to have in case the world outside these walls was as horrible as I'd heard.

The walls I was referring to belong to a wayward children's home called Riverbend and life inside of them sucks. Capital 'S' sucks. Riverbend. I know the name sounds innocuous enough. As if it might be a place where you'd picnic with your 2.2 children (when that was allowed, of course) and your scrappy little dog, but no, there is nothing endearing about this place. And the term wayward is such a cute word. It sounds as if we all got lost on our way delivering muffins to grandma's house. In reality, it's pretty much what you would expect for a government-run hellhole. The kids who are dumped here aren't expected to amount to much. It's your run-of-the-mill freak show minus the bearded lady, and is chock full of the deformed, imperfect, and unlovable.

The building itself, more hospital than dorm, is pristinely clean. The air is always heavy with the sharp smell of antiseptic, as if they are constantly trying to scrub our malformed stink from the tiled walls. The strong cleanser burns in your nostrils and scratches at your throat, making your eyes tear in regular intervals. I never minded it too much. The stench reminded me of home and that's what this place has been for me: home. I've lived within these white sanitized walls for all of my eighteen years. And, just like that, today, the morning of my eighteenth birthday, I'll be thrust into the world alone, cast aside... again. "Congrats on surviving your childhood, now get out," should be printed on the birthday card I won't receive or maybe written on a cake in frosting, the cake that I've never gotten in all my years here.

Although it was still early, I needed to wake my roommate, Wendy, to say sayonara. I promised her that I would remember to say goodbye. She knew being sentimental was hard for me and she worried I'd sneak away, never to be seen or heard from again. Wouldn't that have been a great way to go? *I'd disappear like a ghost in the morning mist*, I thought as I watched her face for a sign that she'd heard me moving around the room.

"Wendy," I whispered, half hoping she wouldn't hear me and I could slip from the room without crying. *Shoot*, I thought, my heart a heavy aching blob in my chest, *I'm never going to see her again.*

Wendy stirred and lifted her head from the warm dent on her pillow. "Hey, Dawn," she said, her smile tired, but beautiful. My name sounded good on her lips. It was the name I'd given myself. Here at Riverbend, since nobody cares, we are allowed to name ourselves. I chose my name around the age of five just before one of the older girls, my pseudo mother, Mindy, had left. One night we'd snuck out after the late headcount. Her pockets were full of contraband snacks, and we'd climbed the hill behind the facility to wait for the sun to rise. I was proud of myself for staying awake the whole time; the errant squawks and chattering sounds made by woodland creatures were good at keeping my imagination and adrenaline pumping, especially in the inky gloom of night. When the sun finally kissed the horizon, it was breathtaking. It was the most beautiful thing I'd ever seen at that point in my young life: the awakening of the day, the magnificent dawn. Mindy suggested that I take it as my name. "A beautiful name for a beautiful girl," she'd said, her face beaming in the soft glow of first light. It was the last gift she'd given me before she was gone forever.

I shook away the depressing memory and smiled down at Wendy. I stroked her curly hair with a shaking hand. Tears threatened to tumble from my eyes, so I looked up for a moment to blink them away. I didn't want to upset her or make things harder for her. For me.

"You leaving already?" Wendy asked and sat up slightly. She leaned on her thin elbows for support. Her movement pushed her head against my hand. It reminded me of the abandoned kitten I'd recently found in the dumpster behind Riverbend. The hungry little kitty had greedily wanted my touch. It practically pulled the fur from its tiny head, rubbing so hard against my hand.

I nodded and gave her my best smile. "Yup. Gotta go." Reluctantly, I retracted my hand and sighed. In my head, I'm really happy to leave, but this is hard, much harder than I'd thought.

"Will you come back for me? Two years, that's not that long. Promise you'll come back for me, Dawn," Wendy said, her eyes wide and wet and pleading.

I nodded again in a silent promise. But it was a lie.

Don't get me wrong, I would love to come back in two years and help her make the transition into the 'real' world as a free woman, but the blue tinge around her lips, darker than it had been in recent weeks, and the rhythmic wheeze of the oxygen pump told me I was right. She would be dead soon. And, selfishly, to protect myself from the pain of losing her, I didn't want to know when it happened, how it happened… why it happened. I just simply could not stand to know and to lose another friend, my sister in bad luck.

Here in Riverbend, it's like the Land of Misfit Toys, only without jolly old Santa, flying reindeer or the happy ending. We are all Bumbles here, damaged and unwanted. We are feared by some, hated by others, and destined to never have love or to be cared for.

I patted my soul sister, my sweet, lost kitten on the head. The purr of the pump quickly soothed her back to sleep. I grabbed my sad bag of belongings and left the room, head down, a thick lump of unexpressed emotion filled my throat.

Outside, I collected my bus ticket and some extra cash from the driver of a black sedan that dropped me unceremoniously at the bus station. He'd thrust them through the half-opened window and mumbled something about buying myself breakfast before he sped away into the morning light. Clearly, he knew that I didn't get to enjoy a last meal of lumpy oatmeal and overripe bananas with my pretend brothers and sisters.

I climbed onto bus number ten and settled into a seat with the hood from my sweatshirt pulled up over the back of my head despite the warmth from the rising sun.

A mother and her toddler took the seat in front of me and I inadvertently made eye contact with the curious, cherubesque little boy. *Mistake,* I thought immediately, and scolded myself for being so careless. I settled my neck deeper into my thick Riverbend-provided sweatshirt and did my best to blend into the dark fabric of the seat.

The bus rolled away from the station, barely full. The little boy popped up in the seat in front of me like a drooling jack-in-the-box, clearly trying to play peek-a-boo with the strange girl who had accidentally shown the slightest bit of interest. He continued to jump up and down in his seat. His mother held him from the back of his t-shirt with a steadying hand. The bus lurched to a stop and the boy almost fell, ass over teakettle, onto the floor, caught at the last second by the deft hand of his mother. An odd pang of jealousy ran through me at this pure sign of love and concern. I've never known that and I probably never would.

The mother got the little boy settled back into his seat. Moments later, he popped up again, his wet smile broad, and his bright eyes twinkling at me over the headrest.

"Colton, sit," ordered the mother, clearly exasperated at her perfect child and his tireless game playing.

"Mama, Barney," the boy said and looked directly at me, his eyes full of excitement at his discovery.

"No, sweetie. No Barney today. We're going to Grandma's house," cooed the mother.

The boy's brow furrowed and he put his sticky looking hand on his mother's head for balance, mussing her hair. "Mama, Barney," he said again and pointed a chubby finger toward me.

"Whatchya looking at, Buddy?" asked his mother as she untangled his fingers from her hair. Then, she pushed herself up in the seat and turned, settling her gaze on me. She gasped audibly and squeaked, "Oh! I'm so sorry! He's really into Barney. You know. That stupid purple dinosaur." She gulped, eyes bulging, clearly embarrassed.

"It's fine," I lied and pulled the hood of my sweatshirt tight over the puffy wine-colored birth mark that covered more than half my face.

Turning away after another apologetic smile, the mother swept the boy's legs from under him with her arm. "Sit,

Colton. Please sit," she whispered harshly into the little boy's ear. "Wanna snack? Here, Buddy." She distracted him with a plastic baggie filled with dry cereal.

My first experience with the outside world and already I was humiliated. *Wonderful*, I thought as images of the dancing dinosaur swirled in my head, and my imperfection throbbed with the heat from embarrassment. Unfortunately, at Riverbend, our main source of entertainment and education was the television, so I was well acquainted with Barney and all of his horrifically annoying friends. I rolled my eyes, leaned against the window and desperately wished for the ride to be over.

2

Hours passed and thankfully the little boy with the dinosaur fetish had slept for most of the trip. I wasn't sure who was more relieved by that fact, me or his mortified mother.

As the trees whizzed by the oversized windows, I reviewed my plan again in my head.

I intend to find my parents. Yes, the very ones who dumped me all those years ago. But, please don't expect a tear-filled reunion with a swelling soundtrack in the background of our gathering. My one goal is to make their lives as miserable as they've made mine. The best part is that they won't expect it or expect me. I'm sure they've forgotten all about me by now. Eighteen years would do wonders to assuage your guilt, I'd imagine.

What do I know about my parents, you ask? Some. Luckily, given my advanced age and knack for learning, I was allowed to hold an unpaid job at Riverbend. I worked in the back-office filing papers and shredding documents; no task too difficult in case I became a spontaneous simpleton. After getting used to my presence and finally trusting my abilities to properly read the alphabet and push the correct button on the paper shredder, Miss Betty, the office manager, would leave me alone to do my work. I secretly learned her patterns and got increasingly brave and started nosing around in the off-limit files, the very ones I'd sworn to never read. One of those files was mine. I was supposed to mindlessly file them into the cavernous cabinets or feed them into the paper eating machine, but when left alone I'd study mine. And what an interesting read it was—very helpful for the girl whose heart seethed with rage and a desire for justice.

From my file, I was able to get the names and address of my parents. I was also able to confirm that I was a Tester. In my case, my parents were fortunate enough to have money which allowed them to pay to have the government take an egg from my mom, a sperm sample from my dad and mix them into a genetic soup. They then implant the goo into an unnamed host and waited for me to be born. Using the host instead of the actual mother gets you the all-important government guarantee against mistakes. Mistakes like me.

I seared all of this information into my memory and have been literally counting the days until I could put it to use. I hope they haven't moved since they threw me away. I still haven't decided exactly what I'm going to do when I find them, but it will be dramatic and unforgettable, I promise you that.

The bus finally pulled into the station in Portsmouth, N.H. and the door hissed open. I pulled my sweatshirt's hood tight around my head again and exited the bus, careful to avoid catching the eye of the other lethargic passengers.

In the bus station, I walked toward a display of maps and found one that I thought would help me locate the street I knew my parent's house to be on. After studying the map, certain of which way to go, I sensed eyes crawling on me like ants converging on a discarded potato chip. Dread filled my belly and I looked up to see that a guard of some sort was giving me a once over. No doubt he thought my eighteen-year-old figure was fetching and possibly his middle-aged spread would appeal to me in some strange way. Feeling irritable and slightly bitchy, I pulled my hood back and smirked at him. Surprise washed through his brown eyes when they surveyed my damaged face and he quickly looked away and busied himself with picking up a loose ticket from the floor of the station.

"Gotchya, jerkwad," I huffed under my breath, a sly smile stretching across my face as embarrassed heat crept up my neck and spread over my imperfection. Fortunately, I was used to the look I'd just gotten; that shifting expression of surprise and disgust all wrapped up into one squint and wince.

I took this opportunity to leave the bus station and be a phantom in the memory of all those who caught a glimpse of me in my big reveal to the randy guard. I felt many of their stares; eyes rolling over my face, lingering on the puffy stain, their thoughts balancing between pity for the girl who could be pretty if only she were dealt a different deck of cards and repulsion for the freak who shouldn't dare to show her face in public. If they only knew, I thought as I headed toward Main Street on foot.

3

It was getting late and chilly so thankfully Main Street was relatively empty as I passed by stores, occasionally catching my reflection in the pristine glass display windows. I half expected the shop owners to come running out their front doors, bells jingling, brooms in hand, to shoo away the hideous creature that dared cross their storefronts, possibly scaring away the last paying customers of the evening. Luckily, that was merely my wild imagination. Being trapped in an orphanage, I created my own expectations for the world beyond the walls. Some I'd been right about, like the little boy and the stupid wannabe cop. Most of the stores seemed warm and welcoming in the fading dusk. I almost wanted to stop in, maybe apply for a job, but a little voice inside my head would speak up before I could turn the knob and warn me away. "No one would hire you," she said, her voice incredulous and knowing.

I kept walking, checking the city map once or twice to ensure I hadn't gone too far. Still on track, I fantasized about what I would do when I met my parents. I wanted them to hurt like I hurt, but I also desperately wanted them to want me. These new feelings were confusing. I'd spent so many years plotting their demise that I couldn't understand where this sudden yearning for acceptance was coming from.

I shook my head and passed the doubt off as the delusional thoughts of an exhausted mind and refocused on getting to their house and exacting my revenge. It wouldn't be long now. As my steps echoed off the empty sidewalk, I realized I was only a few streets away. In my mind's eye, I reminded myself that they could have moved. A new family could live in this house therefore I'd need to do some reconnaissance before doing anything rash. I'd hate to destroy a family who had no connection to me, who hadn't rejected me all those years ago.

I smiled when I saw the street sign I'd been aiming for. I stopped under it and looked up.

"Crescent Lane," I read to the night sky.

After inhaling a lungful of the crisp, fall air, I turned up the lane and mentally readied myself for who or what I might find at house number twenty-two.

4

House number twenty-two was dark when I arrived. A wave of disappointment flowed through my body. I wasn't sure quite what I expected: warm, welcoming lights, the din of a family dinner finishing up? Not that I was an invited guest. I was nobody to no one. My insides were hollow and I fought any potential emotions that might stop me in my quest to gain Intel and formulate my plan for annihilation.

I hurried to a gate that separated the front yard from the back, gently lifted the wrought iron latch, and let myself into the inner sanctum of the backyard. It was dark now, so I could only make out a few features: a swimming pool surrounded by another fence, no doubt to protect the family's perfect child from accidents, an aged wooden playset, and a few chairs encircling a gourd-shaped fireplace. I grimaced at the normalcy of it all and wondered why they didn't think to protect me like they clearly protected the child they kept. I shook off the growing feelings of irritation and continued to the back door.

On the back deck, I tread quietly and tried to stay within the shadows provided by the mature trees. My heart pounded wildly within my chest and I started to question if this was a smart idea. My only knowledge of the real world had been extrapolated from my years of television watching yet here I was, pretending I was a common criminal, searching for a way into a house that I had no business being near.

As my mind whirled with guilt, anxiety, and a smidge of excitement, a light popped on. My breath hitched in my throat. The soft glow cut through the dark, framing me where I stood, a human statue with an ugly purple face.

I stood in my spot, frozen, waiting for the onslaught of barking watch dogs, a man's voice demanding, "Who's out there?" or maybe even the click of a gun's safety button being pushed, readying for action. After a moment, I realized a motion sensor light over the back door had turned on. There would be no torrent of bullets. The light would have illuminated whether it was me or an errant piece of newspaper blowing by its mechanical eye on a breeze.

I exhaled and tried to regain my composure, to slow my heart rate to a reasonable, survivable level. I saw my reflection in the glass and smirked at the foolish looking girl with wild, panic filled eyes; her only fear was being caught before she even did anything wrong.

Since I was graced with the light, I stepped from the shadows and put my hand on the lever to open the door. I took a deep breath and let it out, the cool air swirling in a smoky trail as it passed through my lips.

I pressed the lever down and the cold metal pushed back against the weight of my hand. Locked. *Shit,* I thought, and put my face close to the glass and squinted, my blatant snooping met with darkness.

I searched the recesses of my memory for a situation in my vast knowledge of television crime shows for my next step, knowing that I couldn't stop now that I'd come all this way. I thought for a moment and then recalled an episode of a talk show discussing how not to become a victim of burglary and other crimes. Hiding a spare key in an obvious place was the number one way to get yourself robbed of your well-earned treasures.

I scanned the surface of the deck for possible hiding places, hoping against hope that my parents were working on the day that special aired and that they were blissfully unaware of the hidden dangers of thieves making themselves at home by borrowing an ill-placed emergency key.

On the far corner of the deck, a dried husk of a tomato plant in an oversized pot seemed to be waving to me on the breeze. *There,* I thought and maneuvered around an errant chair from the patio set to check.

I crouched down and lifted the pot, moving it aside from its dark stained circle on the weather-beaten wood.

"Crap. You dumbass." I scolded the tomato plant for lying to me, and for getting my hopes up.

Still crouching, I moved the pot carefully back into place, noting that it might make a lovely missile through the glass door should it come to that, but I wasn't ready to give up on my search for a key just yet. I noticed a small set of steps near the pot and scanned the wood trim with a skeptical eye. To my delight, I saw a glimmer of metal in the dark. One of my parents, possibly my dad in a stroke of genius, had nailed a spare key to the trim just below the planks of the deck. Once hidden by flowers, the cold nights of autumn had shriveled them just enough for me to easily see his handiwork. I plucked the key from the nail and turned it over in my hand. I almost felt bad for them for being so stupid, and for leaving such an important part of everyday safety in such an unoriginal place, as if begging for something bad to happen by tempting the fates. Something bad is going to happen, I remembered as various levels of my plans for revenge flipped through my mind.

I shook my head to refocus and approached the door again. Still dark inside, I inserted the key and turned it. A shiver ran down my spine when the seal on the door popped open. I walked inside—actually walked inside—what was probably my parent's house.

I took a deep breath of the air in the kitchen, my parent's kitchen. It smelled good, clean, not as clean as Riverbend, but lived-in clean, like lemons and soap.

I poked around in the kitchen for a moment, shuffled through a stack of newspapers on the counter, and then opened the refrigerator. I stared at their food. Containers of leftovers stared back at me, begging to be put out of their misery. I helped myself to one, pulling back the rubbery plastic top and sniffed the congealed mass of elbow macaroni and cheese. My stomach growled reflexively. It smelled so good, like homemade, not mass produced like I was used to. I stuck my finger into the plastic container and fished out a crooked noodle. The intense flavor of foreign cheeses coated my tongue. It was intoxicating. I was hungrier than I'd realized. I found a clean spoon in a dish drainer and dug into the container, shoveling it in like Bob the Builder's bulldozer. Scoop, I remembered, smiling like a simpleminded idiot. I shoved another oversized bite into my greedy mouth.

Almost by accident, I finished the container. I instantly regretted it. Not for the calories I had just wolfed down, but for eating someone else's food. Maybe it was being saved for my mom's lunch for tomorrow or my dad's dinner. I set the empty container in the sink and hoped that she would think that he did it and he would think that she did it, the classic sitcom conundrum. If only people would talk to each other they'd realize it was the creepy lurker in their house, not a gluttonous family member claiming the goodies before the other one had a chance.

I wiped my mouth on the sleeve of my sweatshirt and continued my mission: find out who lives here and confirm that they are mine. *Mine,* I thought. That word was almost as foreign to me as the fancy cheeses that had covered those delectable noodles.

I found a hallway off the kitchen and was greeted with frame after frame of smiling faces. Luckily for me, the homeowners had a penchant for documenting every birthday, holiday and vacation, and then took the time to encapsulate their memories forever in an obnoxious trail of glass and wood.

The first picture was a baby. A baby girl. My stomach hitched for a moment and I wished that it was my image in the frame; a sweet, purple faced baby in a pink, lace-trimmed dress, loved, cherished, and remembered forever despite her ugly deformity.

The next picture was a toddler. The same girl, I assumed. This time it was her first birthday, at least according to the cake which was festooned with a giant number one candle. The girl had smeared frosting from her cake all over her chubby face and hands. The parents stood on either side of her high chair, smiling like idiots, clearly proud of their perfect daughter and her imperfect eating style.

I grunted at the picture as the film reel of birthdays continued in the perfectly preserved frames; age 2, age 3, age 4. It was enough to make me sick. The cold noodles roiled in my belly from the heat of jealousy and anger. *Why her and not me?* I thought. The bitterness of my years at Riverbend was hitting me with a flash of heat across my face. My birthmark throbbed intensely with the increased blood flow.

I continued my trip down their memory lane and saw the little girl growing into a preteen, then a teenager. She's pretty, I noted and I squinted at the last image from her seventeenth birthday. I studied her happy, joyful face, shiny brown hair with a slight natural wave, her bright brown eyes, a little pug nose, and a dimple on just the left cheek.

"Holy shit!" I said to the girl trapped in the frame. *She looks like... me!* I thought and swallowed hard to keep the fancy noodles from revisiting in an explosive manner all over their treasured wall of memories.

I paced the hall and reviewed her face at every age and saw an obvious glimmer of myself in each one. The me I would have been had I not been cursed with this devilish mark on my face. *How can this be?* I wondered. *She's practically my age. How can there be two of us?*

The plot thickens, I thought, and wracked my brain for a good explanation for this unexpected interloper and her obvious likeness to me. An idea niggled at the back of my brain and I ruminated on it for a few minutes as I continued the tour of what I'm sure now is my parent's house. Correction, *my* house.

I found a door slightly ajar and pushed it open. It was a bedroom. A girl's bedroom. Clothes in various shades of purple and pink were strewn on the bed, a chair, and on the floor. I stopped in front of a display shelf covered with trophies and ribbons for dance, horseback riding, and volleyball. *Perfection,* I thought and grunted my irritation at them, fighting the urge to break them into tiny pieces and scattering the remnants on the cluttered floor like I was feeding pigeons at the park.

I sat on the bed and fingered the edge of the peace sign comforter that was pushed toward the middle of the mattress. I pressed my damaged face into the soft feather pillow and inhaled the sweet scent of this lucky girl's vanilla shampoo. I closed my eyes for a moment and tried to imagine myself here, growing up in this room, winning my own share of awards. *This little princess has the life,* I thought, my face scrunching up in frustration within the folds of her luscious smelling bedding.

Suddenly, it hit me. I sat up, eyes wide, all my sensing tingling as if I'd been zapped by a live wire. "Holy shit, I have a sister," I said into the dark recesses of my sister's room. The niggling feeling in my brain lessened a bit, but still there was something else, some other realization that hadn't come to fruition just yet. A sharp pang of anger pierced my insides as if I'd been run through with a sword. I put my hand over my stomach and shook my head. Clearly, the ink on my Riverbend paperwork had barely been dry when they'd tried again for an undamaged, perfect child. Although this notion hurt like hell, I wasn't too surprised. They had the means to go for a perfect kid, and who was I to blame them for that? It was the way of the world, after all.

I pushed my wild thoughts aside and continued the tour. I wound up in the master bedroom and was struck by how organized it was. I'd always enjoyed organizing things and this was probably where that desire had come from. From my parents. *My parents,* I thought as I opened a closet and ran my hands along the sweaters and blouses hung in rainbow order.

I found a built-in shelf of books and reviewed some of the titles: lots of Stephen King, Dean Koontz, and other horror writers. I smirked, wishing they'd see the irony in giving away a daughter with a face that any one of those authors would appreciate and maybe even create a character for in one of their books.

Finally, down at the bottom, nearly hidden by the shadows, I found what I had been looking for all this time. My brain practically imploded with the confirmation of what my subconscious was trying to tell me. *The Lost Twin*, by Sherry Jacobs, stared at me as if the title had been printed in flashing neon instead of black and white. I pulled the book off the shelf and flipped it open to read the flap even though I already knew what it was going to be about.

The words on the flap barely registered as my mind tried to make sense of all the clues I'd discovered in my short time within these walls. *I'm the lost twin,* I thought. Already reeling from the fact that I had a sister, I now knew that we were twins. Born on the same day, probably within minutes of each other and yet, here we were, separated by man's law and my hideous imperfection.

Suddenly dizzy, I laid on my parents' bed and put an arm over my eyes, the book still gripped in my hand. The revenge that I'd been plotting all this time was starting to feel ridiculous to me. They did what they had to do. They could only keep one baby and the choice had been obvious. I was damaged and my twin was not. Angry tears burned at the corners of my eyes. This unfair world and the stupid government mandate of "one child per couple" had ruined what might have been. For a brief moment I thought back to the days when parents were allowed to permanently discard their imperfect babies and my noodle-heavy stomach clenched with a painful cramp.

At least I'm not dead, I thought and sat up, my head starting to hurt. I walked back to the shelf and put the book into the empty space. The next title caught my attention. *Hemangiomas – Surgical Options,* by Dr. Carl Spellman. *Why does that word sound so familiar?* I wondered. My usually fast mind had been rendered sluggish, no doubt over-stimulated with waves of shocking information.

A light illuminated the hallway outside the master bedroom and stopped me in mid-thought. I fought the urge to gasp and instead dove under the bed like an Olympian into a swimming pool. *Shit,* I thought and waited to be caught.

Shadows from activity in the hall had my heart racing. I peered under the bed skirt as a flash of movement breezed by the door.

"Mom, you home?" a voice called. The door opened a bit further and the overhead light flipped on. I sensed the room was being scanned by curious eyes. I closed mine, and wished I'd rethought this whole stupid plan. A click from the light switch forced my eyes back open. She'd left. I was still unseen.

I heard the din of a television program coming from down the hall in the living room that I had passed by on my way from the kitchen. I tiptoed from the master bedroom and back down the hall of memories. More lights were on this way and I worked overtime keeping my shadow behind me. Quickly, I poked my head around the corner and caught a glimpse of a young woman sitting on an overstuffed sofa. Luckily for me, her eyes were trained on the bright screen of a cell phone. She smiled, deftly clicking things with her thumbs.

I paused for a minute and watched her, my mouth agape. I wondered if she knew about me. I felt the urge to reveal myself to her, and I desperately fought the deep desire to step from the shadows and show her the truth that had been kept away from her for so long.

A metallic click to the girl's left drew both of our attention. The knob on the front door turned and my bold desire for acknowledgment disappeared. An urgent need to escape washed over me. With her attention still drawn to the door due to the imminent arrival of one of her parents, I slipped quietly through the kitchen, soundlessly opened the back door and disappeared into the dark void of the backyard.

The motion sensor light picked up my movement and I ran like a mad woman toward the gate that I had so brazenly walked through less than an hour before. Bright headlights from an approaching vehicle seemed to aim directly for me and forced me to squish against the side of the house. A leafless pricker bush poked my back and legs through my clothes and grabbed at the skin on my exposed hands. I bit my lip to keep from whimpering, and despite the pain I pushed myself deeper into the shadows.

The headlights disappeared and I slowly released the breath that had been burning in my lungs since I had suddenly forgotten how to breathe. The front screen door screeched open with a rusty whine and I heard the girl, my sister, say, "Hey, Dad," before the door banged shut behind him.

I poked my head around the corner one last time, then scurried onto the sidewalk and down the street, away from the people who I had once wanted to torture, possibly kill. Confusion swirled in my head as I plotted my next move and my heart ached dully inside my chest. It ached for everything I'd lost without ever knowing it, ached for everything my sister had lost and would probably never know. The uncertainty of my future was maddening and for the first time in my life, I wished the government had let my parents kill me when they had first laid eyes on me. Shot me right through my imperfect face.

5

After wandering aimlessly around the labyrinth of streets in this unfamiliar town, I finally found my way to a diner that was still open despite the lateness of the hour.

I winced at the bell jangling over my head as I stepped through the front door, annoyed that all the late-night customers were informed of my arrival without my consent. I plunked into a booth in the back corner, away from the prying eyes of strangers, and pulled a menu from behind the napkin dispenser pushed against the grimy wall.

A middle-aged waitress with a bouffant hairstyle and glasses that hung from a silver chain approached. She had a busy air about her, despite the limited number of customers she was taking care of. "What'll you have?" she asked without looking up from her notepad.

I hesitated for a moment, never having been asked that question before. "Um, coffee, I guess," I answered with a shrug that she didn't notice because she had already started walking away. "And pie," I added. "Any kind of pie."

The waitress scribbled my words into her notepad and disappeared behind the counter and through a swinging door with circular windows that reminded me of the outer hull of a ship. *Put your lifebelts on,* I thought with a smirk as I remembered a line from one of my favorite movies.

The waitress came back with my order and left the bill on the table, clearly too busy to come back again to check on me. I was glad. I had seen enough commercials to know that waitresses usually come to the table at the most inopportune times; mouth full, in the middle of a deep conversation, etc. Not that I had a companion to have a deep conversation with, but I was still glad to know that I wouldn't be bothered again.

I took a sip of the hot coffee and winced at the bitter tang. I ripped open three tiny cream containers that she had left on the rim of the saucer and poured them one by one into my drink. The black brew instantly turned lighter and it somehow filled me with a brief sense of hope, as if showing me that if a liquid that was dark and undrinkable can lighten up and become sweet from something as simple as adding cream, then maybe my depressing day can also be lightened somehow—the proverbial silver lining. My shoulders sank when I realized I didn't know just how it would happen.

I decided to eat my pie, drink my coffee, and use the restroom. Then, after taking care of my immediate needs, I'd try to figure out my next move. After wolfing down my pie in five large forkfuls and slurping down my cream laden coffee, I visited the restroom and did my business. The bathroom was gross, not nearly as clean as Riverbend, and I scolded myself for almost missing the stupid place. I caught a glimpse of myself in the cracked mirror as I washed my hands and was startled. The face looking back at me was the girl from the living room at my parent's house. Somehow the splintered glass had distorted my reflection. It cut off my birthmark entirely and left me with half a face. Half her face. Half a pretty face.

I stared at myself for a few minutes, reveling in the fact that the undamaged side of my face looked like somebody. Another human in this world looked like me, sort of. I smiled and only left when another customer came into the bathroom and broke the spell.

I settled back into my booth and grabbed the check. The total was $4.95 and I could understand why the waitress didn't want to come back to me. It wasn't because I was a hideous freak, it was because I was clearly not going to be her biggest tipper of the night. I left six crumpled dollar bills on the table and stood to leave, but a man with a paper hat, dirty apron, and grungy mop bucket blocked my path. At first, I thought it was accidental, but when he didn't budge at my 'excuse me,' I became concerned.

After looking over both his shoulders, obviously watching out for interlopers, he turned to face me. He appeared to be in his early twenties. He would have been handsome had his face not been ravaged by acne, his cheeks and forehead oily and pockmarked.

His eyes darted over my face as if surveying my birthmark for information. I pulled my hood over the back of my head and squinted at him defiantly.

"You new here?" he asked, his voice low, as if whispering state secrets.

"Who wants to know?' I said, surprised by my playing along in this odd exchange instead of telling him to take a flying leap. Something about his secrecy had my curiosity meter going up.

"You got a place to stay?" he asked, ignoring my question.

"No," I said involuntarily and silently scolded myself for giving this stranger vital, private information. I'd seen enough Lifetime movies to know that young girls are easily taken advantage of, but somehow, some way, I trusted this guy.

"I'm off in thirty minutes. Meet me out back," he said and rolled his mop bucket away, behind the counter, and out of reach.

I stood for a moment staring after him, wondering why I was so intrigued with an order from a stranger. Something about his bad complexion made me feel like we had some sort of covert kinship. *Brother and sister of the clan disgustus,* I thought and smirked.

I decided that I would meet him out back and find out what he wanted. Worst case scenario, he was some murderer or a pimp, not that there would be a big market for a girl with a ruined face like mine. *Whatever.* I headed into the dark night, waiting for my mystery man to reveal his deal. With my Swiss Army knife at the ready in my front pocket, I knew he'd spill his guts one way or another.

6

Thirty minutes later as promised, my mystery man met me on the backside of the restaurant, in the dark, by the dumpsters. *How romantic,* I thought as I eyed him and carefully assessed him for any dangerous vibes.

He seems more nervous than me, I thought as he approached. He tried and failed to light a cigarette that hung from the corner of his mouth.

I squinted at him suspiciously and he pulled the cigarette from between his lips and tucked it behind his ear. I put my hand in my front pocket and squeezed the cool metal of my knife inside my palm, just in case.

He looked around the back lot which was empty except for a motorcycle and a beat-up car with mismatched hubcaps and then turned his attention back to me. He grinned and wiped his shiny brow with his sleeve.

"So, here I am," I said, hoping he'd get on with it.

"So, here you are," he parroted back and laughed at the flash of confusion that passed through my eyes.

"Do you know me?" I asked, suddenly embarrassed that I might have forgotten an old acquaintance.

"No. But you're from Riverbend, aren't you?" He asked with confidence, as if it was written on my puffy purple face.

"Yeah. How'd you know?"

He nodded toward my chest. "The sweatshirt. It's a dead giveaway." He smiled again.

"Oh." I suddenly felt very hot and wished that I had ditched the stupid sweatshirt as soon as I'd gotten off the bus, but it was the only warm thing I owned.

"I've got the same exact one," he said, a twinkle in his blue eyes.

I shook my head. *Did I hear that right?* I wondered and peered at him, wary and relieved at the same time.

"You don't believe me?"

"I don't know," I said and quite honestly, I didn't know. Should I trust him? Even if he had been in Riverbend, it didn't mean he was a good person.

"Look," he said and lifted his stained white t-shirt. A pale scar stretched from between his nipples down to his belly button.

I stepped forward and without thinking, I traced a finger down his scar. "What happened?" I asked, my birthmark throbbing as the blush of embarrassment crept up my neck and washed over it. I let my hand fall to my side and I mentally flogged myself for being so bold with a stranger, a stranger who was a grown man.

He dropped his shirt and grinned. "Heart surgery at two years old. I got placed in Riverbend shortly after that."

I nodded. I'd heard of kids getting abandoned as babies, but I couldn't imagine parents spending two years with a child and then discarding them in exchange for a better, healthier version. "That must've been tough."

He nodded and waved a dismissive hand at me. "Long time ago," he said, but the sadness in his eyes was still evident, despite the twenty or more years that had passed.

"My name's Dawn," I said and stuck my hand out toward him.

He smiled at me, his eyes happy again, and took my hand. His palm was rough as if he worked very hard. "I'm Tommy," he said and after a few pumps he released my hand.

"Tommy?" I repeated.

Now it was his turn to blush. "From Rugrats. Tommy Pickles was my favorite. That's what happens when you let kids name themselves." He laughed.

"You didn't have a name already? When they left you at Riverbend?" Tommy's faced fell and I instantly wished I'd kept my big yap shut. "Sorry, none of my business," I quickly added.

"No. It's okay. I did have a different name, but I wanted to be a new person, you know. If they didn't want me, then I didn't want my name to remind me of them."

I nodded. "Makes sense."

Tommy squinted at me and pulled the cigarette from behind his ear. "Want one?"

I shook my head. He shrugged and tucked it back behind his ear.

"So…" I hesitated, hoping he'd give me a hint as to why he wanted to meet me.

"Yeah, sorry. I figured if you were new to the area, you might need some help. I could lend you a hand. I've been in your shoes. It's not easy."

"Well, I don't have any money so I couldn't pay," I lied. I wanted to hold fast to the meager funds I had been given.

Tommy shrugged. "You wouldn't need to pay me. Someone helped me when I got out so I figured I could pay it forward. That kinda thing."

"Thanks."

Tommy nodded toward the motorcycle behind us. "You ever been on a bike before?"

I shook my head. Bike? I fought the image of me clinging to the backside of this… man.

"You'll be fine," he said as if sensing my anxiety and started walking toward the motorcycle. "You can take the helmet." He tossed it to me before I could protest.

"Where are we going?" I asked him, trying to delay my inaugural ride on what I'd only known as a death machine.

He smirked and straddled the motorcycle. With eyebrows raised and a mischievous twinkle in his eye, he said, "It's a whole new world out here, Dawn. A whole new world."

7

The ride on the motorcycle was much longer and more exhilarating than I'd expected. Whizzing by cars as if they were standing still and taking corners like on a racetrack, I could tell he was trying to show off a bit. I pinched him more than once to indicate that I appreciated his skills, but would prefer to arrive at our mystery destination in one piece.

When the bike finally stopped, we were at the edge of a forest, not another human in sight. I didn't quite know what I had expected, but this was not it.

I hopped off the bike, removed the helmet and shook my hair which was plastered to my forehead and neck from a combination of my nervous sweat and the heat generated from the padding pressing into my scalp.

With me off the motorcycle, Tommy looked around the trees and then gunned the engine, forcing his precious bike straight over a slight rise and into the tree line.

I stared after him in disbelief, still unsure of what his plan was. Fear started to override my curiosity and I wondered if perhaps I should have been a tad more careful with who to trust in this strange new world.

I heard the engine cut out and Tommy returned a moment later with a grin on his red face.

I took a small step backward and frowned at him. Heat coursed through my birthmark as I quickly planned what to do if he attacked. I figured I could throw the helmet at him as a distraction and then I could dig my knife out of my pocket. The rest would depend on his next move.

"Whoa, relax, Dawn," said Tommy as if sensing my uneasiness with being driven to the edge of nowhere by a stranger.

"Tommy, what the hell's going on?" I used his name on purpose. I had seen a television special that recommended using their name in the event that you were cornered by a predator. Something about making sure they knew you were a human and so were they. My mind swirled. Have I been cornered by a predator already?

"Relax. I'm a good guy. Really," Tommy coaxed. His eyes were pleading and soft.

"Start talking," I ordered. My fight or flight instincts were kicking in hard and I worried that if he didn't spill the beans soon, he'd end up in a puddle of blood. His, not mine.

"This is the edge of a Normals' and Testers' camp. I thought you'd like to be with some of your own people especially since you don't have a place to stay. They welcome everyone."

I furrowed my brow. I'd never heard of such a thing. I'd never seen a news report or ad for anything close to what he was telling me. Even though I was starting to believe him, I still needed more information before I'd traipse into the woods with him.

"You live out here?" I swung my arm toward the towering pines and shrugged.

"A lot of us do," he said, his smile returning.

"Normals and Testers, huh?"

"Yup. But if anyone asks, tell them you're a Normal."

"Why?"

"Just trust me. Normal is the way to go," he said, nodding knowingly.

"How do you know that I'm not a Normal," I asked him, my eyes slanting with suspicion. I knew I hadn't told him what I was. *How does he know?* I wondered and tapped my foot impatiently.

"I didn't know for sure, I just guessed. I'm a Tester, too. It's nothing to be ashamed of. There's just a hierarchy here and you get treated… better, I guess, if you're a Normal."

"Why does it matter? Shouldn't we all be under the same Imperfect umbrella? We were all unwanted."

He shrugged. "True. I'm not sure why it matters. It doesn't matter to me. I like girls… um, people for who they are, not how they were created, but that's just me. But, trust me, it matters to the ones in charge, so it's better to play the game. Get the food, get the good tent with soft blankets, and worry about the sins of being a liar later." He grinned again and I sensed he was quite proud of teaching me the ropes of this odd community he was about to drag me into.

He nodded toward my hand that still gripped the helmet. I looked down at it and my knuckles were white from hanging on so hard in preparation for self-defense.

Reluctantly, I relaxed my grip, handed him my pseudo weapon, and followed him into the trees. We walked for a moment on the path of crushed ferns and broken saplings made by his prior excursion with his motorcycle. His bike was hidden behind a large tree, covered with large pine boughs. He knelt down next to it and tucked the helmet underneath. The black helmet disappeared easily into the shadows.

Tommy produced a flashlight from his inner coat pocket. He flicked it on and searched the woods. For a second, I was worried he was lost already, but then I realized by the way he had cocked his head that he was listening to determine if we had been followed. Once he was satisfied with the usual sounds of the forest, we continued on our way, down a well-beaten path that I hadn't notice before.

With our eyes trained on the weak beam of light, we walked in silence for a while. Despite wandering into the woods with a stranger, I actually started to enjoy myself, although subconsciously I would let my hand graze my pocket from time to time and was comforted by the knowledge that I had protection in the form of a Swiss Army knife that was easily accessible should the need arise. The air within the forest was intoxicating to me. Pine trees leaking sticky sap mixed with the pungent rot of deadfalls, decomposing needles, and undergrowth entwined in a lovely earthy scent; it was better than anything I'd ever smelled at Riverbend.

My reverie was broken with the introduction of human noises; clanging pots, murmuring voices, intermittent laughter, and the hustle and bustle of a busy campsite.

"We're here," Tommy announced, breaking our silence.

We stepped from the protection of the forest and were greeted by a mass of tents and wood structures covered with blue tarps. A number of fires carefully surrounded by rocks burned and it appeared that the inhabitants of this mysterious place were in the middle of preparing dinner.

"Food should be done soon," said Tommy as we crossed the threshold from being unseen to being seen.

"Hey, Tommy," yelled a voice from next to one of the fires.

"Hey," he replied nonchalantly, as if he brought strange looking girls here all the time.

"Miranda's in her tent," another voice from the campfire called. The knots in my stomach eased a bit at hearing a woman's name figuring that if he had a woman then he wouldn't need me for any of his… needs.

"Who's Miranda?" I asked and was surprised by the covetous tone my voice had taken.

Tommy laughed as if sensing my jealousy. "Cool your jets, Dawn. She's in charge here. She has to meet every new member right away."

"Member?"

Tommy nodded. We stopped just outside the largest tent on the grounds. Tommy trained his flashlight on the flaps and nodded again.

Heat flushed over my face which set my imperfection to throbbing again. "You want me to go in there? Alone?" My voice squeaked at the very idea.

Tommy smiled. "She won't bite," he said, although I wasn't convinced. The twinkle in his eyes, revealed by the nearby flames, showed his amusement.

I frowned at him and shoved my hand defiantly in my pocket. I curled my shaking fingers around my knife, pushed open the flap, and stepped inside.

The interior of the tent was quite nice, not at all what I expected based on the exterior of the campsite. A woman, probably in her late twenties, sat at a large table with papers spread in front of her.

She looked up at me and although her mouth smiled, her eyes washed over me, instantly judging and inspecting me.

"Who's this?" she asked. I looked behind me, expecting to see Tommy, but I was alone.

"Me?" I asked, feeling quite dumb.

She nodded and had a hint of amused irritation in her blue eyes.

"Dawn."

"Beautiful name, Dawn. Nice choice." She pointed to an empty chair across from her.

I stepped deeper into the tent and sat in the chair as she indicated. Across from me, her curious eyes continued their inspection. Heat from embarrassment inched up my neck and swept across my face. My birthmark screamed from her unspoken judgment and fresh pulses of blood.

"Tommy bring you?" she asked, although I sensed she already knew.

I nodded. "Yes, ma'am."

She smiled, seeming genuinely amused at my formality. "Miranda. Everyone here calls me Miranda."

I nodded again and took my hand out of my pocket. I was feeling safer now that we'd been formally introduced.

"You from Riverbend?"

"Yes."

"First day?"

"Yes."

"You're lucky you ran into Tommy then," she said and poured water into a beat-up plastic cup for me.

I grabbed the water and slurped it down in one gulp. She smiled and poured more for me.

"Thanks," I said and tried to sip at the second serving. I didn't want to appear greedy in addition to whatever else she might already think of me.

"Do you know where you are?" she asked, her eyes moving over my face again.

"At a camp?" I hated how small and stupid I sounded.

She furrowed her brow and nodded. I sensed she was starting to think I was weak of mind in addition to being blessed with the world's biggest strawberry on my face.

"Tommy was short on details," I added, hoping to convince her that I wasn't a complete idiot and that perhaps I could stay here and contribute in some manner.

"You a Normal?" she asked as she trained her eyes directly on mine, unflinching.

I nodded. "Yes," I lied and my body immediately tensed under her scrutiny.

She stared at me for a long minute and then finally broke her gaze. I was sure she was going to out me, call me a liar, and say that she'd read my obvious body language and she would have to cast me out, and banish me with all the other Testers who had lied to better their position.

"Good," she said and wrote something on a sheet of paper in front of her. "We could use more Normals around here."

I sat back in my chair and exhaled. Tension oozed from every crevice of my body all at once.

"Find a tent on the north side of the campsite. Tommy can show you where. There should be some extra blankets and such there. Dinner is in ten minutes so I'll introduce you to the group then." She stood and pointed toward the flaps, excusing me from our tete-a-tete.

"Thank you," I said, wishing I'd dared to ask more questions about where I was, who all these people were, and why they lived in the woods. Instead, I turned on my heel and scurried out like a frightened puppy, anxious to find a safe place to curl up and disappear.

8

Before the dinner bell, Tommy was kind enough to bring me to his side of the camp, also known as the Normals' side. I was shown to a four-person tent that was especially designated for women and had a spare corner. I was also given a stack of items that contained a mattress pad, a plush blanket, and a pillow with a clean pillow case. There was even a toiletry pack with small items for washing up and brushing my teeth.

I wanted to ask where they'd acquired such lovely things and why they were so willing to share them with complete strangers, but I bit my tongue. I was leery of pissing anyone off and risk getting the boot. The last thing I needed was rejection and the punishment of a long, lonely walk in the dark woods. If that happened, I'd be certain to eventually run into unscrupulous people who would no doubt be more than happy to take advantage of someone with nowhere to go and no one to stick up for them.

After rolling out my mat, smoothing out my blanket, and fluffing my pillow, I stowed my new toiletry items in my name brand plastic sack and left to find Tommy. Luckily, he hadn't gone far. He was hanging outside my tent with a gaggle of girls and he was finally smoking that cigarette he'd try to light earlier. One of the women pulled it from between his lips and took a long drag from it. I watched his face to see if it upset him, but instead he smiled at her. It was the kind of smile that made a girl weak in the knees.

Tommy noticed me watching the small group from afar and waved me over. Two of the girls smiled warmly at me. The third, his cigarette buddy, scowled at me, as if I'd interrupted an intimate moment between them.

"Ladies, I'd like you to meet Dawn," he said and twirled his hand toward me as if he was a ring leader and I was his trained monkey.

"Dawn, huh?" said his smoky pal. "That's original," she scoffed and giggled into her hand, clearly proud of her immature dig.

The other girls winced and rolled their eyes. One of them shook my hand, told me her name was Pebbles and seemed interested in my arrival story. The other, her name not offered, also seemed to pay polite attention as I told them of my recent release from Riverbend and my accidental meeting with Tommy. I left out the part of breaking into my parent's house. That deed already seemed like it had happened weeks earlier, not hours. *Funny how much your life can change in mere minutes,* I noted as Pebbles shared how she'd arrived at the camp a few months before.

After Pebbles finished her tale and the five of us shared an awkward moment of silence, Tommy broke the tension with a stupid joke. He also introduced me to the sourpuss to his right. Her name was Queenie and she was more than happy to tell me how Tommy was her man and hers alone.

Tommy seemed nonplussed by her fierce devotion to him. I wondered why he'd neglected to mention the fact that he had a possessive girlfriend when we'd met outside the restaurant, but I shook the notion away when I heard a voice call for dinner.

 followed the small group to the large center of camp where a giant fire burned in the middle. Food was doled out and I was impressed by the quality of the items offered. Corn bread, beans, some sort of gamey meat and peas were all available for the taking. I noticed that the Normals on one side of the fire were served first. The Testers on the far side were fed second although their portions seemed pretty equal to our own.

After the food was gone, everyone remained and talked, sharing stories of their days and accomplishments they had whether working at a job or scrounging up items for the camp from the neighborhoods and stores nearby.

I listened to the stories swirling in the smoky air and scanned the faces of my new family. They all seemed happy enough, well fed, and clean. I thought I could stay here for a while, and my stomach rested easy for the first time all day.

The evening waned and the crowd began to quiet down. They must be all out of stories, I assumed until I noticed Miranda had made her way next to the fire. She held her hand in the air and it was clear that her authority called for their attention.

Once the group was completely, eerily silent, my once calm belly quivered as if sensing something was coming. Something about me.

"Thank you, brothers and sisters," Miranda said, her voice commanding. "We have a new sister in our camp. A Normal sister from Riverbend. Her name is Dawn." Miranda turned toward me as I leaned back into the shadows and hoped that the announcement was enough and I wasn't going to be put on display. My birthmark ached at the prospect of strange eyes probing it and judging me.

She found my face in the flickering light of the campfire and pointed at me. "Come here, Dawn. Show yourself."

I gulped and stood. As I approached Miranda, the combination of the heat from the flames and from my uneasy innards churned up my neck and burned over my face setting my imperfection to throbbing like never before, as if it wanted to jump clean off my face and scurry into the woods.

"Ahh, here she is," said Miranda to the silent crowd. She took my hand and dragged me close to her into the light. "Does anyone know Dawn from Riverbend?" she asked with a wisp of suspicion in her voice. "Can anyone verify that she is indeed a Normal?"

A fresh wave of heat washed over me and I was suddenly lightheaded. Shit. I never even thought that there could be someone here that I would know or who might know me. I caught Tommy's eyes and he seemed to be apologizing to me with them, as if he'd forgotten about this horribly embarrassing ritual for the newbies to the camp.

There was a murmur in the crowd and I worried my knees would buckle and I'd end up falling face first into the fire, my purple blemish, and the rest of me, reduced to ash.

A man in a striped shirt from the Testers' side of the campfire pushed through the crowd and stepped forward. On the fringe of the firelight, I was unable to make out his face. *A man?* I thought. *I don't know any men. Who can this be? And what the hell is he going to say about me?*

"I can speak for Dawn. I, too, was at Riverbend. She's indeed a Normal."

Miranda nodded and seemed satisfied. "Thank you, Bert. You've been most helpful." Miranda turned toward me and held me by my shoulders. She kissed each of my burning cheeks with lips that were wet and warm. "Welcome, sister," she said, and released her grip on me.

With a wave of her hand the group started to clear away from the fire and head toward their tents. I stood by the blaze, unable to move and still a little freaked.

A strong hand touched my shoulder and I nearly jumped out of my worn sneakers. I whirled around and expected it to be Tommy, but instead I was greeted by the other man, the one who had spoken up for me. I recognized his striped shirt and then I recognized his face. His name rushed back to me in an eddy of confused and thankful emotions.

"B!" I yelled and threw myself into his arms. He squeezed me tight, and the heat from his body enveloped me.

I burrowed my face into his neck and drank in the musky scent of his scruffy beard.

"You remember me?" he breathed into my hair.

Reluctantly, I pushed back from his embrace and stared at his face. He was older, three years older to be exact, but then again, so was I. And, he had facial hair and had filled out considerably in the shoulders since I'd last seen him on his eighteenth birthday, which was, of course, his last day at Riverbend.

"Sure, I recognize you! You were one of my favorite people!" I said without thinking and immediately felt the heat of embarrassment whip across my birthmark like a slap in the face.

Bert grinned and his green eyes twinkled in the firelight.

I forced my mortification away and willed my brain to work properly. I'd had a major crush on B at Riverbend and had been heartbroken when he was sent away. He was one of the only boys who treated me like everyone else despite my obvious deformity.

"Time for bed, Dawny-girl," said Bert, his smile bright and relaxed. "Wanna catch up tomorrow? I'll come by your tent in the morning, okay?"

"Sure," I answered and desperately wished we could catch up now. I had so many questions for him, but I sensed bedtime was taken seriously here, since nearly everyone else had left.

"Sally, can you walk Dawn to her tent? I don't want her to get lost," he said and a girl I'd never me before came over and gamely took my hand.

"Good night, B," I called over my shoulder as I was led away by Sally.

"Night, Dawny-girl," he said and disappeared into the dark on the Testers' side of the camp.

As I walked with Sally, still hand in hand, my mind swirled with questions. Why is B here? How long has he been here? Why are the sides separated? Most important, why the hell did he just lie for me?

Luckily for me, Sally was one of my tentmates. Unluckily for me, so was Queenie and her unnamed cohort. I did my best to quietly get comfortable on my mat, and rubbed the soft blankets against my face. I hoped sleep would take me before the other women settled down for the night, but it wasn't to be. I was trapped in a tent with three giggling girls and I was instantly reminded of a television show that had an awkward teenager forced to go to a slumber party with snooty girls who were not her friends.

In my case, the mean girls were Queenie, Sally and no-name, who I decided to call The Giggler since that's all she seemed to do. No matter what nasty thing Queenie said about another person at the camp, The Giggler would cackle and nod her head in agreement. Come to think of it, I don't ever remember her actually saying anything. She'd just giggle, hyena-like with the occasional snort.

After their gossip dried up and it started to get quiet, someone's blanket whipped me in the face. It seared across my birthmark and I scolded myself for not sleeping with that side of my face pushed deep into my cushy pillow. I thought about letting it go and just roll over and act like I was asleep, but I knew from all my years of dramas that you need to punch the bully in the face to get respect. Not that I was planning on punching anyone in the face, but I did want to nip this bratty behavior in the bud, especially if I was planning on staying at Camp Reject, which was my clever name for this place of rag-tag and discarded members of society.

My heart racing, I sat up and squinted at Queenie. Her smug expression was discernible from the small amount of light afforded by a lantern set on its dimmest setting.

"Oh, you're awake," said Queenie, badly feigning innocence. The Giggler teetered and covered her mouth with her hand, her eyes bright and wide over the fleshy barrier.

"Of course, I'm awake," I seethed, "you just hit me with something."

"Sorry, there was a bug," Queenie lied, a defiant smirk plastered on her pretty face.

"Um hm," I grunted. My mind was suddenly devoid of any suitable comeback.

"So, now that you're up, what's your deal?" asked Queenie. Her curiosity had a fearful edge. I'd seen that look many times before.

"I've got no deal. You heard Miranda. I just got released from Riverbend and had nowhere to go. That's it."

At the mention of Miranda, I saw the women wince and exchange glances, as if I'd used some sort of power against them. I then realized that I had the power of knowing who was actually in charge.

"What about Tommy?" asked Queenie, her voice breaking and I suddenly realized what all this immaturity was about. She thought I was after her man.

"What about Tommy?" I asked, not quite ready to let her off the hook just yet, my face still stinging from the blanket assault.

"Do you like him?" asked Sally, speaking up for Queenie who suddenly appeared to be on the verge of tears.

"The truth?" I said and hesitated, partially to continue the torture of Queenie, and partially because I didn't know if I liked him. I barely knew him.

"Yes," said Queenie, her voice wavering. "Do you like Tommy or not?"

I stared at her and searched her face in the muted light. I questioned why she was so worried about it. So, what if I did like him? It's not like he'd go after a girl like me with an obvious deformity when he already had a girl who looked like her. She was so pretty with her blonde hair and clear skin. I wondered what her imperfection was, and no, an awful personality didn't count.

I smiled despite the inquisition. I sensed it made them all uncomfortable. I purposefully looked down at my blanket and plucked at a small pull in the fabric, delaying my response. I almost enjoyed the brief moment of control that I clearly had over my tentmates.

Finally, I took a deep breath and let it out dramatically. They leaned forward expectantly and I fought the urge to laugh, and worried that I'd sound like The Giggler in a fit of madness. "I like him as a friend. I don't know anything about him really. Except where he works and that he has a motorcycle. And lives here," I admitted and swept my arm over the tent to indicate the camp beyond our thin, fabric walls.

Queenie let out a breath that she'd been holding while waiting for my answer. *Bated breath,* I thought, almost laughing at the notion that that was a real thing and not just something written into television shows for dramatic pause.

"That's what I figured," said Queenie, but I sensed she was relieved. "What about that tall drink of water from the campfire. Barf?"

"No, Bert," corrected Sally, looking down at her hands as if she did something wrong in knowing his name.

I nodded. "B's an old friend from Riverbend, but I haven't seen him in years. I didn't even know he was here until he spoke up for me."

"He's a Tester anyway," said Queenie with an air of disgust.

I noticed Sally's body stiffen at Queenie's comment and filed it away in my mind. "Why does that matter?" I asked, wanting to know the answer, but almost not wanting to know. I guessed it was better to hear it from these gossips than from Miranda.

"You don't know?" asked Queenie, her tone incredulous.

"She's new, remember?" said Sally, her voice teeming with anger.

"Right," said Queenie, nodding. "I forgot."

"So? Why's it a big deal and why separate sides of the camp?" I asked.

The three women looked at each other as if telepathically checking with each other to determine if it was okay to tell me the truth. I was getting impatient, but thought I'd give it another minute before I got more demanding.

"Well," said Queenie, "Miranda doesn't want us Normals to go and fall in love with a Tester. It wouldn't be… prudent."

"Prudent?"

"Practical."

"I know what prudent means! I meant what does that mean in general? Why can't you fall in love with a Tester?"

"Isn't it obvious?" asked Sally, pain evident in her voice.

"Not to me," I said, feeling dumb. *What's the deal? What am I missing?*

"Duh," said Queenie, oblivious to Sally's distress, "because Testers' can't reproduce so there's no point in wasting a Normal on a Tester since they can't have a baby!"

My mind reeled. "What do you mean they can't reproduce? Why not?"

Queenie sniggered into her hand. The Giggler followed her with a bellow and a slap of her blanket covered knee. Sally stared at me, her face sad and uncomfortable.

"Have you been living under a rock?" asked Queenie, with an air of condescension in her tone.

"Apparently so," I admitted, knowing that we were quite sheltered in Riverbend. The news wasn't on our approved list of television viewing so we weren't privy to the happenings in the world.

"The government implants Testers with a gene that prevents them from reproducing. It's a failsafe for any mistakes they make so the Tester can't pass it onto another generation. It's the price people pay to have the government make them a perfect kid. Only Normals can reproduce because they were conceived the old-fashioned way, you know, bumping uglies," said Queenie who descended into a fit of guffaws that probably woke the entire camp or at least the handful of tents surrounding ours.

I watched her laugh with my brow furrowed. It didn't make sense, but then again, it did. With so much control, it made perfect sense for the government to find a way to manage what they were creating, who they were creating. "Is this true?" I asked Sally.

A tear flowed down Sally's cheek but she wiped it away before Queenie or The Giggler could notice. She nodded and I wondered which Tester she loved on the other side of the camp.

A man's voice roared, "SHUT UP!" from outside our tent. Queenie killed the light and buried her face into her pillow, still trying to get herself under control.

I burrowed back into my bed and thought about what I had just heard. These girls didn't realize that I really was a Tester and I had just found out that I was going to be unable to have a family of my own, unless I went to the government for help, of course. And, realistically, I never imagined that a girl who looked like me would find a man interested in having a family anyway. But still, the realization was a shock. *Yet another blow to us Imperfects,* I thought.

Fresh tears swept down my cheeks. The salt seeped into my birthmark and bit at the welted trail left behind from Queenie's blanket. The last thing I thought before falling into a deep sleep was that Queenie didn't realize that her man, Tommy, was a Tester too.

10

The next morning, I was surprised to find myself alone in the tent. I sat up and stretched, and grumbled at how sore my body was from a night on a thin pad versus the spring laden mattress I was used to at Riverbend.

A wash of sunlight blinded me when Sally entered the tent holding a paper plate with a muffin balanced on it.

"Oh good, you're finally up," she said and plunked down next to me. "I snagged you a muffin. Miranda doesn't usually let us take food back to our tents, but I told her it was for you."

"Thanks," I said and sat up, and rubbed the remnants of sleep from my eyes.

"No problem," said Sally. She opened her mouth to say something else and then appeared to think better of it. She clamped her mouth shut so hard I heard her teeth clink against each other.

"What?" I asked, figuring she'd been kind to me so I'd throw her a bone.

She shook her head. Then, after eyeing the flap of the tent for interlopers, she whispered, "Bert came by earlier looking for you. I told him you were asleep. I know where he stays though so I can take you over there after you eat. If you want."

"Okay. That sounds good," I agreed.

Sally squinted at me and took a deep breath.

"Is there more?" I asked even though I already sensed there was. There always seemed to be more here at Camp Reject.

"Why do you call him 'B'?"

I smiled and ripped a chuck of muffin from the crusty top and stuffed it into my mouth. My stomach gurgled with appreciation. "It's kinda stupid, really," I said and popped another piece of muffin into my mouth.

"I like stupid," said Sally. She was smiling along with me although I sensed she wanted to know more than she was letting on.

"At Riverbend we could name ourselves and he picked Bert. Like Bert from Bert and Ernie on Sesame Street. By the time I met him I was totally sick of that show. They would run it constantly so I couldn't bear to call him that. Plus, puppet Bert has that weird unibrow thing and I'd always thought B was much cuter than that…" I paused when Sally stiffened at my assessment of Bert's appearance.

She nodded and gave me a weak half-smile. "Let me know when you're ready to go," she said and crawled to her bed to fuss with a small palette of makeup.

I watched her for a moment as I chewed more scrumptious pieces of muffin. I sensed she was irritated, but it wasn't clicking with me. She carefully applied eye shadow and a swipe of blush then peered at her reflection in the small mirror and grinned at her handiwork.

Finally, it dawned on me. Sally had the hots for Bert! *Should I ask her about it?* I wondered. They'd made it sound so wrong last night. Normals and Testers were not to mix. At least not in *that* way. And, I barely knew her. I didn't want to make her more uncomfortable with me than she already was. So, I decided to wait. I'd ask B about the ins and outs of camp life and keep my suspicions about Sally's desires to myself, at least for now.

Sally clicked her palette shut and the sound of the plastic closure brought me back to the present. "I'm ready to go," I said and stood, futilely smoothing the creases from my slept-in sweatshirt with my hands.

"I'm ready too," said Sally, a fresh smile on her made-up face. "Let's go find Bert."

11

Sally and I walked silently through the camp. We passed the giant, stone-lined fireplace where last night we'd all gathered for dinner and the show starring me. The embers still smoked and the scent followed us as we crossed into Tester territory. The tents here were definitely not as nice at ours on the Normal side. Some had extra tarps thrown over the tops to prevent leaks. Others were missing the mesh windows, and had blankets hanging in their place, clearly a futile attempt to keep mosquitoes at bay.

We weaved through the tents and finally ended at the edge of a group of young men speaking in hushed voices. One noticed us and eyed the others, silently urging them to shut up before their secrets were overheard.

Sally seemed oblivious to their sneaky behavior and stepped into the middle of the group, essentially dispersing them with her mere presence. The men milled about for another moment and then headed in different directions with the wave of Bert's hand.

"Hey, Sal, thanks for bringing me my Dawny-girl," he said and enveloped me in a big bear hug. From the corner of my eye I saw Sally look down at her hiking boots, her expression forlorn.

I pushed myself from Bert's embrace and opened my mouth to speak, meaning to point out some endearing feature of Sally that Bert should have noticed, but she was already retreating. "I'll catch you later, Sally," I called to her backside. She nodded but didn't turn around and quickly disappeared back into the myriad of tents.

"Sleep good?" Bert asked. He grinned and his eyes swam with amusement. He didn't seem to notice Sally's heartbreak and I felt a wave of heat wash over my face, my purple birthmark throbbing angrily in the morning sunlight.

"Good enough," I answered curtly. I wasn't quite sure why I was so mad at him. I barely knew him anymore and what did it matter if Sally liked him? A relationship between them would be… unethical?

Bert's brow furrowed. Clearly, he was trying to read the confusion that had spread across my face. "Did you get something to eat? I can go wrangle you up something. I think there's probably some oatmeal left."

I shook my head to clear the muddled cobwebs of sparring emotions. "No, I'm good. Sally brought me a muffin."

"Oh, sweet. I bet that was good."

"It was. Didn't you guys have muffins, too?"

"Nah. We get what's left. Those are gone pretty fast. Just oatmeal for this old boy," he said and thudded his chest with his fists like Tarzan.

"Doesn't that make you mad?" I asked, confusion creeping back into the front of my mind. *Why were the two sides treated so differently? More bothersome, why are there two sides in the first place?*

As if reading my thoughts, Bert took my hand and guided me toward the edge of camp, away from earshot. He nodded toward a platform nailed haphazardly into in a large tree on the outskirts of the tents. "I'm scheduled for watch. You wanna come up with me and talk?"

From the concerned look in his eyes, I knew I had to say yes, even though I was petrified of heights. I nodded in the affirmative and eyed the gnarly boards that were clearly hammered by unskilled hands into the tree trunk. I convinced myself to climb by reasoning that if they could hold a big man like Bert, there was no reason they couldn't hold me, a petite girl who probably weighed fifty pounds less.

Following his lead, I climbed the tree trunk, one board at a time until I reached the platform at the top. Luckily, it had a railing so my fear of teetering off the edge was put at ease. I sat as close to the middle of the platform as I could just in case an errant gust of wind came and threatened to blow me off.

"There, that's better," said Bert, leaning his back against a thick post on the corner.

"What are you watching for exactly?" I asked, my eyes roving over the expanse of trees and ferns that spread out from beyond the reaches of the camp.

"I don't know. This is Miranda's thing. She thinks the cops are looking for her. For us. I think she's paranoid, but it gives me something to do so I do it."

I nodded, understanding the paranoia to a degree. I had felt very exposed in my limited experience in the 'real' world.

"What about you, Dawn? You plan on staying?"

I shrugged. "I guess so. I don't have anywhere else to go."

Bert nodded and I sensed that was the same reason he stayed too.

We were quiet for a moment, and I watched as Bert's eyes tracked movement down below. An amused smile broke across his face when a squirrel popped up from the underbrush on some busy squirrely errand.

"Can I ask you a question and you promise to answer honestly?" I said, surprising myself with the assertive tone that was escaping my mouth.

"Of course, Dawny-girl. I'd never lie to you," said Bert, his eyes suddenly serious.

I leaned forward and whispered, "Why did you stand up for me at dinner last night? You know I'm not a Normal. Why did you risk lying to Miranda?"

Bert's brow furrowed and I worried I'd pressed him too far. He didn't owe me anything and here I was, pushing for answers that I probably had no business knowing.

Bert licked his lips and rubbed the scruff on his cheeks with one hand. "I didn't want you to end up here," he said, sweeping his hand over the platform, "on watch for no reason, sleeping in a shitty tent, bugs crawling on you, eating oatmeal for weeks in a row. I wanted better for you, I guess." He blushed behind his hand.

My eyes widened and I nodded. "Th… Thank you," I stammered and studied the grain of the wood on the planks under my legs.

"Life isn't easy," he continued, "The real world doesn't want us. This camp barely wants us. It really sucks." His eyes were woeful.

I nodded and patted his knee in a weak attempt to comfort him. "What do you mean when you say the 'real' world doesn't want us?"

"Oh, Dawny-girl, I hate to be the one to tell you all this stuff, but I guess someone has to." He took a deep breath and looked like he was carefully choosing his words, as if his information was going to be too much for a newbie to handle. Finally, he exhaled. "For starters," he said, "Testers aren't allowed to have jobs."

My brow furrowed. "They're not?"

He shook his head and pressed his lips together. "The government won't allow it. So, there are places like this." He swept his arm toward the campsite that buzzed below us with activity. "The Normals go out and work, and we stay here and run the camp. We cook, clean, scavenge and most importantly, watch out for the cops." He grinned as his last point as if it was his favorite task over the more mundane ones he'd mentioned.

I sat quiet for a moment and let this new information sink in. "No Testers can work. Like, at all?" I shook my head. It was an incredible notion. "How are people like us supposed to survive if we can't earn money?"

Bert chuckled softly. "I guess that's they're point. They don't care. That's why there are tons of places like this," he nodded down below. "Some camps are made up with only Testers, but they aren't nearly as nice or well run as ones that have Normals mixed in. The money really helps keep things… livable."

"Livable," I repeated like a dumb bird.

He nodded. "I stayed in a Tester only camp when I first got out of Riverbend. We had to do some bad things to survive." His eyes glazed over at the memory of a life he clearly regretted. He lifted his head and gazed at me, a small smile creeping into the corners of his lips. "We have a good arrangement here with the Normals, you know? Miranda, she's smart and runs things really well. We're lucky she lets us be a part of camp. Separation is important though, since technically Testers and Normals aren't supposed to live together. So, she keeps that bit of separation between the two camps, makes us a bit lower class, to keep the police from having a problem with it, you know, in case they find us way out here."

I nodded.

"Miranda's master plan is to make matches between the Normals because they can… well… make more Normals. She wants to grow an army, one baby at a time. Although this is an agonizingly slow way to do it, she knows she'd have control over them from birth and could have the parents raise them knowing their lot in life was to rise up with her and her anti-government crusade.

I squeezed my eyes shut for a moment to keep them from bugging out of my head. *An army of babies, born in the woods. Okay?*

"There's something else," he added and looked away again, his cheeks flushing. "They did something to us. The government. They added some secret gene to all of us test tube babies to prevent us from procreating. Clearly, they didn't want us out in the world running wild and making more little mistakes."

Absently, I put my hand over my stomach. The mere idea of the government preemptively taking away something so precious was invasive and too horrible to believe.

Sensing my reaction, Bert grabbed my hand and gave it a reassuring squeeze. "Sorry, Dawny-girl. At least now you know everything."

I wondered how many of the people at the camp knew all of this. Bert had asked me to keep it all to myself as if it were a secret. I questioned how he knew and how he was privy to so much insight into Miranda's plans.

After Bert unloaded, I felt comfortable enough with him to tell him about my visit to my parent's house and how I might have a sister. I left out the fact that she might be my twin since the idea sounded even too fantastic to my own ears even though I'd seen the proof myself in live, living color.

I also omitted that my dark and twisted fantasy in meeting them was to hurt them or punish them so they'd suffer as I had suffered. I didn't want Bert to think that I was deranged or damaged in more ways than he could already see with his beautiful green eyes.

"Hey, guys," a voice called from below us. Both of us winced at the discovery of our hushed meeting.

"Hey, Sally," Bert called down. "Just reminiscing up here," he lied, looking at me with stern eyes. I nodded confirmation of his fib.

"Sorry to bug you, but Miranda was looking for Dawn."

"Be down in a minute," said Bert. We stood and got ready to climb down the makeshift ladder. Before I could descend, Bert grabbed my arm and pulled me close. Whispering harshly into my ear, he said, "Don't worry about me. I'll be okay."

I stared into his eyes for further explanation, but I sensed he wanted to leave it there. My stomach flipped from his proximity to my face and the intensity of his gaze, his green eyes bright in the sunshine. I thought for a moment that he might kiss me, a first for me despite being eighteen, but we were interrupted again by Sally, her voice more urgent this time in her request for me to go see Miranda.

The spell broken, Bert released me and started down the ladder so he could catch me in the event of a misstep. I made it down in one piece although I was breathless for several reasons.

"Catch you later, Dawny-girl," said Bert as he quickly walked away from us, and disappeared into the maze of tents.

"That looked pretty serious. Everything okay?" asked Sally after he was out of earshot. I sensed she was looking for dirt, or maybe wondering if we'd been talking about her.

"Nah, we're good. Just talking about old times," I lied and started the walk back to the Normals' side of the camp, my head nearly exploding with all the new information Bert had just unloaded on me.

12

"What took so long?" demanded Miranda when Sally deposited me in her tent and quickly vanished outside.

"Sorry, I was catching up with B, uh, Bert," I said, and instantly wished I could take that information back, as if it would be frowned upon, especially by my present company.

"Oh yeah. Bert's a good soldier." She gave a knowing grin that made my stomach twist with suspicion and nervous energy.

"What did you need me for?" I asked, hoping to change the subject.

"Riverbend." She pointed to a large sheet of paper on the table.

I stepped closer and was surprised to see the paper was actually a technical blueprint of Riverbend.

"This one's a few years old," she explained, running her hand across the thin, creased surface. "I was hoping you could review it and mark any changes to the building or grounds around it. Since you're the newest escapee, I thought you'd help me." She smiled at me although her eyes remained sharp and serious.

"Sure, I'm happy to help." I grabbed a loose pencil from the surface of the table. I squinted at the blueprint and after orienting myself with obvious landmarks, I was able to point out a few changes that had occurred with a recent upgrade.

"Perfect. That's great," cooed Miranda as she studied my corrections to her blueprint.

"Why do you need to know this anyway?" I asked, curiosity getting the better of me.

Miranda's head snapped up so quickly that I wondered if she'd sprained her neck. "That's none of your business at this point," she said, her voice cold. "Don't worry, Dawn, once I get to know you better, I'll let you know your role in any upcoming… activity."

I nodded and half-smiled at her, not wanting to piss her off, especially since I was suddenly realizing that she was probably going to use this new information, my information, for nefarious purposes. I wasn't one hundred percent sure how I felt about that. Clearly the government sucked and was unfair to people like us, but the mere idea of her planning and plotting was unsettling. I didn't like the idea of it or the idea that she might include me in whatever she was planning.

"You can go. Grab some lunch. I heard we're having rabbit stew today," she offered, a pleased expression moving across her face, and softening it a bit.

"Sounds great," I lied and left her tent to look for Sally, and hopefully something less cute to eat for lunch.

Lunch was a horror show of humiliation. I couldn't find Sally, and Tommy had left for work at the diner, so Queenie and The Giggler worked overtime to make me feel unwelcome. To top things off, despite my protests in the lunch line, a large scoop of rabbit stew was handed to me. The steaming bowl almost made me gag as I retreated to an empty spot around the campfire which had roared to life once again.

I managed to choke down a few saltine crackers before 'accidentally' spilling my soup into the dirt and scurried away with my proverbial tail between my legs to the medium comfort of my tent.

I stayed tucked away until I heard dinner being called and the mass of murmuring humanity outside my tent herded toward the food which smelled delicious on my empty stomach. I prayed it was something less woodsy.

Much to my surprise and pleasure, someone had scored a few chickens and they were roasting over the fire. A large shaved branch had been unceremoniously jammed through their rear end and neck hole, but I was glad the sight of their roasting bodies didn't bother me as much as the rabbit.

Somehow, chickens weren't meant to be pets, but a rabbit could be your bosom friend. Not that I had any experience with either animal—most of the food at Riverbend was canned, expired, and definitely not forest fresh.

I found Tommy and Sally and sat with them, taking the last seat and blocking Queenie and The Giggler from our little group. Tommy and Queenie exchanged glances that were hard to miss. Her squinted eyes and tight lips exuded bitterness. His open face was mildly apologetic and his friendly smile quickly reappeared when Queenie huffed off into the dark, The Giggler quickly following on her heels.

I worried I'd pay for this misdeed later in our tent, but I was content for the moment and tried to push my forthcoming punishment and ridicule to the back of my mind as Tommy, Sally and I made small talk.

After the food was gone, Miranda made her way to the center, and like a ringleader at a circus, she made a few announcements to her devoted troop of misfits. Most of them didn't really apply to me so I was only half listening when she mentioned a few names. Bert was among those named and my ears perked right up. Sally also straightened, her back rigid, and her head cocked toward Miranda. The cords on her neck stuck out so far, I thought I might be able to pluck them like the strings on a harp.

"So, you might have realized those guys are not here tonight. There's a reason for this. They were on a mission in town and were arrested," said Miranda, pausing long enough for the group to let out a collective gasp.

I looked over at Sally and was not surprised to see her crying softly into her hands. Instinctively, I put my arm around her. She leaned into me and her thin body shook against mine. My heart broke for her and for her unrequited love for Bert. My heart also ached for Bert, in jail, probably scared and hungry with no hope for release assuming the camp didn't have the budget to post any bail for him and his fellow inmates.

"Their arrests will not be in vain," announced Miranda, her voice strong and echoing off the tents and trees surrounding us.

A middle-aged man from the Testers' side of the camp stood. "What are we going to do, Miranda?" he asked, concern etched in his creased face.

"Nothing. We'll have to see if they get released. It pains me, truly, but that's all we can do for now," said Miranda, a glimmer of power reflected in her eyes from the flames licking in the campfire behind her. "Dinner is done. Sleep well and we will come together tomorrow to make some plans." She dismissed the group with a wave of her hand.

Despite the bedtime mandate, I stayed behind to comfort Sally. Tommy stayed too, eyeing the crowd as it dispersed. When the group had thinned to just us three, Tommy leaned in close and whispered, "Don't worry guys, they don't keep Testers in jail for long. They don't want to take care of them. Old Bert is probably eating like a king and sleeping like a baby tonight." He grinned and Sally's shaking slowed. I smiled at him and mouthed 'thank you.' He nodded and stood, offering me a hand up.

I took Tommy's hand and together we half lifted Sally to her feet. She swayed and then locked her legs, recovering enough to walk back to our tent. I hoped Tommy was right, that Bert was okay and was being treated well by his captors.

After tucking Sally into her makeshift bed, I huddled under my covers and made myself a promise: I would go to Miranda and demand that she makes a plan for his rescue. Tester or not, he was an integral part of Camp Reject and he mattered. He clearly mattered to Sally and he mattered to me. If Normals had more pull at this camp, I was planning on using it, no matter what the consequence.

14

Morning broke and I was up early enough to see Tommy off to work. Queenie was with him and was pawing at his chest like a playful kitten. He grabbed her hands and stopped her petting when he saw me watching. A crimson blush crawled across his pale cheeks. Queenie also noticed me and squinted in my direction as if warning me off. I waved at them and continued onto Miranda's tent; hell bent on getting some answers.

I marched into Miranda's tent unannounced and wasn't surprised to find her poring over a new set of papers that were spread out on her table. She looked up as I approached and smirked.

"That didn't take long," she said as if she'd been waiting all night for my arrival.

"You expected me?" I asked, still uncertain if I was reading her correctly.

"You Riverbenders always stick together," she said and nodded as if she approved of my level of devotion.

"I guess we do," I agreed. "So, what's the plan to get Bert and the others back?"

"There's no plan," she said nonchalantly, as if her people got arrested and returned unscathed all the time.

Maybe they do, I mused as I carefully formulated my next question. My cautious preparation came out with a surprised, "What do you mean?"

"Bert and his boys were on a mission for me. They were meant to get picked up."

"Meant to? Like, tried to get arrested?"

"Like, yes," she mocked me. "They're doing reconnaissance from the inside."

"Why would you risk them like that?" I demanded. My tone was much harsher than I'd practiced.

Miranda laughed. "You've been here for all of two days and you want to lecture me on how to run things? I'm planning a siege here, not planning a party," she scoffed at me.

I was taken aback. Clearly, I'd overstepped my bounds. I knew I needed to tread lightly around Miranda if I wanted to stay on her good side, better yet, if I wanted to stay here.

"Sorry," I muttered and looked away from her icy stare. I needed to regroup and rethink my approach. Finally, after she released me from her laser-like gaze, I was able to think again and speak in complete sentences. "Listen, I know you're working hard for us and I'm nobody to anybody. But, would you mind explaining this to me? Please?"

She inspected me and seemed to sense the healthy level of fear that was coursing through my trembling body. With an irritated sigh, she relented and pointed to the chair across from her. I sat and leaned forward to show her that I was fully invested.

"Bert and his boys were meant to get arrested to see if the police know anything about us. We've had to move camps quickly before and it wasn't easy. The logistics of it all is, quite frankly, mind boggling. There are so many moving parts. I needed to know if they'd heard of our encampment or if they'd caught wind about what we're planning. What I'm planning. Legally, they'll only be able to hold the boys for a few days, which will be long enough for them to overhear anything that might help us."

Tension oozed out of my body as her solid explanation washed over me. She was right. I didn't know how things worked here or on the outside world. I'd only learned some of the ugly details of life from Bert yesterday so who was I to question her? I nodded and smiled. "Thank you. I feel better now," I said and instantly wished I hadn't added that last part.

Miranda smirked, her eyes twinkling mischievously. "So glad to put your mind at ease, Dawn."

I sat staring at her, unsure of the protocol. *Am I supposed to get permission to leave?* I wondered as the awkward moment dragged on. Heat pulsed through my birthmark setting it on fire.

"Do you need something else?" she finally asked, thankfully giving me my exit.

"No. Thanks again." I hurried toward the daylight shining through the tent's billowing flaps.

"Dawn."

I turned on my heel. *So close*, I lamented and fought the urge to flee as if I hadn't heard her say my name. "Yes?" My voice sounded small and weak in my ears.

"I'll be calling on you soon for a favor. Can I count on you, Dawn?" Her steely face showed me that there was only one answer to her question.

I nodded. "Yes," I agreed, a wave of youthful stupidity washed over me making me feel even more pathetic and inexperienced than before.

"Good enough. You may go." She waved a dismissive hand toward the exit, her expression grim, despite winning my feeble agreement.

15

Days passed with no word from Bert or his crew. I spent the first day of his absence on kitchen duty scrubbing white protruding growths from the skins of old potatoes. The next day, I sorted bins of questionably acquired fruits and vegetables, on the lookout for anything suitable for human consumption.

On the plus side, I met new people while working in the meal prep area. The head chef was a man whose disability was even more noticeable than my own. His name was Kirk (yes, like Captain Kirk) and his alien hands, claws really, were the flaw that had him growing up in a wayward children's home from somewhere in the Midwest.

Kirk had a playful smirk and a sharp sense of humor that I assumed had kept the bullies at bay while maneuvering adolescence and then adulthood with his imperfect hands. Although defective to the world, to me, his hands were quite miraculous. He was more adept at using a kitchen knife than any chef I'd ever seen on television. He could skin a critter faster than you could look away. I liked him and actually looked forward to the time I spent with him.

My other job was to comfort Sally. She had been a mess since Bert disappeared. I'd told her what Miranda had told me about his purposeful arrest, but it didn't seem to make her feel any better or miss him any less. I was surprised that she was so open with me about her feelings for Bert, especially since Normals weren't meant to connect with Testers on that level. I worried that if Miranda caught wind of Sally's infatuation with him, she'd be banned from seeing him. I couldn't even imagine what kind of a wreck she'd be if that was ordered from the top.

Excitement came to the camp on day three when a wiry, bearded man with an overstuffed black backpack emerged from the woods and headed directly for Miranda's tent. Even though he was being quite stealthy, weaving between trees and then tents, doing his best to avoid prying eyes, I noticed him and his methodical approach immediately. I stared at him because he was new to me and because he seemed somehow… familiar, as if I knew him from somewhere. But where? I'd been sequestered in Riverbend for eighteen years and then visited only a handful of places before I landed here at Camp Reject.

The man caught me gawking and stopped to stare back at me, his gaze cold and unflinching. His eyes roved over my face and I thought I saw his back straighten when they lingered on my half-purple mug. He ogled me long enough to get me to turn away. I pulled my hair across my cheek in a weak effort to hide my birthmark from his invasive eyes.

By the time I dared to look back he had disappeared into Miranda's tent and I didn't see him again after that. It was as if he'd materialized from thin air and then quickly disappeared, a figment of my imagination. No one else spoke of the slinky character either. Come to think of it, Miranda had not come to dinner on that third night and I remembered one of her lackeys bringing plates of food to her tent before the rest of us ate.

On the fourth night of Bert's absence, dinner was interrupted by hoots and hollers from the perimeter on the Testers' side of the campfire.

Craning my neck, my eyes scanned the crowd who were now on their feet, and I spotted what had caused the uproar. It was Bert! Bert and his crew had made their way back to camp. They ate up the attention; hugging pretty girls, fist bumping guys, getting clapped on the back, and grinning like goofy Cheshire cats.

Bert caught my eye and gave me a wink. Heat exploded over my imperfection and it pulsed like crazy as the blood rushed to it. My own smile was hard to control despite my burning discomfort. A slight breeze offered a cooling wave of relief. As it washed over me, I walked toward him, suddenly feeling greedy and wanting one of those hugs for myself. Before I made any headway through the crowd, I noticed Sally from the corner of my eye. Fresh tears rolled down her pale cheeks and her body shook from the shock of seeing Bert again after his liberation.

I grabbed Sally's arm and started to drag her toward the waning crowd hoping to get her a hug too. Our forward progress was halted when Miranda intentionally stepped in front of us. She glared at me and her frown told me she knew more than I thought and Sally's ill-placed desires would not be met, at least not tonight, and not right under her upturned nose.

I guided Sally back to our seats on the log next to the fire and we sat like scolded children on time out. Miranda raised her arm for silence. The group responded quickly to her gesture and settled back into eating, serving the returning men food from their own plates. Miranda called Bert to the center and shook his hand.

Cold fish, I thought and eyed Miranda with disdain. In the very least, Bert deserved a hug for going to jail for her and her stupid secret mission.

"Friends," said Miranda, the condescending tone in her voice undeniable, "Bert and his men are back."

The group cheered briefly, but she silenced them with a curt nod. "I need to speak to each of them independently before you reacquaint yourselves with them. I expect you not to ask them where they've been or what they've been doing. It will all be revealed within the next few days, but for now I prefer to keep the sensitive information they carry between the camp leaders."

Leaders? I thought. *Who's leading besides Miranda? Maybe the mystery man from the other day?*

Bert looked at me, his expression apologetic, as if he was sorry for not being able to speak to Sally and me first. I shrugged slightly and hoped he understood my limited ability to communicate with him in front of Miranda and her eagle eyes.

Dinner broke and I headed back to my tent with Sally on my arm. Her crying had dissipated and she was now sniffing and wiping at her face with her sleeves.

"Glad to see Bert again?" I asked her although I already knew the answer.

She nodded and sniffed again for good measure. Sally looked around and then whispered, "I know I'm not supposed to like a Tester so much, but he's really special."

"He is," I agreed, and squeezed my lips tight over my teeth in a grimace, silently acknowledging the unfairness of it all.

16

The next morning, after seeing Tommy off to work and avoiding the sideways glare of Queenie and her cohort, The Giggler, I wandered beyond my usual kitchen duty tent and found myself close to the Testers' side of the camp. I wasn't exactly certain of what I planned on doing, but I was, in the very least, hoping to bump into Bert.

My plan was thwarted even before it began when Sally jogged up behind me. Her face was bright, and her cheeks flushed. Clearly her well of tears had finally gone dry after a good night's sleep.

"Hey, Sally," I greeted her as a wave of guilt passed through my body as if I was caught red-handed trying to steal her boyfriend.

"Hey, Dawn," puffed Sally. "Miranda. Wants. You," She choked the words out between breaths of pine scented air.

My stomach was suddenly heavy with anticipation and dread. "What for?"

Sally shrugged and sucked at the air. "She didn't say."

I believed her. *Best not kill the messenger*, I thought, amused at myself for finally understanding what the old adage meant.

We left the perimeter of the Testers' side of the camp and headed back toward Miranda's tent.

"Did you see Bert?" Sally whispered; her eyes eager.

A crimson wave of guilt washed over my face, setting my birthmark ablaze. "I… I…" I stuttered, not sure if I was overstepping some imaginary line.

"It's okay," said Sally, as if sensing my discomfort, "I know you guys are old friends. And, Bert and I aren't… anything, really. I just want to know that he's okay."

I nodded and was thankful that she let me off the hook. "I didn't get a chance to see him." I suddenly wished I had something good to report to her.

She shook her head. "Sorry. When you left, I figured that's where you went. After Miranda flagged me down, I waited a few extra minutes to find you so you could get some time with him, but guess I was too early."

I smiled at her and for the first time I appreciated her friendship. It was something I hadn't expected so soon after leaving Riverbend.

We arrived at Miranda's tent and Sally peeled off on another errand leaving me alone at the billowing flaps. The guy standing watch outside nodded at me and I went in, dread still heavy in my belly.

Miranda sat at her table, reading from a new pile of files placed smack dab in the center. When she saw me, she tossed the one she'd been looking at back on the top of the pile and smiled at me.

Her smile wasn't comforting in the least bit. It seemed more… sinister, menacing, threatening… all of the above. The trepidation that had been sitting in my stomach like a lead balloon shifted and I suddenly worried that I'd need to visit the latrine. My nerves were working their way out of my body from either the top or bottom. I still wasn't certain which way, but I could feel it coming.

"Dawn," said Miranda, her smile breaking, her face more relaxed as if she sensed my discomfort and wanted to ease my mind and stomach before she had a real mess on her hands.

"Morning, Miranda." I hated how pathetic and weak my voice sounded in my ears.

"I hope I didn't take you away from anything… important." She smiled again and I had a good idea that she had seen me heading off to the Testers' side of the camp, obviously to see Bert.

"No," I lied. "Do you need something from me?"

She eyed me carefully for another moment. I shifted my weight from one leg to the other to keep from passing out under her steady glare. Finally, she broke her gaze and bobbed her head toward the mass of files on her desk. "See these?"

I nodded.

"These are from Riverbend."

"Riverbend? Why do you need files from Riverbend?" I blurted. My mind swirled with more questions, but my tongue and mouth were unable to form them, frozen from the rush of confusing information.

"I collect all sorts of data. I like to know the people in my camp and these files help me do just that." Her face was smug and knowing.

I wondered what she was talking about. *Who else was from Riverbend besides me, Tommy and Bert?* Statistically, there are probably a few others, but who cared what some government-run orphanage said about us?

"Would you be surprised to know there was one about you in this pile?" she continued and waved her hand over the stack like Vanna White turning a letter on Wheel of Fortune. I sensed she was lying. Actually, I knew she was lying because I had shredded my file myself right before I had been discharged. Didn't I?

"Yeah, I'd be surprised, I guess," I said, still not sure what was happening. Was she trying to blackmail me? I doubted there could be anything too dire in my file if, in fact, she did have it. I had been a good kid and a hard worker. I toed the line but did what I was told. I wasn't some rabble rouser like some of the other kids I'd known that had gotten their exit tickets punched early.

I just wanted you to know that I have it and that I'm able to keep secrets. Well, I keep the secrets if you're on my team. Correction, I only keep secrets for people who are on my team." Although her mouth remained in a pinched scowl, her eyes twinkled and gave away how pleased she was with herself.

I nodded and started to understand. She *was* blackmailing me, but I was still confused as to why I would be of any value to her. Suddenly, a hot dart of realization seared through my brain and I worried I'd fall down. I quickly blinked away the swimming sensation in my head and realized that if she did have a file on me, she knew that I was a Tester, not a Normal. Shit. Does she know? Vomit burned in the back of my throat and beads of sweat popped out on my forehead and temples and I fought the urge to wipe them away with the back of my hand, not wanting to bring her attention to it in case she hadn't noticed my physical reaction to her coercion in the dim light inside the tent.

In our awkward silence, she studied my face and seemed almost amused by my bewilderment and visible distress. "So? Are we on the same team? Dawn?"

I nodded. "Yes. Same team," I agreed and waited for the axe to fall.

Miranda stood and came toward me. Involuntarily I flinched and hoped she hadn't seen it. She stopped in front of me and put her arms around my shoulders. She rested her head against my cheek. My birthmark burned under her hot skin. Her embrace was tight and purposeful. I tried to reciprocate and put my hands on her back as if we were old friends.

Miranda took a half step back and looked directly into my face. "Same team, Dawn. Remember that," she said and released me. She returned to her table and resumed reading from the stack of files. "Oh. You may go," she said and waved me off as if the blackmail and intimidation had never happened.

I turned on my heel and bolted, disappearing through the flaps as if I was being chased by a horde of angry bees. I made my way back to my tent and instead of going inside I walked around the back of it and threw up into the dirt. Twice.

17

Still shaken from my encounter with Miranda, I decided to skip dinner. Sally offered to bring me a little bite to eat if she was able to sneak something, so I gratefully accepted and stayed curled in a small ball on my makeshift bed, and rubbed the plush fabric of my blanket against my cheek as if I was reverting to the simple comforts of my childhood.

After dozing for a while, I became aware of movement inside the tent. I opened my eyes and expected to see Sally bearing edible gifts, but was instead surprised to see Bert. His smile was broad and his hands were full of biscuits.

I sat up and let my blanket fall into a puddle of folded fabric onto my lap. Bert handed me the baked contraband. I made a little nest in my lap out of the blanket and set the biscuits carefully inside. I took a nibble from the last one, suddenly very hungry.

Bert's eyes glistened and his smile somehow seemed broader than before. "Glad you approve," he said and nodded toward my pile of goodies.

"Thank you. How'd you know?"

He smiled slyly. "Sally. She told me what happened earlier so since I'm the conquering hero, I was allowed to take a little more at dinner tonight. I figured I'd share the wealth. With you," he added and a wash of red covered his handsome face.

"Does Sally know you're here?"

"Does she need to? I wasn't aware I was supposed to let her know all my moves." He grinned again. This time the twinkle in his eye was boyish and mischievous.

A little twinge of nervous energy fluttered to life in my belly. I quelled the butterflies with another, bigger bite of biscuit and gave Bert a sheepish grin in return. "No, I guess not," I agreed.

"Listen, Dawn, Dawny-girl," said Bert, his tone suddenly serious, "Miranda would kill me for even being over here, especially in a girl's tent, but I just had to tell you what I learned on the inside."

My stomach clenched at the mention of Miranda. Not again, I thought and held a hand over my belly, hoping to keep everything inside this time.

"When we were held up in jail, I met someone."

"Met someone? What does that mean?" For a second I remembered an episode of some random drama where the guy dumped the girl because he'd 'met' someone. As if the mere act of meeting someone on the street – or in jail – were grounds for dumping your partner. I wondered why my mind had gone so quickly to this odd place. Bert wasn't even my boyfriend. He was just an old friend. If anything, he was more Sally's boyfriend than mine. *Maybe that's it,* I thought. I was having guilty feelings because I was in a tent… alone… with a cute boy… and he wasn't *my* boyfriend.

As if reading my expression, he quickly corrected himself, "No, no, not like that! I met a guy who I think is related to you."

I let the words wash over me for a brief moment and absently took another bite of the biscuit that was quickly being squeezed into powder in my hand. "You met a relative of mine? In jail?"

"Not in jail, exactly. At the jail."

"At the jail," I repeated. Clearly the dumb parrot was back in full swing.

"Yes." Bert licked his lips and cocked his head toward the door of the tent. Chattering people were approaching, but their voices became softer as they continue to walk by.

"Who?"

"I think he was your dad."

"My dad?" The biscuit in my hand officially met its demise as I involuntarily squished the life out of it.

"Yes. He was one of the cops who guarded the cells. He asked me if I knew you. He knew I'd lived in Riverbend from our initial round of questioning. I overheard him talking about you to another cop. I almost think he did it on purpose, like he knew I was lying or something and wanted me to overhear that he was your father." Bert shook his head as if still trying to makes sense of all this himself. "It had to be you. He described a girl who looked just like you. I heard him say that he'd gone to Riverbend on your release day to get you, but you were already gone."

I shook my head and still couldn't believe the words that were coming out of his perfect mouth. "You sure it was me? He said she looked just like me?"

Bert brushed my birthmark with the back of his hand. I let him, surprising even myself. "It was you. No doubt. He was looking for you."

Bert licked his lips again. He leaned down so his face was even with mine. He met my gaze and before I could speak again, he kissed me. His lips were warm and wet and… intoxicating. "We'll talk more soon. I gotta go," he said in a husky whisper and disappeared through the door of the tent before I could respond.

Holy shit, I thought. My face was still hot, and my imperfection throbbed at regular intervals from the heat of Bert's touch. I didn't know what was more amazing, the fact that my dad was looking for me or the fact that Bert had just kissed me… and I liked it. I liked both of those things… a lot.

18

Sleep was hard to come by after my encounter with Bert. I stayed up late and listened to the rhythmic breathing of Sally, Queenie, and The Giggler who I now knew was named Wilma. I kept the name The Giggler for her in my mind though since Wilma was too awful to say aloud.

As the sun started to rise, I nibbled at the last of my gifted biscuits and let my thoughts wander wherever they wanted. Finally, I fell into a deep sleep just as everyone else had begun to stir.

Hours later, I was awake, pulled from my slumber from a combination of the tent getting hot from the late autumn sun and from murmuring voices that seemed to be right outside. I knew it was Tommy and Queenie and they sounded to be in a bit of a tiff. I decided I could hide until they were gone or I could leave now and save Tommy from another undeserved scolding.

I decided on the latter and exited the tent, stretching my body as soon as I could stand upright. Queenie's face dropped when she saw me, no doubt knowing that I'd overheard her immature dressing-down of Tommy; her being jealous of yet another girl in camp and how it was All. His. Fault.

Tommy grinned when he noticed me and I thought I saw a wave of relief wash through his eyes, as if the verbal onslaught from Queenie might finally come to an end.

"Hey, guys," I said and stood next to Tommy, my hands on my hips, and ready for Queenie to turn her negative attention to me.

Without hesitation, she started right in. "Sleeping late, Lazy Bones?" she sneered at me. "Or just lying around eavesdropping?" she added, her eyes slanted and suspicious.

"Eavesdropping," I said and smiled, quite proud of myself for giving it right back.

Tommy laughed and Queenie punched him hard in the shoulder. "Ow. Relax," he said to her and rubbed his assaulted arm.

"Well," huffed Queenie, "you picked a horrible day to skip breakfast. You missed all the excitement," she chided, and her eyes glistened with malice.

I turned to Tommy and shrugged. He opened his mouth to speak but Queenie jumped back in. "Miranda outlined her plan of attack this morning."

"Plan of attack?" I repeated, my brow furrowing at the mere notion.

"We're hitting Riverbend. Hard and fast. Lights out. They won't know what hit them," she said punching her fist into her open palm. She giggled and smirked, clearly anticipating a bad reaction from me.

"Victoria Mae!" said Tommy, his voice loud and agitated. "That's enough. Just go," he ordered and pointed up the main path of the camp.

Queenie cowered a bit at his tone, but quickly straightened and stuck out her bottom lip in an exaggerated pout. "Meanie badini," she said and marched away.

We watched her retreat until she was out of sight. Then, I turned back to Tommy, full of questions. "Who the hell is Victoria Mae?" I asked.

"Queenie. She's actually a Perfect, but she lives here with us."

"*She's* a Perfect?" I asked, my mind swirling at the notion of that little snot rag being considered perfect.

"Long story short; we met at the diner, fell in love and she ran away from home to live here in Shangri-La with me." His eyes were tired as if the magic between them was long gone. He continued, "She gave herself the name 'Queenie' so she'd fit in better, as if she'd named herself like Testers and Normals get to. I know it's stupid," he said and looked down at his dirty sneakers.

I nodded, and my heart ached for their horrible decision and for us having to live with it. "So, more importantly, what did she mean about Riverbend? What's Miranda planning?" I gulped, and my mind swirled with the faces of the friends I'd left behind.

Tommy shrugged. "I'll tell you what I know. I don't get to go. Just Testers. They're more… disposable. You should ask Bert. He'll have to go."

I swallowed hard. "Bert," I repeated, the stupid parrot roosting yet again.

"Yeah. All those guys that just got back, they'll go and so will the rest. That's how we stay afloat out here. Some of us work, like me. But mostly, we raid places and steal shit to keep going. Riverbend's the first political type place we've hit. I'm sure Miranda has a reason for that. She's been talking about starting some half-assed revolution or something, but she'd need a lot more people than what we have here. We'd have to meet up with other camps…"

"A revolution?" I interrupted. "Do they use weapons? Will they hurt people?" I fought the urge to gasp and covered my mouth with my hand to keep it inside. What about kids like Wendy? Sick kids who would have no way of defending themselves from an attack and certainly wouldn't be able to survive in a remote camp with no electricity.

Tommy shrugged again. "If they have them, I'm sure they'll bring them. I wish I could go, but she needs my paycheck," he lamented and dug inside his front shirt pocket and pulled out a bent cigarette.

I shook my head. "No. She can't."

Tommy produced a lighter from his pants pocket and angled his head down to light the smoke. He took a big drag and blew it off to the side, away from me. He nodded. "She's going to. Tomorrow night."

"Tomorrow night? Seriously?"

"That's what she said at breakfast. Maybe it'll get delayed by a day, but I doubt it. She's pretty thorough in her planning." He smiled as if he were proud of Miranda and all she'd accomplished to keep Camp Reject up and running.

"I've got to talk her out of it," I said and started walking toward her tent. Visions of Wendy and other disabled kids I'd left behind danced inside my head. And, Bert, what if he got caught or worse, got hurt. I had to do something to stop this madness. Too many innocent lives were at stake.

"Good luck," called Tommy, "you'll need it."

19

I stormed into Miranda's tent, Hurricane Dawn, ready to level some serious damage to her rebellious, careless plans. I was surprised to find her in close conference with the strange man I'd seen sneaking into camp a few days ago. This time, I immediately recognized him. It was easier now because he wore a familiar light grey uniform; required garb for all security guards at Riverbend. Clearly, he was a traitor to the government who employed him.

I eyed him suspiciously and then turned my heat seeking laser beams onto Miranda. She flashed a warm smile at me. It flustered me so much that the speech I'd been working on since leaving Tommy had disappeared and I was left bumbling for the right way to explain why she needed to stop. I opened my mouth to speak and all that came out in a whiny, little girl utterance was, "Riverbend? Why?"

Miranda flinched, but I sensed she fought hard to keep the soft smile on her face, her first maneuver in my manipulation. She put a hand on the arm of the security guard and rubbed it up and down in a loving way. "Come back in a few minutes, would you, baby?" she cooed, her voice calm and soothing. The guard nodded and gave me a glance of disdain before he left. He slapped at the flaps of the tent and melted into the sunlight.

My stomach roiled with anger and nervous energy now that we were alone. Involuntarily, my mind churned with the images of what Miranda probably had to do with that guy or to that guy to get him onboard her crazy train. I shuddered and shook my head, hoping to spill those R-rated images out of my innocent brain.

With her hand, Miranda motioned to the chair opposite her table. I wanted to stand to show her my strength and resolve, but my body clearly wasn't aware of that plan as my feet shuffled me toward the chair, and my butt greedily plunked down, taking the weight off my Jell-O filled knees.

She leaned across the table and for a moment I thought she might reach for my hand and give it an understanding pat. I purposefully stuck my hands under my thighs to keep them from disobeying like my legs and put themselves out for her sad attempt at comforting me.

"I know how you feel, Dawn. Riverbend was your home. It's where you grew up. But we have to be realistic here. We need things. We need food and supplies. We need people. The government is cracking down on places like this camp. We need resources to keep going. Winter is on its way and we have to head south with enough to keep us going until we meet up with a camp I've been in contact with down in Florida. It'll be a long trip, but it's necessary for our survival. Riverbend will be the last big haul and then we're gone. The

Normals will pack up camp while we hit Riverbend. We'll rendezvous after and get out of Dodge. Simple as that."

"Simple as that," I repeated, my mind numb from hearing all the information from her own mouth instead of just unconfirmed rumors from Tommy and Queenie.

"Yes. Simple as that. I could use your support here, Dawn."

"My support?" I repeated.

"Yes. You know Riverbend. You know the kids."

"Why does it have to be Riverbend. Why not some store or restaurant?"

She leaned forward and squinted at me as if I was stupid for questioning her plan. "Riverbend is their way of rubbing our noses in what we are," she said, venom seething below her calm exterior. "They aren't helping those kids out of the kindness of their hearts. They don't have hearts. This way, we're stealing what they owe us. It *has* to be a government target to mean something to our cause. It's the only place that makes sense. A store wouldn't be a blip on their radar. Riverbend would be a big friggin' blip. And, I think you'd be a great asset in there, on the front lines, so to speak." A corner of her mouth rose in a half smile that showed she had it all figured out.

I gasped. "You want me to go with you?"

She nodded, a grim smile on her thin lips. "Of course."

I shook my head. "No. I can't. They're my friends. My family…"

"Dawn. Nobody there loves you. We love you. We need you. You're important here." This time, she did put a hand across the table, reaching out toward me like a mother trying to console her silly put upon teenage daughter, as if she'd asked me to go to the grocery store with her to buy a gallon of milk.

"I have friends there," I insisted. "Sick ones."

"Like Wendy?" she asked and tilted her head toward me, clearly waiting for a reaction.

I nodded; my eyes wide. "Yes. Wendy. She was my roommate. She's really sick."

Miranda squeezed her lips together and thought for a moment as if calculating how much of her plan she should reveal to me since I didn't seem to be handling it very well. Finally, she took a deep breath and said matter-of-factly, "Wendy's problems will end when we cut the power."

"Cut the power?" I whispered. My mind immediately thought of Wendy's oxygen pump, the machine that kept her alive. If the power was cut for any extended period of time, Wendy would… die.

"Your Wendy will fly off to Neverland with all the other Lost Boys and Girls," said Miranda, a smirk of pride on her face, as if she was letting a butterfly go from its Mason jar prison. "She'll be free, Dawn. All of them will be free. One way or another."

"So many will die. A lot of them are sick," I continued, hoping that if I said it enough times and with the proper emphasis, she might understand the enormity of her plan.

"Dawn, it's called 'collateral damage.' It happens in situations like this. You have to be okay with that. That's how we get by."

My eyes welled with tears. I didn't want to think of sweet little Wendy as 'collateral damage.' She was my friend. My sister of circumstance. She didn't deserve to die for a few boxes of powdered potatoes.

"You're still such a girl, Dawn," Miranda chided, shaking her head.

I let myself cry for a moment, and the release seemed to be clearing my mind. Cohesive questions began to form as my blubbering subsided. "How did you know about Wendy?"

Miranda smirked again and nodded toward the stack of files that had been moved into a corner on the floor of her tent. "Ryan, the security guy who just left, he brought me those files so I could see which kids we want to focus on... retrieving."

"Retrieving? You mean kidnapping," I corrected, my sadness quickly turning bitter. My birthmark throbbed from a flash of heat in my face and my tears burned a salty trail over my imperfection. The irritation made me cranky and bold.

Miranda nodded. "Not untrue. But we know there are kids who would love to be with us. To work toward a goal with a… family. Our family."

"So why do you need me if you have those files?" I questioned, not wanting to be part of a mass execution and kidnapping of innocent children.

"You know them. They'd follow you. You also know the layout of the building, and could maybe guide us to areas with extra supplies. The guards know you too. You wouldn't stand out if we sent you in first to do some reconnaissance."

"I'm not being the Pied Piper of this," I argued. "No way," I shook my head at her and crossed my arms over my chest.

"You will," said Miranda, her confidence shaking my resolve.

"And just why would I do it?"

"And so begin the negotiations," said Miranda. A slim smile crept across her face reminding me of a classic Disney villain. "Brava, Dawn. There's hope for you yet," she said with an odd hint of pride in her tone.

"Negotiations?"

"Is there anything you'd want? For example, are there any extras at camp that would make your life easier? Name it and it's yours."

I shook my head. *Is she nuts?* I wondered. As if more tater tots at dinner would make me more willing to slay young children as they slept in their beds.

As if reading my face, Miranda continued, "No? How about privileges then? Remember those files? I know about you, Dawn. I know you're not a Normal. I've seen it in black and white, kiddo. You can keep your cushy tent and I'll keep your secret. How does that grab you?"

Shit, I thought and swallowed hard. This was even worse, even deeper than I'd imagined. I was surprised that she was able to keep that tidbit under her hat for so long. She'd saved it knowing I'd be an unwilling participant in her raid.

With her eyebrows raised in anticipation, she asked, "Need more?"

My back stick straight in my chair, I held my breath and wondered what other secrets she had in her back pocket. I gave her a slight nod and my stomach went sour when she grinned at me. *Shit. She's winning,* I thought and silently scolded myself for even entertaining her insanity.

"How about a person?"

This time, I couldn't keep myself contained. "A person?" I repeated, the stupid parrot in me returning for yet another session of copycat.

"How about Bert? I'll give you Bert."

Involuntarily, my head snapped back as if I'd been slapped and my eyes blinked so many times, she must have thought I was having a stroke. "B… Bert," I stammered. "What do you mean, 'you'll give him to me'?"

"Just what I said. You're in on the big picture of camp life, right Dawn? Normals get paired up with Normals so they can make sweet little Normal babies to keep fighting the good fight. Testers can't have babies, so they're paired with other Testers since procreation isn't an option. Shooting blanks on that side of camp, remember? But, for you, in your case, I'd make an exception. You get Bert. I keep your secret about being a Tester. Hell, at the new camp, we'll tell everyone that he's a Normal too. You guys get a nice tent to yourselves. Life goes on. A very good life when you have a good man by your side, might I add." She smiled, quite pleased with her genius little deal.

My mind was blown for several horrific reasons. *How did she know that I liked Bert? I barely knew! What the hell just happened?* My swirling thoughts were interrupted by a flash of sunlight as Ryan strode back into the tent unannounced. Still all piss and vinegar, clearly. His cocky nature was off-putting to me, but Miranda seemed unbothered by it.

Miranda gave him a quick nod and he stopped just short of the table, a grey blob of masculine energy at the edge of my peripheral vision. "Dawn," she said, refocusing me on the offer at hand, "take some time. Think about what we've discussed. We leave tomorrow night at dusk. I expect you to be there."

I stood carefully and tested my vibrating legs for their ability to walk and then slunk out of Miranda's tent, feeling much like the proverbial dog with his tail between his legs. *What the hell am I going to do? I really want all of those things. But the cost is so high. Lives.* My friend's lives were literally in my hands. The only thing I knew for certain was that I needed to decide: was I a team player of Miranda's Camp Reject or Riverbend?

20

After leaving Miranda's lair, I hid in my tent for a while to rest, but instead of napping, the conflict of what I'd been asked and offered sped through my mind in a continuous race that never crowned a winner. I decided that before I made any decisions, I needed to speak with Bert. After all, he was a big part of this, even if he didn't know it yet. The idea of him being promised to me was nice. The kiss we shared in this very spot was amazing. But was that stolen kiss enough to allow myself to do the unthinkable?

I also tried to reason a way for all the kids to come with us, even the sick ones. But I knew the conditions at camp were not good enough for them. Electricity was non-existent, so life-preserving ventilators or other medical machines would be unusable, obsolete in our minimal way of life. *Simple as that,* I thought, quoting Miranda's easy way of looking at this impossible situation.

On my way to the Testers' side of the camp, muddled, confusing thoughts raced through my mind. This time I didn't worry if I was being followed or spied on. Miranda had probably already anticipated that I'd go talk to Bert and could already predict with reasonable accuracy what we'd discuss and eventually decide to do. She'd win and I'd have to live my life knowing that I was a murderer of ailing children for the promise of larger rations and the attention of a cute boy. *Sick. I'm sick,* I thought.

I spotted Bert sitting on a log next to a small fire. He was surrounded by other guys and my birthmark burned uncomfortably from a fresh wave of embarrassment that washed through my body and over my damaged face as I walked up to them.

"Hey, B. Hi, guys," I said and gave them all a little wave. I trained my eyes on Bert and said, "Can we talk?" Instantly, I cringed, hating that I sounded so… average. A murmur went through the group as if Bert was in trouble. *Clearly all these guys watched too much daytime television,* I thought, remembering that the line 'can we talk' was always the start of a fight on any drama.

Bert stood, his face bright, obviously enjoying the attention from his crew. *Maybe my attention too?* I thought as another wave of heat passed over my face, which set my imperfection to throb at level ten.

Bert ambled over to me. His cocky manner reminded me a bit of the traitorous Riverbend security guard and I wondered wildly if Miranda had put some extra testosterone in their breakfast to get them ready for the mission to come.

"Hey, Dawny-girl," said Bert. He grabbed my hand and led me to a private spot on the edge of the camp. He sat on a log big enough for both of us and patted its mossy bark.

I sat next to him and was quiet, unsure of how to start.

"I take it you spoke with Miranda?" he asked, kindly giving me a prompt to get this awkward conversation started.

I nodded.

"You going?" he asked, his eyes a mix of curiosity and caution.

"I don't know yet," I admitted.

Bert looked down at the ground and picked up a small stick. He began tracing shapes in the mushy dirt and pine needles. His pale cheeks developed a crimson hue from his efforts and, still looking at the ground, he asked, "She tell you I was going?"

I nodded. Even though I'd worried about him getting hurt physically, I'd only been thinking about myself from a mental standpoint. It had never crossed my mind that he'd go and that it might be hard for him to deal with the consequences too. My eyes welled with tears.

Dropping the stick, Bert brushed his hand on his pants and put it on my cheek, wiping away my tears with his thumb. "Don't cry, Dawny-girl. It'll be okay."

I sniffed and pulled away from his hand. The heat from his skin made my birthmark pulsate with every heartbeat and I wanted to focus without the annoying distraction.

"What else did she tell you?" he asked, his eyes trained on my wet, damaged face.

"She promised me things." I said and hated the way it sounded as it passed through my lips, as if I was easily bought.

"Me too," he said and shrugged as if it was a normal way to do business out here.

"Like what?" I asked, suddenly wondering how much of my deal he already knew.

"An upgrade. I'd get to be a Normal at the next camp. Better tent. More food. That sort of stuff," he said and picked up the stick again. This time he broke it into smaller pieces and rolled one between his hands as if warming them with the spongy wood.

I nodded. "Me too. She knew I was a Tester from those stupid files. Did she tell you that?"

"Nope."

I searched his face and believed him. "Did she promise you anything else? Anyone else?"

Bert's brow furrowed. "Anyone else? What's that mean?"

Suddenly it dawned on me: *Did Miranda know about me and Bert from Bert? Was that kiss last night his part to make this deal work out? Does he even like me? Or, was he working an angle for Miranda?* Heat surged in my chest, crawled up my neck, and burned beneath my birthmark. I imagined it was pounding so much now that Bert could probably see it move if he would look at me. *Why isn't he looking at me?*

"Why'd you kiss me last night?" I demanded.

Bert looked up at me and smiled although his eyes showed his confusion. "I wanted to," he said and this time, I saw the blush wash over his face.

Pink's a good color for him, I thought involuntarily and shook my head to regain focus. "Nobody put you up to it?"

"What the hell are you talking about, Dawn? I've loved you since I left Riverbend. You were so adorable, but I was so much older… it wouldn't have been right. But you're a woman now… ahh, forget it." He threw his shard of stick into the ferns.

"You liked me back then?" I asked, incredulous.

He nodded and looked away again.

"B. I liked you too. But I thought you looked at me like a little sister."

Bert shook his head. "Does any of this matter? We're together now, aren't we?" His dark green eyes were filled with hope and fear.

I smiled and nodded. "Yes. You were part of my deal with Miranda," I admitted and hoped he wouldn't be mad. A brief thought of Sally popped into my mind, but I brushed it away.

"Me?"

"You."

"Hmmm. Sounds like a good deal to me," said Bert with a hollow chuckle.

I laughed quietly too and grabbed his hand. It was hot, despite being hidden in the shadows of the tall pines that surrounded the camp.

"What am I going to do?" I asked him, suddenly serious. Clearly, I already had him, but I'd have to do something horrible to keep him.

"I'll follow your lead, Dawny-girl. Whatever you wanna do, I'm in." He leaned in and kissed me square on the lips.

I hadn't expected the kiss, but I managed to fake it enough to enjoy it. We melted into each other and for a moment the world was quiet. Dire, life changing questions were momentarily on hold and we were going to be okay.

21

The mood at dinner was quite jovial considering the circumstances of what was to come. Excess perishable food was doled out so there'd be less of it to move. According to Miranda's evening speech, Riverbend would be a treasure trove anyway, so it made sense to fill up so everyone would have plenty of energy both for the raid and for the big push toward Florida.

I sat with Sally on the Normals' side of the large fire and caught Bert staring at me a few times from across the flickering flames. I tried to be game and smile back at him, but my heart was aching. With the mess I was dealing with, I'd selfishly forgotten that Sally's feelings were involved here too. She also loved Bert and was bound to be hurt when she found out he'd been promised to me. *Well, promised to me if I agree to go along with Miranda and the other Testers on the raid,* I remembered, my soul sinking into despair at the mere thought of it.

Dinner broke and I'd hardly eaten a thing. Sally took notice and encouraged me to stuff my pockets with fruit. She was busy shoving an apple into her pocket when Bert came over to say goodnight.

"Hey, ladies," he said, addressing both of us, obviously trying to act casual.

"Hey, Bert," said Sally. Her face blushed when she realized she'd been caught stealing the apple by Bert's keen gaze.

He nodded toward her contraband and patted his own pocket. "I got two," he said and winked at her.

She beamed at him and then at me, clearly relieved that he wouldn't tell on her.

"Heading to bed?" he asked us, but his eyes were trained on me.

I nodded and tried my best to smile at him although I was certain that I looked sullen and withdrawn.

"Well, good night then, Dawny-girl," he said and turned away.

"Night, Bert," yelled Sally as he disappeared into the shadows. Without turning, he lifted his arm, gave her a wave and was gone. Sally grabbed my arm and turned us toward our tent. "Isn't this an exciting time, Dawn?"

"Exciting how?" I asked. My brow furrowed involuntarily.

"You know. Moving, hitting Riverbend… all of it." She gave my arm a squeeze.

"I don't think that's quite how I'd describe it," I started but decided I was too exhausted to explain why I wasn't as giddy as she was.

"Is it because of Riverbend?" she asked, as if reading my mind.

I sighed and leaned into her a bit. "Yeah. I have friends there still. My best friend, Wendy, is on a pump and I'm worried she won't make it if they cut the power." My eyes welled with tears and I couldn't go on.

Sally nodded beside me and I felt her stiffen as if ready to support more of my weight should I need it. When we neared our tent, Sally steered me toward the back of it and whispered, "You have options, Dawn."

"Options?" I repeated, my annoying pet parrot returning.

Sally nodded. "Have you thought about your options, you know, if you don't go? I'm sure Miranda promised you the moon, but what if you turned her down? Do you really think she'd kick you out?" Sally's eyes were wide, and filled with girlish hope and helpfulness. It broke my heart a little to know that I hadn't been offered the moon, just her boyfriend.

I opened my mouth to respond, but spied a shadow moving on the side of the tent well within earshot. I made eyes at Sally to shut her up and then tiptoed to the corner to see who was trying to quietly eavesdrop on our private conversation.

As I rounded the corner, I was unsurprised to find Queenie crouched down doing a terrible job of pretending to straighten the side of the tent, as if it was her nightly routine to check the spikes and push them into the earth if they'd popped out a bit, and with her bare hands no less.

"What's up, Queenie?" Sally asked from behind me.

Queenie stood and her eyes roved over our conspiring faces. "Nothing. Just… looking at something. I'm good." She walked away, quickly disappearing into the shadows.

"Shit. That was close," whispered Sally.

I nodded and wondered how long Queenie had been squatting there and how much she'd overheard. *I guess I'll know if Miranda comes marching over here or summons me to her tent,* I thought and went to lie down. After settling into my bed, I closed my eyes and wished this stressful night would end and the answers to my problems would come to me in my dreams.

22

The answers I desperately needed did not come to me in my dreams. As a matter of fact, sleep itself was hard to come by. I think I dozed for a bit after everyone had clambered in for the night, but a hot wash of panic overtook me shortly afterward and I lay in a slick of sweat for at least an hour before I heard a slight rustling at the door to our tent.

I squinted into the dark and saw a figure make its way inside. I watched as the figure glanced at each of the sleeping women and then fixed its eyes on me. I huddled into my blankets for a moment until my eyes focused on the face… then the smile. I waved at him. Silently, he nodded and backed out of the tent while I peeled myself from my wad of damp of blankets and tiptoed outside. Success was mine and I had barely made a sound.

"Hey, B," I whispered when we were clear of the tent and far enough away to keep from waking anyone else.

"Hi, Dawny-girl," he breathed and took my hand.

"What's up?" I asked and prayed that he didn't sense how nervous I was despite my clammy palm and my obnoxious heart which was pounding like Animal on his drum kit.

"I needed to see you… to speak to you."

I nodded and noted that there was still a glimmer shining in his eyes despite his serious tone.

With his eyebrows raised, he blurted, "Let's get out of here."

My brow furrowed. Did he want some privacy to make some moves on me or did he mean leave as in *leave*? I was suddenly rendered mute at the mere prospect of either situation.

As if sensing my confusion, he squeezed my hand and put his free hand under my chin and lifted my face to his. "Let's go find your dad," he added quietly.

I shook my head. *He's risking way too much for me*, I thought. "What about Miranda?"

"Screw Miranda." He grinned. It was boyish and charming despite his strong language.

"Is that our only option?" I remembered Sally's interrupted thoughts from earlier in the evening. Maybe there was still a chance I could talk my way out of going. But, in that case, even if I wasn't there, the raid would still go down and Wendy would still be cut off from her life support.

He nodded and his eyes glinted in the moonlight. "We could sabotage the raid somehow, but that would just put off the inevitable. We could go back to the police station and turn Miranda in, but then everyone at camp would go down with her. I think we should find your dad and tell him what we know. He might be able to stop her and at least spare the Normals who were left behind from being picked up. Eventually they'd figure out something went wrong and could move the camp on their own. I'm sure a new leader would emerge. Maybe even that little wench, Queenie."

I cringed. The idea of Queenie leading anyone was horrible, but it was better than the alternative of my friends at Riverbend suffocating slowly in their beds. "When do we go?"

"No better time than the present."

"Right now? With nothing?"

"Just the apples in my pocket," he said and patted his coat.

I took a deep breath and was about to nod when the snap of a fallen twig grabbed our attention. We both turned toward the sound and squinted into the dark. I hoped it was a woodland creature doing its nightly business, but it sounded big. Human big.

Bert's hand tightened on mine and for the first time, I sensed he was afraid—afraid that we'd be thwarted before we even got our plan off the ground. As the interloper approached, the silhouette was illuminated by the bright moonlight and it appeared to be a female with hair blowing in the slight autumn breeze. My stomach lurched at the prospect of it being Queenie. Maybe her spying had become more brazen.

Bert released his grip on my hand when the culprit was in full view. We both exhaled and my racing heart eased a bit.

"Sally," I breathed into the crisp air. "What're you doing out here?" A wave of guilt washed over me when I realized she'd just caught us alone, together, in the woods. Her man and her best friend. It was one of the oldest clichés around.

Sally approached us and scanned our faces as if trying to confirm what she'd seen and overheard in the dark by reading the guilt in our eyes. I shifted my weight away from Bert so our pose didn't look as intimate as it had a moment ago.

"Take me with you," said Sally, her eyes filled with tears and urgency.

"Did you hear us?" asked Bert. I could see him searching the tree line for others.

"I heard Dawn leave the tent. I wasn't really asleep yet," she admitted, her blush apparent even in the dark.

"You want to leave with us?" I asked, making sure she understood it was now or never and now meant without anything.

She nodded. "I hate it here and I couldn't bear being here without the both of you," she said and started to softly cry.

Bert wrapped his arms around her shaking shoulders and whispered into her ear. "Of course, Sally. You're always welcome."

I nodded and patted her back. "We wouldn't want to go without you either," I said and hoped she knew how much I meant it.

Bert released Sally and she took a reluctant step back. "Which way is out?" she asked.

Bert pointed toward the Testers' side of camp. Slowly, quietly, we wove through the tents of slumbering people and smoldering campfires and skulked our way to safety. Once we arrived at the border of the camp, we looked up at the guard tower and were relieved to see that the appointed guard was fast asleep. His head was tucked between two rungs of the makeshift wall to support his neck, and his grumbling snores were audible from where we crouched in the shadows.

Satisfied that we were safe, Bert waved us on and we disappeared into the dark forest. We would have hours to escape the trees and make our way back to town to find my dad. Despite being enveloped by the gloom of the woods and having an overwhelming sensation of nervous energy swirling inside me, I knew this was the right plan. Correction: the only plan. My dad would stop the raid at Riverbend and I would finally have a family—a family who apparently wanted me and who had never wanted to throw me away.

We picked our way through the maze of trees and ferns. Despite repeatedly slipping on pine needles and tripping over

invisible tree roots, I smiled, and knew that I was on my way
to freedom. And, on my way to being… wanted.

23

The night gradually gave way to the breaking day and we were still scurrying through the woods like confused squirrels. Picking our way through a dark forest with only a single flashlight that Bert had thankfully brought with him was a lot harder than I had anticipated. We'd gotten turned around several time and made horrible time.

When the trees thinned to ferns and a scourge of sunlight struck my face, I knew we were close to the road—the very road I'd been on with Tommy and his flying machine. I wondered what Bert's plan was for when we got to this point. Three people would not fit very comfortably on a motorcycle, I surmised as we reached the pile of cut pine boughs.

s I waited for Sally to catch up to Bert and I, I surveyed the clearing beyond the trees and was happy to see that it was free of humans: Normals, Testers or otherwise.

Bert stood next to me, panting a bit from our jaunt through the woods and he cocked his ear toward the direction from which we had just come. "Did you hear that?" he asked me, his brow furrowed.

I quieted my own heavy breathing and listened. Between the occasional squawks from irritated birds I thought a heard a girl. "Is that Sally?" I asked Bert although we both knew the answer.

Bert grabbed my hand and we rushed back into the trees. We paused occasionally to listen for the voice again. It grew louder with every footstep we took back into the forest.

Finally, we happened upon Sally. She was sitting on a log and holding her ankle with both hands. She was rocking back and forth, and had a pained grimace plastered on her face.

"Oh, thank God," she whimpered when she saw us come into view. "I've been calling forever," she added with a well-timed sniff.

My stomach clenched with guilt for not hearing her or even noticing that she'd fallen behind. After seeing that she was going to be okay, my guilt was quickly replaced with stress knowing that this delay might result in getting us caught before we even had a chance to save the kids at Riverbend.

"What happened?" asked Bert. He knelt at her side and pried her hands away from her ankle. He inspected it with knowing eyes and gentle hands. A pang of jealousy washed through me and I beat it away with a fresh wave of guilt when I saw the concern on his face.

"Is it bad?" asked Sally. She winced when he touched a dark purple spot above her ankle bone with his thumb.

"It looks broken," said Bert.

"Shit," Sally groaned. She rested her head on his shoulder. Jealousy came crawling back, and settled deep in my chest. I tried and failed to ignore it.

"We're almost there," I said and waved toward the road. I stopped talking when Bert shot me look that could only mean 'shut up.'

Bert shook his head. His face looked as though he was completing a complicated math problem. Finally, he looked me directly in the eyes. "She's got to go back," he stated firmly.

"You go. I'll make it back or someone will come through here eventually and find me. Go. I'll be fine."

Sally's tone was filled with a false sense of bravery and I knew what Bert was going to say next before he even said it. *I'm going to have to do this alone,* I thought. My belly was heavy with mixed emotions of fear, urgency and that ugly little jealous fellow who was growing larger and denser by the moment.

"I'm taking you back, Sally." Bert tucked Sally's hair behind her ear and stared steadfastly into her eyes. "There's no other way. Dawn will have to go on alone." He turned away from Sally who was clearly relieved at the change of plans, and said, "Can you do it, Dawn?"

I nodded, although I had serious doubts about my chances of success. Before I could say anything, Bert continued, "This actually might be a good thing. With three of us gone, that might tip off Miranda to our plan. If Sally and I turn back up, if they've even noticed we're gone yet, we'll be buying you more time to get to your dad's. Plus, this injury will cause a big hubbub in camp so everyone will be even more distracted. Sally and I will have to come up with a lie for how this happened." He nodded at Sally.

My imperfection prickled with heat at the depth of her pleasure in being the center of attention and for taking Bert away from me in such dramatic fashion. I secretly wondered if she'd done it on purpose. If she'd hurt herself to gain his attention, and to keep him from leaving and being with me.

Bert turned to me and swept me into an embrace. Although being so close to him was comforting, it almost felt sad, as if he was saying goodbye forever instead of goodbye for now. Then, I thought about what I was supposed to do. I'd go live with my family and Bert would be moving on with the camp or getting arrested at Riverbend. Either way, our time together was coming to a premature end. The very thought of being separated from him made me want to quit, and go back and let the whole Riverbend thing happen as planned. *Wendy might already be dead*, I rationalized as I pressed my face into Bert's chest. The heat from his body seared into my imperfection in a way that was almost intoxicating.

Bert released me and tenderly kissed my lips. *Another goodbye*, I thought and fought tears from sprouting from the corners of my eyes. I pushed all the negative thoughts away as best I could and watched as Bert picked Sally up in his strong arms and turned in the direction of camp.

"Good luck, Dawn," said Bert. "You can do this." Sally waved at me over his shoulder. On her face was a smug grimace, as if she'd run a physically exhausting and painful marathon, but won first prize anyway.

I watched them until I could no longer see the flash of movement from their intertwined bodies. When they were officially gone, I finally let the tears flow. *This is not how it's supposed to go*, I lamented. I sat on Sally's log to catch my breath and formulate a new plan, a plan that involved just me.

24

I spent a few minutes cursing Sally's weak ankles and my
bad luck, and finally pulled myself together enough to decide
what to do next. I really wanted to see Bert again so I had to
do everything I could to stop the raid at Riverbend. I hoped
that if I told my dad the plan in time, he could pull a
switcheroo and instead, have the police raid Camp Reject
before they had a chance to bring Miranda's hammer down
on Riverbend. The only problem with that plan was that all
my friends in the camp could be arrested, including Bert and
Sally and Tommy, too, unless he was at work. But, I
reasoned, since his motorcycle was still in the brush, he
probably had the day off and would also be picked up if the
camp was compromised.

Shit, I thought as I made my way back to the tree line. I
eyed Tommy's motorcycle, still hidden away and wondered
for a moment if I should take it. But, the little nagging voice
in my head reminded me that I didn't even know how to
drive a car, let alone a motorcycle. I would have to get back
to town another way.

After a last survey for prying eyes, I edged out of the
trees and walked on the road's shoulder toward town. The
road was pretty desolate which was disconcerting. I felt

exposed and alone all at the same time, as if everyone and no one were watching me. The ones who were ogling me were no doubt planning horrible things for me. I questioned if I'd even have the guts to flag someone down for a ride should a car pass by. *They're probably dangerous*, I thought, remembering yet another television program that showed how hitchhikers are targeted as easy victims, ripe for the taking.

I walked for at least an hour before any vehicle came. The first one was a white, souped-up pickup truck with obnoxiously oversized tires. The driver slowed next to me and from the corner of my eye I saw the window silently slide down. The man behind the driver's seat called to me as he rolled to a stop. Reluctantly, I had turned toward the open window to answer his shout when he suddenly hit the gas and drove off. I figured he was repulsed by my imperfection as it visibly throbbed in the mid-morning heat.

The second vehicle, another truck, didn't even bother to slow. It sped by and spewed me with little rocks and left a trail of dust in the air that made me cough and left grit in my teeth.

Another hour passed and a recognizable sound came tearing up behind me at a high rate of speed. *A motorcycle*, I thought as the sound registered in my dehydrated brain. For a brief moment my heart stopped, and I was gripped with fear.

I had the urge to run into the trees and hide, safely camouflaged behind the lush ferns. But the motorcycle came up so fast behind me that by the time I'd formulated my escape plan, the helmeted driver was already off his bike and striding toward me.

Fear surged through my body in a dizzying wave. I was rendered inert. My aching feet shook in my sneakers and were stuck in the dirt like garden stakes labeled with Nike instead of lettuce or carrots. The driver removed his helmet and a familiar mouth grinned at me. "B!" I yelled and threw myself onto him. My body trembled with relief and exhaustion.

"Dawny-girl," he purred, holding me tight against his chest. "You didn't think I'd let you do this by yourself, did you?"

Tears flowed freely from my eyes and when I looked into his face a warm rush of gratefulness and love washed over me. I grabbed his rough cheeks with both hands and kissed him hard on his thick, warm lips.

He reciprocated and we stood on the side of the road, kissing like fools for what seemed like forever. Finally, the spell was broken by the sound of an approaching engine. Bert handed the helmet to me. "Put this on," he ordered. He grabbed my hand and guided me toward the waiting motorcycle.

The car passed by us without slowing and Bert's shoulders fell as if a thousand pounds had fallen off them.

"How'd you get Tommy's bike?" I asked, wondering if he'd stolen it or if Tommy was privy to the details of our great escape.

Bert's once cheerful face was suddenly grim. "Tommy knows. He noticed we were gone because Queenie reported your absence to Miranda."

"Miranda knows?" My mouth hung open like an old barn door on its last rusted hinge.

ert nodded. "Sally and I going back to camp was the best thing that could've happened. I told Miranda that you caught Sally and I… well, doing stuff, and you ran off. I said Sally and I went looking for you, but then Sally got hurt so we went back. So, all she thinks is that it's a love triangle thing." He blushed, as if the mere idea of admitting all of that to Miranda was too much for his macho image.

My mind whirled and I began to pepper him with questions. "Was she pissed? Did she believe you guys?"

Bert held up a hand to slow my interrogation. He nodded and swallowed hard. "Sally and I made sure she believed it."

I squinted at him. "How'd you do that?" I asked. The little green guy in my chest started punching things.

"Come on, Dawn. Please don't make me tell you. Let's just say that she believed us and we're in trouble because Testers and Normals shouldn't mix in such a manner." He blushed again and I worried that Miranda would be sick enough to make them prove their love in front of an audience.

I crossed my arms over my chest and tried to soften my expression, knowing he'd done whatever he did with Sally for me. Correction, for us. "Fine. Do you trust that Tommy won't tell anyone the truth?" I asked, changing the subject to something less horrifying.

Bert nodded. "Tommy has a thing for you so he was cool with me taking his bike and going after you. Miranda wanted me to find you and bring you back anyway so it's not like he had a choice. The bike's communal property, but Normals get dibs if they have a job to get to."

I shook my head. "Tommy's with Queenie. There's no way he likes me that way," I insisted.

Bert shrugged. "He and Queenie are on the rocks; they have been for quite a while. She was talking about going home."

My mouth dropped open. *How had I missed all of this perfectly good gossip?* I oddly started to miss good old Camp Reject.

"It's okay if you're flattered by Tommy liking you. He's a good guy," said Bert. He looked away, over my head and I saw his Adam's apple bob up and down as he swallowed hard again.

My brow furrowed. "Not as good as you are, B," I said and grabbed his cheeks again.
"I want to be with you and no one else," I said and pecked him on the lips.

He smiled down at me and my knees nearly buckled. His warm, green eyes and satisfied smile were the most beautiful things I'd seen since leaving Riverbend.

Another engine whirring around a bend in the road broke our tender moment and urgency took over. "We gotta get outta here. You never know if Miranda would send others to find you," said Bert. He pushed a spare helmet onto his head, straddled the motorcycle and kicked it to life with his foot.

I climbed behind him onto the vibrating motorcycle and wrapped my arms around his trim waist. He got the bike into gear and we took off toward town. Inside my helmet I smiled, grateful for his help and knowing that since we had the motorcycle, we were just a few minutes away from changing everything.

25

I directed Bert to turn into Tommy's diner. On the drive, I decided that it was probably best to have him wait for me there. I'd seen enough after school specials to know that a man tooling up to a father's house with his barely legal girlfriend on the back would lead to the beginning of a very long evening. Not to mention the fact that said father was a cop. That added a whole other layer to this already stressful situation.

After explaining my thoughts to Bert, he reluctantly agreed to let me walk the few blocks to my parent's house. I'd left him in the same booth I'd sat in when I'd met Tommy. *Full circle, some would say,* I thought as I watched him stir a third sugar packet into his coffee through the large front window.

Realistically, I needed the short walk from the diner to coordinate my thoughts. I had been told that my dad wanted to meet me, but the little nagging voice in my head advised me differently. She also told me that it was possible that dad would have open arms, but my mother and my sister could be another story. And, maybe, my sister didn't even know about me. I could be stirring up a shit storm just by showing up. Then, the long-lost daughter would get to drop the bomb that she'd been hanging out in the woods with an illegal camp of lawbreakers who were going to raid a government facility and leave dead children in their wake.

As I neared the house, I paused for a moment next to the tall arborvitae trees that lined their neighbor's property. I tipped my head toward the sky and let the warm autumn sun wash over my face. Eyes still closed, I breathed in through my nose and exhaled from between pursed lips. I imagined a passerby would think I was doing some odd type of yoga right here on the sidewalk. The errant thought made me smile and gave me a boost of confidence. I was ready to ring the doorbell and meet my family.

Slowly, I stepped from the safety of the trees and was in front of their house. A freshly washed police car was parked in the driveway, with swirling bubbles still visible on the dark pavement beneath. I was happy that it was Saturday and hoped that a weekend day might increase the odds of everyone being home together. I turned onto their brick path that led to the main door and took a second to straighten my shirt. As I tugged at the back hem to adjust it properly, something hard struck at my wrist. With a sharp jerk, I was turned away from the house and spun around in a blurred flash of fabric, muscle and a whiff of men's cologne. I opened my mouth to protest, but the searing pain from my bent wrist was so intense no noise came out.

My body was twisted and the angle of the sun momentarily blocked the face of the person who was hurting me. Confusion swirled through my mind as it ran through a possible list of attackers.

Finally, in my squirming attempt to get loose, I was bent forward enough to see the bearded face of Ryan the Riverbend security guard. Miranda's henchman's face was strained as he tried to contain me while I continued to wrestle against his vice like grip.

Despite my valiant efforts to free myself, he managed to grab my other wrist and held both of them tight in front of his chest. He pulled me close to him, and twisted my hands right under his chin. His hot, acrid breath burned in my nostrils. A flitting image of a wolf in a nature special I had seen flashed across my field of vision and I remembered that some animals would chew off their own leg in a desperate attempt to get themselves free from a trap. Although the idea of gnawing off my own arm didn't appeal to me, the idea of giving his arm a good chewing did and I leaned forward to bite at one of his meaty hands.

"Shit, Dawn! Cut it out," he growled as I nipped at his flesh.

"LET. ME. GO," I ordered.

Ryan ignored my demand and stretched my hands even higher. He yanked them over my head, which painfully strained every muscle in my upper arms. He turned toward the road and started dragging me from my parent's front yard. The irony of being kidnapped on a cop's front lawn wasn't lost on me as my arms burned from the abuse.

Ryan managed to drag me back to the sidewalk and toward a grey sedan with a Riverbend decal on the side that he had parked a little way up the street.

As we neared the car, the backseat opened and Bert jumped out.

"Shit, Ryan, I told you I should get her," he said. His tone ping ponged between exasperation and worry.

"Help me, Bert," I pleaded to him although my brain screamed about his obvious betrayal. Pain seared from my shoulders and upper arms and radiated into my neck and back.

"Move," Ryan grunted at Bert as he dragged me past him. Ryan pinched both of my wrists into one of his giant paws and squeezed them together. In one swift motion, he put his free hand on the back of my head, released my hands and shoved me by my cranium into the black abyss of his sedan. I did an Olympic caliber dive onto the backseat and landed with a thud on my aching wrists, deftly averting a face plant on a metal seatbelt buckle. Bert quickly jumped in after me and slammed the door. Ryan climbed into the driver's seat and shifted the idling car into gear.

Out of breath and unable to speak, I righted myself and glared at the back of Ryan's head. Then, I turned my angry heat onto Bert. He grabbed one of my hands and inspected it for damage. I pulled it from his grasp and angrily swiped at the hair that had become stuck to my sweaty temples and cheeks in my struggle to get away, peeling it away from my throbbing imperfection like layers from an onion.

Bert looked at me with eyes that told me to remain calm, but that moment had clearly passed after I'd been so rudely and unexpectedly man-handled by Ryan.

I glared at Bert and, voice shaking, I demanded, "What the hell's going on?"

Bert's shoulders slumped and he nodded toward Ryan. "I'll let him explain," he said and turned away from me to stare out the window at the colorful homes flashing by.

26

After driving in silence for ten minutes, my initial questions ignored, the welcoming neighborhoods faded into a constant blur of trees and desolation. Finally, Ryan pulled over to the side of the road. He turned in the seat and set his dark, authoritative eyes on me.

I stiffened and shivered involuntarily. My sweat from our struggle had cooled and the air conditioning that blew on me from a vent over my head was turning me into a frozen fish stick, common fare at Riverbend.

Noticing my convulsions, Bert offered to put his arm over my shoulders to help warm me, but I declined his offer with a curt shake of my head. I still had no idea what was happening and I didn't know if I could trust him and I definitely didn't want to reward him with backseat snuggling if he was a dirty, double-crossing liar.

Question swirled in my mind as Ryan's beady eyes roved over my ruined face. Why did he stop me from seeing my family? Was Bert working with Ryan? Did Miranda send him? Did she know of our plan?

Ryan rubbed his rusty beard and exchanged a glance with Bert. It made my stomach turn to see them have some sort of silent collusion. It broke my heart to think that I couldn't or shouldn't trust Bert. Clearly, he'd kept their relationship a secret from me and that was damning.

Ryan cleared his throat and his eyes shifted back to me. I squinted at him and bit my lip to keep from spewing obscenities that would make a sloshed sailor blush. "Sorry about the dust up back there, Dawn," he said. His apology seemed sincere although hearing my name come from his mouth made my skin prickle, as if it wanted to jump out the window and slither away.

Bert tried to grab my hand. I stuck it under my thigh to keep it from him. His shoulders slumped again and I sensed he knew that he'd royally screwed up.

I eyed Ryan and nodded, prompting him to continue.

"I followed you guys to the diner and hoped to stop you there, but I was too late. Bert wanted to get you, but I had to be quick, before you did anything stupid."

"Before *I* did anything stupid," I huffed. *This guy's a piece of work*, I thought and fought the urge to bite him again.

"Stupid might not be the best choice of words," he acknowledged, "but it was imperative that I stop you before involving your father."

I gulped and eyes bulging, I turned to Bert. His eyes reflected his guilt, as if he'd spilled our whole plan to Ryan in the few moments he was alone with him in the coffee shop.

As if reading my thoughts, Ryan continued, "Don't blame Bert. I already knew the plan. I found Sally crying in the woods on my way into camp and she sang like a canary. You can't blame her, though. She's wrapped around Miranda's thumb. Guess that shouldn't be a surprise since they're sisters and all," he said. He shook his head and grinned as if he'd told a humdinger of a joke.

"S… sisters?" I stammered. *Boy, I've got a lot to learn about this world*, I thought as I reviewed my relationship with Sally in my mind and pondered how much I'd revealed to her over the short time I'd known her. *And Bert,* I thought, *did Miranda want to give Bert to me to keep her sister from having him even though she knew it will hurt her?* Brutal.

Bert's usually healthy complexion paled after hearing the news that Sally and Miranda were sisters. I imagined that he, too, had told Sally some things that he was regretting about now.

Ryan's grin widened at our obvious discomfort. "Guess you hadn't figured that out yet, huh?" He smirked and the urge to bite him on his fat hand swelled within my chest.

My voice flat and cold, I said, "No, I wasn't privy to that information."

"Shit. That Miranda, she's everywhere," said Ryan. He shook his head and slapped the seat, and his eyes were filled with respect for our fearless leader.

"So, why did you stop me? For Miranda?" Angry heat seethed under my birthmark and it started to throb making it harder to hide my irritation at his obvious admiration.

Ryan's grin disappeared and he sat straighter in his seat. He shook his head. "Not for her. For you."

Bert's eyes widened and he nodded at Ryan's comments as if he was buying them hook, line and sinker. *Clearly, he's gone insane or was easily brainwashed by this galoot*, I thought as I struggled to understand exactly what was happening.

"Miranda made contingencies," offered Bert.

"Contingencies?" I repeated, my pet parrot back and in full swish.

Bert opened his mouth to speak again, but Ryan held a hand up to stop him. "Let me tell her, Bert," he said firmly. Bert nodded curtly and sat back in his seat. Although his annoyance was clear, he trained his eyes on Ryan, his lips pursed.

"Miranda suspected that you might not agree with her plans for Riverbend so she's got it set up so your dad will take the fall for the raid."

My brow knitted at the ridiculousness of what I'd just been told. "What? How?"

Ryan shrugged. "Don't know. But I've seen her do it in the past. Before Riverbend, I worked security at a place up north and she was able to clear it out and then she got some director guy in charge to take the fall for it. I'm not sure if he even knew what happened. It was wham, bam, sayonara, man." He chuckled and his healthy respect for Miranda and her manipulative skills weighed heavy in the air around us.

"You knew Miranda from before?" asked Bert. Clearly that detail had been left out of their earlier conversation because he seemed as surprised as I was at that fact.

Ryan nodded. "I'm her inside guy, so to speak. I get the job at the facility on her radar and then I feed her info. Like those Riverbend files she had. Those were from me," he said and stopped short of thumping his chest like the ape that he was.

"So where does this leave us now?" I asked. "If I can't tell my dad, she'll still hit Riverbend and my friends will die. And, there's no guarantee that she won't frame him anyway."

Ryan squinted and he leaned over the backseat as if he needed privacy for his next statement. "She's not the only one with contingencies," he said. His eyes grew wide and he stared at us expectantly with unblinking, shark-like eyes.

"What does that mean?" asked Bert. He looked at me and I tilted my head slightly in agreement of his question although my heart was still unwilling to give him an inch.

Ryan smirked and licked his lips with a darting tongue. I was surprised it wasn't forked like the slimy snake that he was, although if he had a good plan, my opinion of him might have to change… maybe. "I've rearranged a few things that will probably make you pretty happy, Dawn," he said and awkwardly winked at me.

I had to fight the urge to gag at his overt indicator. His wink made me feel like I was a toddler who was just told that I could stay up an hour later than bedtime. It was as if he thought he'd just offered me a grand gesture and he was my magnanimous uncle who prided himself on being the 'fun' babysitter.

"Please explain," I urged when he didn't elaborate on Bert's question.

Clearly satisfied that he had us on edge, Ryan said, "I've got all the medical equipment hooked up to an internal generator so when Miranda cuts the power, the kids who need it will still have it. So, nobody has to die. Nobody has to be framed. Nobody gets hurt except for the pantries at Riverbend."

A flash of grateful heat washed through my entire body. My heart was suddenly warm, as if it had been removed, dipped in a bowl of hot water and then returned to my chest, repaired and whole and very pleased to be back in its fleshy home.

Ryan grinned. "Great idea, right?" he asked, clearly hoping for a pat on his hairy back.

Bert looked at me and could clearly see that I was overcome and was currently unable to speak as waves of relief pounded on my tense shores. I let him pull my hand from under my thigh. He gave it a squeeze and held it up to his cheek. He nodded his approval at Ryan and said, "It's perfect, Ryan. Just perfect."

***

After taking a few moments to pull myself together, I was finally able to properly thank Ryan for his good idea and implementation. By the way his face lit up, I sensed that he was hungry for praise, probably something stingy old Miranda wasn't super generous with, even if he was her 'inside guy,' a phrase that made my stomach turn from the obvious, poorly hidden innuendo.

"Where do we go from here?" Bert asked after I was finished with my thorough petting of Ryan's ego.

Ryan appeared confused for a moment and then his bearded mouth creased into a huge grin. "Back to camp. Miranda bought Sally and Bert's love triangle, Romeo and Juliet mumbo jumbo so we'll just go back. She knew Bert went after you and sent me after Bert. Round and round we go, huh, Dawn?" He winked at me again.

My empty stomach turned sour as my name oozed from his mouth like jelly squishing from the sides of an overstuffed sandwich. I felt sticky just hearing it pass through his bushy mug. Despite my distaste for all things Ryan, I managed a smile and my mood did ease a bit when Bert squeezed my hand in support of the new plan.

"You wanna go back, Dawn?" asked Bert, his eyebrows raised in speculation.

I shrugged. "We don't have a choice. I can't have Miranda bringing down my dad. He's got nothing to do with this. I'd hate to cause him and his family any more pain than they've already had."

"To camp we go," said Ryan. He put the car in gear and turned in the direction of Camp Reject.

"What about Tommy's motorcycle?" asked Bert when we sped by the diner and it quickly disappeared from view in the rear window.

"Don't need it," said Ryan, his eyes wide in the mirror. "Camp is being packed as we speak. It's just something extra we'd leave behind anyway."

Bert nodded and gave me a weak, tired smile. I hadn't noticed how worn down he was from the shenanigans of the day. I worried he'd be too exhausted for the raid tonight which might cause him to make a mistake and possibly get caught… or worse. Instead of voicing my concerns, I lifted his hand and held it to my marked cheek. I let the heat from his skin melt into my imperfection. I closed my eyes and wished that this simple moment could last forever.

27

The ride back to camp didn't take very long thanks to Ryan's lead foot. He ditched the car in a dirt turnout and we walked on foot through the forest back toward camp. Once we were on the perimeter, Ryan took off to find Miranda, no doubt to get his stroking from her for finding both of us and returning us in a timely fashion.

Once Bert and I breached the edge of camp, I was taken aback by the sparseness of it. The tents were gone, and the wooden structures that were once covered with tarps were now piles of discarded scrap wood. The fires were cold and without even a wisp of smoke. Errant stones that once neatly lined the large fire in the center were askew, as if kicked by busy feet and then left in disrepair.

The Testers who still milled about the camp seemed lost, as if there wasn't anything to do but wait.

Bert and I walked toward Miranda's tent and I couldn't help but feel like I was heading to my own execution. The only thing missing was dire music and townspeople with sad, tear-streaked faces and eyes filled with anguish for the futures that were going to be snuffed out forever by a hail of bullets or a hangman's noose.

We were ushered into Miranda's tent, the only one left, by a Tester I didn't recognize. Bert called him Marlboro and nodded a greeting as we passed by him.

After our eyes adjusted, I noted that the insides of Miranda's tent were picked clean. Even her trusty table was gone, probably packed away with the files on all of my Riverbend friends.

Ryan and Miranda stood together in the center of the tent and he was whispering into her ear. The gesture seemed quite intimate, despite the slanderous expression on Ryan's face when he saw us walk in.

I turned to Bert and rolled my eyes. Ryan was a putrid human being, but I knew I had to force my mouth shut in order to keep all of our secrets from being discovered by Miranda. I hated that Ryan had something over me. I detested it almost as much as I loathed the idea of going to Riverbend tonight.

Miranda gently pushed Ryan away from her ear and turned to Bert and me. She grinned and squinted at us and I immediately worried that Ryan hadn't kept up his end of the bargain. I squeezed Bert's hand and waited for the proverbial axe to fall.

"Well, hello there," said Miranda, her voice solicitous. "Having a hard time deciding, are we, Bert?" she asked and nodded toward our interlaced fingers.

Bert's grip on my hand released a tiny bit and I fought to hang onto his hand. I didn't want her to win, at least not with this. "Hey, Miranda," said Bert. His face burned crimson and his palm felt clammy in my solid grip.

"Miranda," I said and nodded at her. I was unable to say anything else. Angry heat swelled in my chest and I worried I'd say something stupid.

"So? Have you decided about tonight, Dawn? Are you coming with us?" asked Miranda although her eyes showed that she already knew my answer.

I nodded again. "Yes. I'll come."

"And, you've chosen Bert as part of our deal?" she continued, her expression smug, as if she hoped to upset Bert at the notion of us using him as currency.

"Yes. Bert and I will stay together at the next camp. As Normals. With all the benefits."

Miranda nodded. "And what about Sally? Kicking her to the curb?"

Bert glanced at me, his eyes pleading and desperate. He squeezed my hand and I knew he needed me to answer for him. "Sally'll be okay. I'm sure you, as her sister, can find her a suitable mate. She'll need a Normal anyway, correct?"

Miranda flinched and broke her laser beam gaze away from us long enough to glare at Ryan. He rubbed his scraggly beard and shrugged as if he didn't know how I knew Sally was her sister. After giving him a silent lashing with her steely eyes, she turned back to us. "Correct," she said and grinned. "Touché, Dawn. I knew you were special. We'll make sure to put your negotiation skills to good use at the new camp."

I nodded, although I didn't like the idea of having to work so closely with Miranda at the next encampment. Hell, I didn't even know if I'd be staying at the new place. Maybe I'd just wander back north after I was off her radar.

"Onto bigger and better things then?" asked Miranda.

Bert and I nodded. He gave my hand another squeeze in appreciation for helping him get off Miranda's giant gaff hook.

"Go grab some dinner. There's not much left, a few canned goods maybe. We're leaving at dusk." Miranda turned away from us and went back to Ryan. She ran her fingers through his hair in a way that made my stomach twist in revulsion.

Bert and I turned and scurried through the tent flaps and into the freedom of the cool air outside. We walked quickly toward a group of Testers crowded around a cardboard box half full of canned food. As we perused the remaining cans, tension from escaping our meeting unscathed left my body, but was quickly replaced with a sense of dread from the task still to come at dusk.

After the canned food was gone and just before the sun was extinguished from the early evening sky, the group of remaining Testers left the old camp behind. We wended our way through the forest and into a clearing that I'd never seen before.

Parked in the growing dark was an old, oversized box truck. It had been scrubbed of any identifying features and was quite stark against the backdrop of towering pine trees. As we filtered from the tree line, a Tester I sort of recognized climbed from the driver's seat and handed the keys to Miranda.

With a glint in her eye, Miranda dropped the keys into Ryan's waiting hand. She curled his fingers over the keys and for a moment, I thought she was going to kiss his closed fist, but thankfully, the wistfulness in her eyes was replaced with a determined glare as she surveyed her rag tag crew of thieves.

"The time is now," she said, her voice clear and strong. "We've been repressed, rejected and hated our whole lives. Tonight is our moment to shine and to show those who persecute us that we will not be silent. We will not go away. We will get our vengeance and we will not be ignored."

The crowd cheered softly. Miranda grinned and held up her hand to quiet the group. With a nod of her head, Ryan yanked on a small rope attached to the rear door of the truck and it effortlessly rolled up. The metallic sound echoed in the small clearing and I noticed how everyone's eyes darted around as if on high alert. They seemed to search the road and trees for an onslaught of police, FBI and SWAT teams.

Ryan started tapping men and women on their shoulders and nodded toward the back of the truck. Wordlessly, they climbed into the back and disappeared, one by one, into the black abyss.

Ryan came to Bert and I last. He put a hand on Bert's shoulder and rested it there, as if they were old buddies helping each other move. "Sorry—Miranda's got shotgun," he said and smirked at us.

As if I'd want to ride next to you anyway, I thought and shook my head at him and his clear delusion that he was a comedian and worthy of our company.

Bert shook Ryan's hand from his shoulder. He grabbed my hand and led me to the back of the truck. In one large step with his long, lithe legs, he climbed into the opening and vanished into the inky black. I surveyed the waist-high bumper and wondered how I'd climb up when a familiar hand shot out from the shadows and offered me a solution to my problem of being vertically challenged.

Bert yanked me up and I was able to climb into the back. From the moonlight, I could see flashes of white from my fellow Testers' shifting eyeballs. They quickly disappeared when the door behind us was rolled down and slammed shut. As the locking mechanism was engaged, a grating, metal on metal sound sent a shiver down my spine. We were stuck, with no way out. The raid was going to happen, whether we wanted it to or not.

***

The ride to Riverbend was bumpy. Without seats or seatbelts and sitting on the cold, metal floor, we were jostled to and fro on every bend in the road and at every stop light. I wondered if Ryan was driving badly on purpose to stir us up a bit, and to keep us frosty.

Bert held my hand the whole way. At one point, he nuzzled my neck. His soft hair brushed against my birthmark, sending waves of heat through my entire body. It was an odd time to be aroused, but teenagers in the dark can't be trusted, I mused as I felt his lips crawl up my neck and onto my cheek, desperately hunting for the warmth of my mouth.

When he hit his target, I kissed him back and then stopped him from taking it too far by giving him a slight shove with both hands on his muscular, heaving chest. Even with the pitch black surrounding us, I sensed eyes on us and I didn't want to give everyone a show before the main picture started—the main picture being the robbery of a government facility, of course.

The truck rumbled to a stop and we heard both front doors of the cab open and close. I took a deep breath and blew it out between pursed lips. Suddenly, I regretted not letting Bert get close to me. *If we get caught we might never have another chance to be together,* I thought and squeezed his hand and hoped he could sense my repentance with the gesture.

The lock on the back was disengaged and the door rolled up slowly, intentionally quieter than in the clearing when we'd loaded up.

Ryan and Miranda stood in front of us and from the lights shining from Riverbend they appeared to be milky, ghostly silhouettes. I fought the urge to giggle at the creepy image by clapping my free hand over my mouth. The giddy nervousness within me must be a coping mechanism, I reckoned as we all took our turns jumping from the back bumper of the box truck into the vacant parking lot behind the facility.

After we were all out of the truck, Miranda nodded her head and as if it were practiced, the Testers split into three groups. Bert and I didn't move. With our jaunt into town, we hadn't been around for her briefing so we weren't quite sure which group we were supposed to join.

Miranda addressed the leader of each group and reviewed her instructions with them. She even made them repeat her directions multiple times as if they were studying for a final exam.

The first and smallest group consisted of only three men. They were the electrical group. They were to mess with the power grid and get it shut down before the rest of us went inside.

The second and largest group was on kitchen and medical duty. They were to ransack the pantry for any dry edibles and then hit the medical unit for supplies that would be useful at our next campsite keeping a special eye out for wound care items, antibiotics, and gauze.

Bert and I were placed in the third group. Our job was to visit the dormitories and collect the children from Miranda's handwritten lists. We were instructed that only the children on the lists were permitted to leave with us. "No strays," she'd emphasized with a purposeful glare at me.

My heart was as heavy as a cinderblock when I read the lists. I recognized a handful of the names. Most of them were boys and of course, Wendy, my old roommate, was not included. *No surprise there*, I thought as I remembered that she was too weak to come with us anyway.

With a nod of her head, the electrical group vanished into the shadows. We were instructed to wait until the facility went black and then we were to move in at the entrances Miranda had marked on her building map which she'd unrolled and laid on the ground for us to review. Miranda was planning on staying at the truck with Ryan. They were going to monitor the air waves to listen to both Ryan's walkie talkie for news of our infiltration and the police scanner for word of our invasion. If we heard three sharp blows of the truck's horn, we were to beat feet and rendezvous back at the truck. Anyone who was delayed would be left behind.

After only a few minutes of waiting in the cool air, Riverbend went dark. It was almost breathtaking as the last wisps of sulfur swam away on the slight breeze and the darkness took over. Our eyes adjusted quickly and we made our way to the designated door.

At the dormitory's side door, Bert tried the handle and the automatic lock that had kept me safely inside for eighteen years was turned off. We were able to maneuver our way inside without issue. As a group, we decided to split into teams of two, each of us taking a floor. I'd purposefully taken floor two knowing it was Wendy's.

Bert and I stopped at each closed door and read the names on the placards by flashlight and compared it to the wish list provided to us by Miranda. We'd been instructed to tell the candidates who we were and ask him or her if they'd like to join us as if it was some honor. If they said yes, they could follow along silently in the hall until we were done and ready to leave. If they said no, we were to duct tape their mouths and zip tie their hands to their beds. Classy, right?

The first two boys who happened to be roommates both nodded their wide-eyed approval and tiptoed behind us in the hall. A smaller boy in the next room shook his head no so we taped and tied him and ignored his muffled pleas as we snuck out of his room.

My skin prickled in anticipation as I neared the last door in the hall. I instructed Bert to stay with the choo choo train of nervous children and let me go in alone since the name on the door was not on our list. I pointed at the placard and I watched Bert read the name and nod his approval, his eyes begging me to hurry the hell up.

I entered Wendy's room, my old room, and was struck with how it smelled exactly the same; like medical tape mixed with high octane disinfectant. I couldn't hear the gentle whooshing of her oxygen pump, but assumed that with the internal generator, maybe it would sound different.

I eyed my old bed and was relieved to see that it stood empty. A stained, bare mattress was all that was left of my residency here. I walked toward the dark lump in Wendy's bed and paused briefly when a wet sucking noise broke my concentration.

I cocked my head to hear better and heard the noise again. When the reason for the sound registered in my over stimulated brain, goose bumps rose on my arms and a small gasp escaped my throat.

I rushed to Wendy's side and scanned the machinery, too afraid to look at her face. Screens that were usually lit with soft green lights were completely black. I pushed the button that I knew turned the pump on and off, and my finger was greeted with a soft click and then nothing.

I pushed several other buttons to try to reset the machine and get it working again, but to no avail. Clearly, the machine lacked the one thing it required to provide the air that Wendy desperately needed to live: electricity.

My mind buzzed with anger and confusion. How is this possible? Ryan promised all the kid's machines were hooked up to an internal generator. How could he have missed Wendy's?

Before I was provided an answer, a hand grabbed at my arm and pulled it down toward the bed. Reluctantly, I let my gaze follow and I was able to see Wendy's face. It was illuminated with an angelic glow from the meager amount of moonlight that crept in through blinds that were crooked and hanging askew.

I put my hand on Wendy's chest and smiled at her. Hot tears rolled down my cheeks and over my imperfection, which set it ablaze as if every nerve ending had soaked up the electricity that should have been provided to my old friend.

"Dawn," Wendy croaked between gasps for air.

I nodded and reached down to move some brown curls away from her face. "Yes, Wendy. I'm here, sweetie," I cooed and hoped hearing my voice would soothe her in what were probably her last minutes in this horrible place we called home.

"What's. Happening?" gasped Wendy, her eyes were large and wet and full of confusion.

"I came back for you, Wendy," I lied. "Keep breathing, you'll be okay," I lied again and worried my expression would give it all away.

"You came. Back?" Wendy asked. The blue tinge surrounding her lips seemed to darken with every word she spoke.

I leaned down and hugged her as best I could as her body stiffened and fought for enough air to keep her thin frame alive. I continued to hold her even after the convulsions stopped. "I'm here, sweetie, I'm here," I whispered into her ear even though I knew it was too late and she couldn't hear me. *She'll never hear another thing again,* I thought and quietly cried into the soft curls that were splayed out on her pillow.

"Dawn," an urgent voice whispered from behind me.

Without turning or releasing Wendy from my embrace, I growled, "Leave me alone."

A hand gently grabbed at my shoulder and tried to pry me from the bed and from Wendy. "Dawn. It's time. We've got to go," urged Bert.

Finally, I released Wendy and with my fingertips, I closed her glassy eyes and fixed her hair around her pale, young face. I tucked the blankets around her and kissed both of her cheeks. She looked like she was sleeping although I knew in my heart that she had been murdered by Miranda and Ryan. I turned on my heel to leave Wendy's room, and this place, this horrible place, forever. A strong wave of anger burned within my chest and momentarily took over the deep wave of sadness that had threatened to stop me in my tracks and render me another casualty of this stupid, careless, unnecessary raid.

Back in the hall with Bert and our new recruits, I waved my arm toward Wendy's closed door and said, "Someone's got to pay for this." I stomped my way back to the exit and into the moonlight with a new sense of purpose, my sights clearly focused on revenge.

29

Back outside, Bert and I herded the children we'd kidnapped through the parking lot. We were the last group to return, and Ryan waited for us by the back bumper. He helped heave the kids into the jam-packed truck, instructing them to find a box to sit on and to get comfortable since we were going to be leaving soon.

After the kids were safely hidden away, I turned my angry heat onto Ryan. In the moonlight, his rusty beard lifted at the corners of his mouth when grinned at me. I glared at him and without warning I struck him hard across the face with my closed fist. His walkie talkie flew from his hand and landed in a mangled heap on the pavement by his feet.

"Shit," Bert muttered from beside me. He grabbed me from behind and hugged my arms close to my body to prevent me from swinging at Ryan again. Ryan held his jaw with one hand and shifted it back and forth as if assessing it for damage.

Ryan bent down and snatched his screeching walkie talkie from the ground and silenced the pained static with his thumb. Then, he set his gaze on me and sneered, his expression was a combination of amused respect and mild irritation.

"Problem, Dawn?" Ryan asked. Clearly, the deluded, wise-assed comedian had returned to the party.

"You're a… a… liar!" I sputtered and fought Bert's vice-like grip on my torso. My desire to wipe the parking lot with Ryan's smug, bearded face was overwhelming. But Bert held strong and I finally stopped struggling. My joints felt like they were suddenly filled with Jell-O as a plethora of emotions zipped through my quivering body.

"Moi?" Ryan smirked and pointed at his chest with the walkie talkie's bent antenna.

"C'mon, Ryan," Bert said and loosened his grasp on me. I wondered for a moment if he was going to let me go so I could kick Ryan's ass.

"What? What exactly did I lie about?" Ryan asked. In the moonlight, amusement flickered in his eyes.

The wild anger inside me surged again and fire swept across my face making my birthmark throb. "The internal generator," I growled. "You never turned it on."

Ryan smirked at me and shook his head. "You're so stupid, Dawn."

"Watch it, Ryan," said Bert. I felt Bert's heart rate increase through my back as he squeezed me tight against his chest, clearly readying for me to make another attempted launch toward our condescending leader.

"Why am I stupid?" I spit through bared teeth.

Ryan shook his head again. "Guess I'll spell it out for you. There was no internal generator."

My body quivered and I worried I might pass out. Bert readjusted his grip as if anticipating my nose dive and held me on my feet. Synapses in my mind fired so fast that I could almost see them explode inside my head like fireworks as Ryan's lie and the dire, irreversible consequences of it sunk into my brain.

"You asshole," I whispered into the chilly night air.

Ryan shrugged as if it was all in a day's work for him. As if the children he'd been hired to protect and keep safe were expendable in the name of his and Miranda's selfish mission.

A door opening and closing from the front of the truck interrupted our confrontation. Miranda eyed us all suspiciously. She pointed toward the cab of the truck. "They're on their way. The scanner's going nuts. We need to motor."

When Bert and I didn't move from our entwined pose, she turned toward Ryan. "Everything good? We've got to go."

As if on cue, the reflection of police lights was visible on the horizon. The red and blue lights bounced off the tall pine trees as the armada approached from the high road above Riverbend. Seconds later, the whine of multiple sirens followed.

Miranda nodded at Bert. "Get her in the truck," she ordered and walked back to the cab of the truck shutting herself inside.

"You heard her," said Ryan. He clicked off his walkie talkie and stood next to the back of the truck. Bert maneuvered me to the opening and lifted me without letting go of my arms until I was inside and out of reach of Ryan. Bert climbed in after me and the last thing I saw before Ryan slammed the door shut was the purple bump from my sucker punch erupting on his pale cheek.

30

We drove for what seemed like hours. The sound of softly crying children was almost comforting as we sat in the back of the truck and waited for information on our next move. Based on the length of time we'd been driving, I assumed we'd gotten away and were headed toward the next camp. My mind kept drifting back to Wendy. I wondered if they'd found her yet, dead and cold. I wondered who else would weep for her besides me. In my years at Riverbend I'd known of children who had died, but I'd never witnessed it firsthand and it was more awful than I had imagined. Her final struggle to breathe weighed heavily on me, as if it was my fault. *I should have fought harder to stop the raid*, I thought. I shouldn't have believed Ryan and his line of bull about the internal generator. I wished I wasn't so young and stupid and trusting.

After dozing off and on, I woke with a start when the back door of the truck was heaved open and we were greeted by Ryan's beaming face. *Ugh,* I thought, *his smile is so over-practiced and cheesy, he could make a sandwich.* I glared at him from droopy eyelids and wondered why he was so cheerful considering the damage we'd just caused.

"Pee break," said Ryan as Testers and children filtered by him on their way out of the truck.

Bert stood for his turn to get out and I grabbed his hand and pulled him back. I had some questions for him and I didn't want anyone in earshot when I asked them. He gamely sat back down despite the obvious stiffness in his legs and back. He folded his body next to mine and groaned like an old man settling into a recliner. I gave him a weak smile although it was hard to do so. I was feeling very betrayed and again was questioning who I could trust and unfortunately, he was going to be on the receiving end of my suspicion yet again.

After everyone had cleared out and Ryan had also disappeared on a urine-filled adventure, I exited our ride with Bert's assistance and found a picnic table a good distance away from the truck.

After Bert assured me that he was okay to wait for the restroom, I stared at him and opened my mouth to speak, but the words I needed to say were being stubborn. I closed my mouth, shook my head and hoped they would come before it was time to load back into the truck.

Noting my awkward discomfort, Bert grabbed one of my hands. "Are you okay, Dawn?" he asked, his brow creased with concern.

I nodded and fought my quivering lip from revving up again as it had many times on the way to this nearly abandoned rest area.

"I'm sure Wendy didn't feel any pain," Bert offered, but his eyes showed that he didn't really believe his statement.

My throat tightened and I cleared it a few times to regain the ability to form complete sentences. My soul hurt so much that I didn't know if I would ever be the same and I probably didn't deserve to be.

Finally, feeling the pressure to get these words off my chest before we ran out of time, I made another attempt to speak with an encouraging squeeze on the hand from Bert. I gazed at our entwined hands and then shifted my eyes up and stared Bert square in the eyes. "Did you know about the internal generator?" My judgment burned like a wild fire as I watched him squirm.

Bert looked as if he'd just received one of my right hooks. He shook his head and furrowed his brow. "No. Of course not."

My icy glare still stuck on his confused face, I prodded, "Are you sure? Don't you know quite a bit about how things like that work?" I tried to keep my tone as neutral as possible, but it sounded accusatory and bitter in my ears.

"Well, I thought the notion of an internal generator sounded hokey, but I trusted that he was telling the truth. Just like you," he added quickly.

"So, you thought there was a chance he was full of shit yet you went along with the plan anyway?" I seethed and released his hand with a jerk of my wrist.

"Dawn. Come on. You can't possibly believe that I'd want any of those sick kids to die?"

I shrugged and turned away from him and dabbed at my wet cheeks with my collar.

"Seriously. Dawn. You can't think I'm like him," said Bert.

"Wendy's dead." I sniffled in the cold air.

"I know," Bert said softly.

As we sat silently at the picnic table, a minivan with a man and woman in it pulled into an empty parking spot next to us. The windows down, we could hear a muffled news report on the radio. The couple turned off the car and got out. Arm and arm, they walked toward the small building with the restrooms. "Twenty-four dead at Riverbend," said the woman, shaking her head. "So sad."

The man nodded. "Hope they catch those troublemakers," he said before they disappeared inside the building.

I turned back to Bert, my mouth agape. "Did you hear that? Twenty-four dead!"

Bert's complexion was ashen. He nodded, and his eyes were wide with shock.

"Oh my God," I muttered and put my face in my hands. My birthmark was ablaze with heat from the combination of my sweaty palms and the salty wash of my tears being pressed into it.

Bert slid next to me on the bench and rubbed my back in a weak attempt to comfort me. Through my shirt, I felt that his hand was shaking at the news of what we had done.

***

Before we had the chance to fully pull ourselves together, we were approached at our private spot by Ryan sporting a smug expression and an icepack for his cheek.

"Might want to hit the head," he suggested. "We shove off in five minutes," he warned and turned back toward the truck.

"Ryan," I called, my tone bordering on an angry panic.

He came back, but stood a few steps away from me, out of reach, as if he didn't want another bruise for his collection.

"What's up, Dawny-girl?"

I grimaced. "Don't call me that," I ordered. *Only Bert is allowed to call me that*, I thought, and glared at Ryan for being such a repugnant toad.

He grinned and was clearly proud of himself for getting under my skin yet again. "Sorry." He smirked, and then involuntarily winced and held the icepack tighter to his cheek.

"We just heard that twenty-four kids died at Riverbend on that radio," I said and nodded toward the idle minivan.

His eyes still full of amusement, he shrugged. "That all?"

My mouth fell open, momentarily rendered speechless. *What an emotionless dick,* I thought.

From my side, Bert growled, "Those dead kids are on you, buddy."

Ryan shrugged again. "Collateral damage, kiddos. You'll see when you get more experience, there's a price for everything." Ryan turned on his heel and started to walk back to the truck. He stopped in mid-step and took a few paces back in our direction. "Now, get your asses in the truck. The police won't care who was in charge of this. If you desert and get caught, you're just as liable to be called murderers as Miranda and I are. Accomplices, that's what you are. Kidnappers, too. Remember that if you get any bright ideas," he said, his cockiness spilling out of him like a toddler carrying an overfilled cup. He turned toward the truck and left us alone, our minds spinning with our limited options.

***

Bert and I sat at the picnic table for a few minutes and stared at each other with bewildered expressions. Our only distraction from our impossible situation was the incessant buzz from the mosquitoes that were implementing their own coordinated attack. Funny, I noted, the bugs weren't an issue deep in the forest at our old camp, but here, on the edge of humanity, they were in a regular feeding frenzy.

Finally, after swatting at yet another nuisance, Bert turned to me with a question in his eyes. I looked down at the peeling paint on the picnic table and was almost afraid to say what I was thinking. I hoped Bert would agree with my assessment of our options and not try to argue for what he believed was best for us.

Bert reached across the table and lifted my chin with his fist. "Whatchya thinking, Dawn?"

I sighed and let my chin rest on his hand. "I'm scared to say," I admitted and shook my head to release him from his burden. I was surprised at myself for being so candid, but, in reality, time was of the essence. I could see the others had made their way back to the truck and were milling about, waiting for the lot to clear before they clambered back inside the void for the ride to the next pit stop.

"Just tell me," he urged. His eyes were sympathetic and understanding.

I exhaled and squeezed my eyes closed. "I think we need to stay with the group." I paused and when Bert didn't immediately disagree, I opened my eyes and was surprised to find him nodding in agreement.

"I think so, too," he said. His expression was grim.

"You do? Why?"

Bert shrugged his shoulders. "You heard Ryan. He's a jerk, but he's also right. We're on the hook for this, too. The cops might believe you were coerced, but not me. I've been with the group for too long, and been in scrapes with the law before, I'd be screwed just like everyone else."

I nodded. I hadn't even thought about that part. Selfishly, I'd only been thinking about myself. *Something to work on,* I thought. "Let's go to Florida, get some rest and our bearings. Then, maybe we can make plans to get away."

Bert slapped the table in a combination of enthusiastic agreement and one last mosquito kill.

We stood and watched the couple in the minivan leave after having completed their business in the rest area restroom. The husband's squinted eyes roved over us and my stomach clenched. He seemed to be memorizing our faces, but I shook off the notion, assuming instead that he was simply irritated by the mass of humanity he got to share his pee break with. *Anyway, he probably hasn't been privy to seeing a girl as lovely as me,* I thought as embarrassed heat flashed over my imperfection. I grabbed Bert's hand and we walked toward the others.

***

Back in the dark abyss of the bowels of the truck, I was able to fall asleep as we rumbled toward our next destination. After what must have been a few hours, I was drawn from my awkward slumber by the gentle pawing of my face. Little hands were probing by cheeks and worked their way into my hair and then back down over my birthmark which was given a squeeze that had me fully alert.

"Dawn? That you, Dawn?" said a small voice.

"Yes. I'm here," I answered. My mind quickly filtered through my memory banks to see if I could remember who the little voice belonged to.

"We goin' home, Dawn?" the voice asked in eager anticipation.

Ah, Georgie, I remembered. Georgie was a little boy who had been returned by his parents just shy of his third birthday when he was placed on the autism spectrum by the family doctor. Technically, he probably just nudged the spectrum, but it was enough for his parents to drop him at Riverbend in the nick of time, before it was too late to qualify for a replacement. Georgie had fixated on the fact that his visit to Riverbend was temporary and he'd be picked up by his loving mom and dad any day to go home. So, every day, for the last three plus years, he would ask anyone who made the mistake of making eye contact with him if today was the day he would be going home. It was incredibly sad and yet another example of how limiting offspring to one and allowing parents to replace an unwanted kid with a perfect version was demented and sick. I realized with a lump in my throat that I had neglected to say goodbye to Georgie when I was given the happy birthday heave-ho.

"It's me, Georgie," I said and put my arm around his trembling shoulders.

"We goin' home, Dawn? The boys who came to get me said we was goin' home."

I squeezed him tight to my chest and rested my cheek on his soft pile of sandy curls. For a brief moment, an image of

Wendy flashed in my mind and I fought hot tears that burned in the corners of my eyes. His hair smelled like hers. Of course it did, they used the same government provided shampoo. I pushed my nose deeper into his curls and took a long drag.

"We goin' home, Dawn?" Georgie asked again. His body was pushed closer to mine as we went over a large bump in the road.

"Yes, Georgie. We're going home."

Bert, awakened by our conversation, put his strong arm over my shoulders and pulled Georgie and I closer to him. I continued to whisper words of comfort into Georgie's ear until his breathing was even and shallow and I knew he was asleep. Our small huddle felt nice, wonderful really. It was as if we were a family—a happy little family on a road trip to somewhere safe and fabulous. With a satisfied smile on my ruined face, I fell into a deep, dreamless sleep.

31

After a few more pit stops, we were finally at our destination. Ryan pulled up the back door of the truck and the south Florida heat smacked us in our faces in a blistering wave. Our adjusting eyes squinted against the bright sun as we made our way from the interior of the truck and into a crumbling parking lot that adjoined a deserted circus.

We were assembled by Miranda and Ryan and I felt like they were showing us off as if we were their children meeting a grandmother who was a stickler for good manners. *A messed-up Brady Bunch*, I thought and fought the cynical smile that crept onto my lips.

A slender man with a freshly shaved, authoritative nature looked at each one of us and then he peered into the back of the truck and nodded his head at the supplies Miranda was taking the credit for rounding up, as if she'd done it alone.

She started to speak and the man held up a hand to silence her. She abided by his gesture although I didn't miss the sideways glance she gave to Ryan after the man turned his attention away from her to continue his survey of our group.

Finally, he stood in front of us and opened his arms wide. "Welcome to Paradise City. Where the grass is green and the girls are pretty," he said with an amused smirk.

Bert elbowed me. Grinning, he whispered, "Guns and Roses," into my ear and continued to mouth lyrics to the song as if he was at a concert instead of at an illegal encampment.

I nodded. I had a vague recollection of that song. I'd probably heard it performed on a television variety show.

"I'm Malcolm," the man continued, "consider this your home. What's ours is yours."

Miranda stepped forward. "Thank you, Malcolm," she said. She opened her mouth to say something else and Malcolm shushed her with a mere glance from his ice blue eyes. She stepped back into the line, her face ablaze.

"Testers are welcome to find a spot in the Big Top. Normals, there are old game stations that you're welcome to bunk in. There should be sufficient materials inside to make a proper place to sleep." With a grand sweep of his arm, he pointed us toward the gated entrance that was being held open by a woman wearing a bright sun dress. Her wispy blonde hair was tied in loose braids that fell over her shoulders.

As we passed through the gate, one by one, the woman smiled warmly at us. "I'm Grace, welcome," she murmured to everyone as they passed the threshold into our new home.

Bert and I walked by the giant tent that we assumed was the Big Top with its grand although faded red and white stripes. Hand in hand, we found a small wooden structure that had washed out paintings of ducks on the exterior. We opened a small hinged door on the left wall and crawled inside. We found a lantern, a pile of clean blankets and two fluffy pillows. There was even a can opener and a few cans of food stacked in a pyramid in the corner. Next to the cans, I found a small metal bucket that was half full of multicolored rubber ducks. As Bert busied himself repositioning the pillows and blankets, I made a neat row of ducks along the ledge that was on the wall directly across from the door. The bright, happy faces brought a smile to mine as I imagined the children who had played this game so many years ago and had probably won a prize.

"Nice ducks," said a voice from the open door behind me. Involuntarily, my body cringed as if I had been hit square in the back with a closed fist.

Bert saw the interloper first and I saw his shoulders slump. "Hey, Queenie," he said, his voice flat and irritated.

"Tommy and I are next door," she said as if it were important information that we should have… and that we'd care.

"How's Tommy doing?" I asked. A smirk crawled across my face and a satisfied heat burned in my imperfection.

Queenie squinted at me. "He's fine," she huffed. "I'm fine, too, in case you were wondering."

"I wasn't," I said and I heard Bert choke on a stifled laugh.

"Glad to see you haven't changed, Dawn," sneered Queenie. "Usually doing bad things makes people different. Guess you're super special," she added and her head disappeared from our doorway.

Bert patted my thigh and gave me a sympathetic look as if Queenie's words were going to be too much for me to handle after the ordeal we'd been through.

I shook my head and lifted his hand to my lips and gave it a peck. "I'm fine. She's a brat."

Bert nodded and stood as much as he could in our small little shack. "I'd like to see Tommy. How about you?"

I nodded and let Bert give me a hand up. He crawled through the small door first. Before I exited, I surveyed the area that we would be calling home. "This might work," I said to my meager collection of ducks and crawled into the sunshine.

32

Tommy was quick to greet both Bert and I. He enveloped me in a giant bear hug and gave me an extra squeeze at the end. I eyed Bert to see if he'd noticed, but he seemed oblivious so I let it pass as our little secret.

We told Tommy what had happened during the raid and about Wendy. Tears welled in my eyes and I fought them from rolling down my cheeks because Queenie was nearby pouting and eavesdropping, per her usual routine. I didn't want to give her the satisfaction of seeing me cry. Tommy vaguely remembered Wendy from his years at Riverbend and it warmed my heart to know that there was another soul on this planet who could carry on her memory now that she was gone.

A clanging bell broke up our reminiscing. Startled by the loud noise, Bert and I looked at each other with alarm in our eyes. Tommy put a reassuring hand on my shoulder. "Lunchtime." He nodded toward the swarm of people heading into the Big Top.

I patted my chest to slow my thumping heart and joined the others as they filtered into the oversized tent. Slowly, we made our way through a chow line that consisted of meat cooked on a barbeque grill. We also helped ourselves to cold noodle salad and freshly sliced fruit that were displayed neatly on a table. Lastly, we passed a few coolers filled with ice. We stopped and scooped up a bottle of water for me and a can of cola for Bert. Our plates full, we took our seats at the top of the bleachers next to our old friends and some new ones.

Before we ate our food, Malcolm walked out and like a master of ceremonies he hushed the jabbering crowd with a dramatic wave of his hand. "Sorry if the bell startled you newcomers," he said. An amused smile spread on his mouth and his eyes crinkled at the edges. After a brief chuckled from the crowd, his face became serious again and he continued. "The laws in Florida are much different than what you have up north. Here, we're allowed to congregate if done so with peaceful intentions."

Malcolm's gaze shifted to someone in the front row. I craned my neck and was not surprised at all to see that he was giving Miranda and Ryan the royal stink eye. She blanched at his gaze and seemed to make herself shrink into the crowd that surrounded her on the lower bleachers.

He turned his warmth back to the hungry crowd. "Eat, my brothers and sisters. Today we enjoy a feast to welcome our new family." He nodded at some of our people and smiled. "Enjoy," he finished and strode toward the barbeque grill to finish cooking for the waiting line of Testers.

After Malcolm's speech, the mood in the tent was light and we happily started to eat. The meal was delicious. The meat was juicy and tender. The fruit was so fresh that I imagined it had just been picked from a nearby tree. It was certainly an improvement over the canned garbage we had access to at Camp Reject.

After eating, my eyes wandered to the far side of the Big Top where the Testers were allowed to set up their beds. From the top of the bleachers, it struck me how the mismatched blankets and bedrolls reminded me of Georgie and his patchwork blanket that he'd carried with him at Riverbend. It was his last connection to his parents. He'd carried it with him everywhere, for at least two years, until it mysteriously disappeared one day with the linens and never returned. *He'd cried so much over that stupid blanket*, I thought and searched the sea of faces for him.

I spotted him sitting in the dirt with a few of the other children we'd rescued from Riverbend. They seemed out of place and tiny in the giant canvas structure. A pang of guilt washed through me and set my birthmark ablaze when he pulled his knees up to his chest and rested his head on them. He looked so… sad.

I motioned to Bert that I'd be right back and I descended the bleachers with my sights on Georgie.

When I hit the bottom and was steps away from my little friend, my neck was grabbed from behind in a Spock-like pinch and I was steered off to the side like a rambunctious kid being guided through the glass section of a department store. I tried to shake the hand from my neck, but the grip was strong and I acquiesced to it, thinking there was no way anyone would dare hurt me here, in front of a large crowd.

Finally, in a corner that offered a bit of privacy, I was released and I turned to see who had stopped me from going to Georgie. Based on the meaty hand and man-like grip, I had assumed it would be Ryan, but instead Miranda stared at me with slanted, suspicious eyes.

"Miranda?" I said and hated how small my voice sounded. *Something else to work on*, I thought and crossed my arms over my chest. I straightened my back in hopes of strengthening my resolve.

"Dawn," she said and looked over her shoulder before continuing.

"What?" I said, my impatience growing.

Her eyes showed surprise at my quick change in demeanor. A flicker of emotion crossed over her face and it spoke volumes. She hated it here already. She despised being just another number in camp. And, most importantly, she hated not being in charge.

A wan smile crept across my face and I covered it with my hand. I didn't want to piss her off. She still had things over me. Namely, she could out Bert and I as Testers and we could lose our little duckie palace before we'd even had a chance to sleep in it.

"I wanted to talk to you about the raid. To… to make sure you were okay."

My brow furrowed and I fought the urge to wrap my hands around her stupid neck. "Okay with it? I'll never be okay with what you did. And what Ryan did."

She nodded as if I'd said exactly what she had expected. "Dawn, you realize Wendy wouldn't have made it out of there no matter what we did," she said matter-of-factly.

Hearing Wendy's name on her lips made me cringe. The fabulous lunch that I just ate burned in my throat and I worried it would make a guest appearance on our feet. I fought back the urge to spew vomit and a torrent of swears at her. "What do you mean?" I growled.

"Even if she made it to eighteen, she wouldn't have made it on the outside."

I shook my head. *How can she be so horrible?* I thought and wiped a hot tear from my imperfect cheek.

"Who would've taken care of her? She'd have been sent on her way with maybe one can of oxygen. She wouldn't have made the car ride to the bus station."

Blinking back tears, I tried to speak, to argue with her sick logic, but nothing came out. It was as if I was in a dream and I wanted to scream, but was too frightened by the circumstances to make a peep.

"We saved her, Dawn. She's free now." Miranda reached for my shoulder and pulled me close to her.

Confusion washed through my brain. *Why is she being kind to me, comforting me?* Then, my brain quickly switched gears and was suspicious. *Is she being kind to me?* I wasn't sure. Nothing made sense.

I let Miranda hug me. As awkward and weird as it was, it felt good to be close to someone, even if it was her. I'd never had someone act as though they cared about me or my feelings except for Bert.

Our embrace was interrupted by a small tug on the bottom of my shirt. Miranda released me and we both looked down to see Georgie standing at our hips. His large brown eyes stared up at us expectantly. "We goin' home now, Dawn?" he asked.

I squatted down so my face was even with his. I looked him directly in the eye and said, "We are home, Georgie. We're home."

33

After the meal was finished and everyone went on about their business, I went back to my shack and tried to take a nap. I was unsuccessful because my mind whirled with thoughts and ideas that I couldn't control. With an arm draped over my eyes, I tried to think about my purpose. *How can I be useful here?* I wondered. I knew that I wanted to make a difference and to have my life matter. But how?

My mind drifted back to little Georgie and his long-lost blanket. I was haunted by the sorrow in his eyes when he repeatedly asked about going home. What can I do to make this a home for him?

Suddenly, I was hit with a wave of genius. I would make this his home by replacing his mother… with me. It made perfect sense. Since I couldn't have children of my own, I could adopt him in spirit and become his mentor, his teacher… his mom. And, I reckoned, not just Georgie. We'd brought a number of young children over from Riverbend and they all needed to be nurtured and loved just like him. I would take this task upon myself and bring them up properly so they could have the life they deserved. *Something Wendy would never have*, I lamented.

My heart surged with energy. It was light and full. It told me that I was on the right track. I would tell Bert that I had decided to stay at our new camp. I would teach the children how to read and write. I would take the place that should have been taken by a parent. I'd keep them from Miranda's clutches in case she was planning something insidious, like a coup or another raid. I would teach them right from wrong. I would teach them how to love and be loved. I would teach them what it was like to be… wanted.

Book Two

The Big Top

1

Some say that the best way to get over an old love is to find a new love. Sally had done just that in spades. We'd been in Florida at Camp Big Top for a few months and shortly after our arrival she was paired with Hunter. Hunter was rumored to be the son of Malcolm, our fearless leader and his partner, Grace. But that rumor was unconfirmed since Hunter was born off the grid and unregistered.

Luckily for Sally, Hunter was gorgeous. His lean, muscular body looked like it had been chiseled from a hunk of marble by Michelangelo himself. And, in the hot Florida sun, the sweat on his shirtless torso sparkled and set off every abdominal muscle in a dizzying display of tan, well-defined flesh.

From the constant smile plastered across Sally's face, I knew she was quite pleased with the pairing and her pining for Bert had stopped the moment she'd laid eyes on her chosen mate. Hunter was a Normal like her and, in addition to being a living, breathing, breathtaking piece of art, he was funny and warm as well. They'd taken to each other quickly and at night, with their shack right next to ours, we often overheard how much they enjoyed each other's company.

Don't get me wrong, I didn't mind eavesdropping on their budding romance, but it did create a problem for me. A big one. With every groan and giggle emanating from next door, Bert's hands would reach for me in the dark with a new sense of urgency. His kisses had become harder, more frequent and increasingly desperate.

I felt guilty for keeping him at bay, but I reasoned, I was only eighteen and I was still quite inexperienced in the dude department. And, quite frankly, the thought of being that close to him scared me more than I'd ever admit.

To make matters worse, Tommy and Queenie seemed to be in an unspoken competition with Sally and Hunter and their nightly dalliances. To my innocent ears, Queenie sounded bossy and condescending as she instructed Tommy on how to do things just right. I felt bad for him, although he clearly didn't mind her verbal abuse. He'd put up with her mouth for this long already, I guessed he wasn't going to change horses now.

In the beginning of our stay, life at Camp Big Top was fulfilling for me. During the day, I'd taken a role as a teacher to the children we'd stolen from their beds at Riverbend and to the unregistered children who were already here before we arrived. I was also a maternal figure to them, giving them hugs when they were needed or tenderly fixing boo boos acquired on the rusting relics of fair rides that had been left to rot in the humid Florida weather.

Georgie was a fixture by my hip on most days. I'd finally convinced him that this was home for now and it seemed to settle him down. He enjoyed playing with the other children in the outdoors and was even learning how to cook with the Testers who ran the makeshift kitchen within the Big Top. He loved repetitive tasks like husking bushels of corn or scrubbing fresh dirt from piles of potatoes. It gave me such pleasure to see him doing well and embracing his new life in our newfound home.

All the kids seemed to be finding their way in our fresh environment which unfortunately left me blowing in the breeze when the learning day was done. Bert was able to find a job. Another perk to Florida living was that the construction business was booming. They didn't seem to care if you were a Tester or a Normal. As long as you had a strong back and could swing a hammer, you were hired. He'd leave camp every day with Hunter with a smile on his face and a spring in his step. Earning an honest day's wage would do that for a person, I suppose.

Tommy found a job at a nearby diner and was gone a lot too. Instead of looking for work herself, Queenie decided to make the most of Florida's near constant sunshine and worked on her tan by lying around in her bra and panties and soaking up the rays while she waited for Tommy's return. Of course, she said it was because she needed to stay off the grid in case her parents were looking for her. I seriously doubted they were. I'm sure they were enjoying the break from their perfect brat.

After a few more months had passed into our time at Camp Big Top, due to Bert's job and the kid's amazing ability to disappear when they were called for lessons, I was finding myself idle and in search of something meaningful to do. Sally and I would hang out quite a bit and we found ourselves getting closer now that the Bert-Dawn-Sally awkward love triangle had been broken thanks to her match with Hunter.

I still had a lot of questions for Sally and didn't quite trust her one hundred percent after finding out she was Miranda's little sister, but occasionally I dared to venture into uncharted territory with her and ask questions that I probably had no business knowing the answers to.

One Monday, after the boys had left and Queenie was busy slathering herself with some oil she'd stolen from the kitchen, Sally and I found ourselves alone and free to talk.

"Can I say something?" Sally asked, her eyes twinkling.

I sensed it was going to be a tidbit regarding Hunter and probably concerning a body part that I really didn't want to know about, but the glint in her eye was making me curious enough to let her proceed in her bragging. I nodded gamely, "Sure."

She hesitated and it lasted for such a long moment that I thought she'd chickened out or simply changed her mind about sharing her secret with me. "Well," she finally started and immediately looked away, "were you mad when you found out that Miranda and I were sisters?"

I shook my head. *Not where I thought this conversation was going to go at all,* I thought and forced my brain to change gears. I cleared my throat. Brow knitted together in contemplation, I responded, "I guess. I was surprised. I wondered why you'd never mentioned it before."

Sally looked at me, her eyes suddenly wet and pleading. "I wasn't supposed to tell you. My job was to make friends with the new recruits to see where their allegiances were. I'm so sorry. I still feel like crap about the whole thing. I'm a sucky spy and lying makes me sick to my stomach. I wouldn't have been able to do it forever."

I patted her back between her hunched shoulders. "It's okay," I consoled her. "I was a stranger. Miranda needed information. That's the world we live in. I get it."

Sally smiled at me and the relief in her face was evident when her eyes brightened again. "Did you ever hear the story of how I ended up with Miranda?"

I shrugged. I'd never thought that far. It was odd to have siblings living together since families are only allowed one kid. So, why did their family get to have two?

Sally took a deep breath and launched into her story. "My parents had Miranda. Then, my mom accidentally got pregnant with me. I was a total surprise, I guess. Anyway, they had to give me up and Miranda, being seven years old at the time, remembered the whole thing. That's why she hates the government and raids their places. She wants to get even for forcing our parents to give me away. When she was eighteen, she raided my place and stole me away. We've been on the run ever since. Almost ten years now."

"Wow. I had no idea. Do your parents know where you are? Do you guys keep in touch with them?"

"Nope. Miranda told them what she was planning to do to rescue me and the shits turned her in. She snuck away that night after she overheard my dad on the phone with the authorities. Her original plan was to free as many kids as she could, but since my dad blew her plan to smithereens, she snuck in and just stole me. I'm grateful for it though. The facility I was in wasn't very nice. This place is much better. And, now, of course, I have Hunter. So, it makes all the struggle and sacrifice worth it."

"So, you're both Perfects, then?"

Sally nodded and looked around as if making sure we were still alone. "But please don't tell anyone. Miranda likes to keep that quiet. She prefers to be considered a Normal. And me too," she added with a conspirator's air.

I nodded. Her secret would be safe with me. For now. And, Camp Big Top was pretty nice, I had to agree with that. But her admission got me thinking about my own family. Should I try to contact them now that things from Riverbend have blown over? The raid happened months ago and my name was never mentioned in any of the newspaper articles written about it. My slate was clean.

"Why so quiet? You're not mad, are you?" asked Sally.

"No. I'm not mad. I had no idea. It makes me understand Miranda and her motivations a lot better so I thank you for that. I'm actually glad there's a reason for her actions. It makes her less… cold."

"She's not cold," said Sally, her tone suddenly defensive.

"Right," I lied. "Sorry. I just mean that her love for you drove her. It's kind of… nice." I said and fought my body from cringing from my blatant fib.

"She does love me," agreed Sally. "And, I have a feeling she got me hooked up with Hunter. Malcolm and Grace were taking the credit for it, but I'm pretty sure it was her."

"Has Hunter told you if they're his parents?" I asked and crossed my fingers, hoping I wasn't getting too greedy on my search for useful information.

Sally shrugged. "We haven't talked about it. I think he looks a lot like them, but I haven't asked him."

In an effort to lighten the mood, I playfully elbowed Sally in the arm. "Wanna go swimming?" I asked and nodded toward the half-filled dunk tank that was recently filled by a whopper of a rain storm.

"You bet," she said. She stood and yelled, "Ready, set, GO!"

We raced toward the dunk tank. For a fleeting moment, we giggled like children who didn't have a care in the world.

2

After dinner the clouds above our encampment roiled dark and angry. Despite our brief experience with Florida, we sensed they were filled with piss and vinegar and were preparing for an unrelenting attack so instead of our usual evening campfire and hang out we all went to our separate bunks to take cover before the storm raged.

After successfully warding off Bert's nightly and expected advances with promises of 'soon,' I fell into a deep sleep that was rudely interrupted by a rumble of thunder, vicious flashes of lightning and arguing voices. I lay still under my blankets and angled my head toward the plywood that covered the small window above me to figure out what was going on.

Sensing my movement, Bert lifted his head and grunted. "They at it again?" he grumbled and pushed his head back into the warm dent in his pillow.

'They' were Queenie and Tommy. 'They' were having another knock down drag out fight and we got to be front and center with an angry Mother Nature as a fitting accompaniment. Between crashes of thunder, louder now as the storm approached, I understood the gist of their fight. According to Queenie, Tommy was a disrespectful cheater. *With who?* I wondered as I continued to eavesdrop.

Queenie screamed that she was taking her stuff and moving elsewhere. I craned my neck to hear if Tommy begged her to stay. He didn't. A wan smile crept across my face and my imperfection burned at the thought of her moving across the camp, away from Tommy and away from me.

Bert's hot hand touched the center of my back and broke my brief fantasy of a Queenie-free environment. "Go to sleep, Dawn," he murmured and his hand slipped down my spine as he returned to dreamland.

I snuggled into my blankets. Oddly, my heart raced as though it had been pumped full of adrenaline and I knew sleep would be the furthest thing from my mind tonight.

3

Despite the noise from Queenie's screeching and the storm's violence finally dying down, my overcharged brain kept me deprived of sleep for hours. When Bert woke with the sun and started to get ready for his job, a wave of exhaustion hit me hard so I decided to sleep in, even though it meant I'd miss out on today's breakfast, which usually consisted of fresh fruit lifted from a nearby orchard that would nary miss a bushel or two of their bounty.

When I finally crawled from my makeshift home hours later, the area surrounding me was barren. All the kids were off playing or working and the adults who were able to contribute were off doing what they'd been assigned. A pang of guilt washed through me for my selfish laziness which set my imperfection ablaze. I put my hand against it to cool the fire, but with the mugginess still in the air from last night's storm, it did little to calm it.

I glanced over at Tommy's shelter and noted that the decorations Queenie had made for the door had been ripped down, shredded into little pieces, and left to disintegrate in the heavy drops from last night's rain storm. His door was ajar and I could also see that her gaudy pink blanket she'd demanded to have had disappeared in the night along with her loud mouth.

A smirk spread onto my lips as I imagined the quiet, comfortable silence we'd be able to enjoy at tonight's campfire. Another pang of guilt rushed over my body when I realized that Tommy might not be as happy as I was with her dramatic exit. *Even if he's upset for a while, it's better for all of us in the end,* I mused as I turned from the scene of last night's ruckus and walked toward the Big Top to see if there were any uneaten scraps available for me to scrounge for my empty, gurgling stomach.

Inside the Big Top, breakfast had already been cleared away, but I was able to grab a pilfered orange from a large bucket that still sat half-full on the serving line.

I sat at an empty picnic table and peeled my orange. A burst of juice hit me in the face and I chuckled at the inconvenience and tapped at the droplets with my collar. From the corner of my eye, I caught movement and was surprised to see Grace waving a napkin at me.

"Morning, Dawn," she said. Her voice was calm and soothing, and her smile was welcoming.

"Good morning, Grace. Thanks," I said with a nod as I took the napkin from her outstretched hand.

"Mind if I join you?" Her raised eyebrows showed her expectation of my acceptance of her request.

“Not at all,” I said. I was surprised and a little bit honored that she would take a minute out of her busy morning to spend time with me. Usually she was knee deep in cooking, ushering in new friends, or working with Malcolm behind the scenes.

She smiled at me again and this time, I sensed something brewing behind her hazel eyes—a question or maybe something else. My stomach clenched with concern as if I were in trouble of some sort, and I instantly felt like a little kid waiting for a scolding. I briefly wondered why I had such a guilty conscience, despite my efforts to live right and follow all of the rules. *Post-traumatic stress from my run-ins with Miranda,* I mused as I waited for Grace to speak.

“I heard there was a bit of a dust-up last night?” she said.

Although it was a question, I knew that she probably already had a good idea what had happened and I wondered why she’d need confirmation from me. After thinking for a moment, I nodded and smiled, suddenly not wanting to offer up too much information before it was asked.

“Care to discuss your side of things?” she pressed; her eyes slanted in suspicion.

My brow furrowed. *My side?* I thought. *I’m an innocent bystander in the fireworks from last night. Why does she think I was involved?*

Grace reached across the table and patted my hand that was still holding a wedge of orange that had been poised to enter my mouth but had stopped halfway home. “I’m sorry,

Sweetie. I guess you don't know the whole story then." She shrugged and stood.

Confusion clouded my mind. "Wait," I said and slid down the bench toward her. "What do you mean? Are you talking about the fight between Tommy and Queenie?"

Grace took a step toward the table and lowered her head. "Yes," she whispered.

I shook my head. "Why do you think I was involved? I was trying to sleep." My voice cracked on the last word and I sounded guilty in my own ears. *Guilty of what?* I wondered as I waited impatiently for her to explain.

Grace sighed. "This is the problem with all of you young people." She sounded slightly irritated, which surprised me since she was usually so kumbaya. "Queenie thinks that Tommy wants to be with you and now she's convinced herself that you two have something going on. Frankly, by the way you've been freezing out Bert, I wondered too." Her eyebrows were raised at the last revelation, as if showing her power by sharing how much camp information, private information, she was privy to. I instantly had flashbacks to my interactions with Miranda at Camp Reject. It seemed the personal goings on, or not goings on, was everyone's business.

My stomach cramped. It was hard enough for me to put one of my sticky hands over it to ease the knot that was forming in my intestines. I was utterly flabbergasted. *Why does Queenie think this about me and who the hell has Bert been complaining to?* My imperfection burned with flames of embarrassment and anger. In addition to feeling completely betrayed by Bert, I was irritated that Grace wasn't at all who I thought she was: hippy, dippy, trippy on the outside, a shark with bite on the inside.

Grace smirked at my confusion and I felt a surge of hatred reel up from inside me. She was Miranda all over again—in my business and causing drama where it shouldn't exist. I was over it. Finally, I was able to find the words to defend myself. "My relationships with Bert and Tommy are nobody's business," I sputtered and swung my legs over the bench seat of the picnic table.

Grace took a step back as if she was afraid I was going to strike her. Her retreat gave me a great sense of satisfaction and the knot in my belly loosened a little. "Not that it's any of your business, but Tommy and I are just friends." I thought about stopping there, but she'd lit a fire that wasn't so easily quenched so I continued, "And, Queenie's a spoiled brat who doesn't deserve a nice guy like him."

I marched toward the flap of the Big Top and smacked it open. Before it slipped closed, I turned back to look at Grace. Even though her shoulders were slumped in defeat, it was disconcerting to see a thin smile creep across her rosy lips.

4

I was still fuming when I got back to my makeshift home. Too amped up to go inside and be trapped by the limited square footage, I paced around it instead, circling my little abode like an agitated tiger in a zoo.

I was distantly aware of people glancing at me as they hurried about their business, but no one dared approach me. Clearly, the irritation from my confrontation with Grace was still etched on my face. My imperfection burned as it soaked up the intense mid-day Florida sunshine and from my own internal fire.

Exhaustion began to settle in after thirty minutes of grumbling under my breath and stomping around my shelter like a mad homeless person. I started to feel silly and thirsty. I swiped at the sweat on my forehead with my sleeve and chuckled at myself for the display that I had just blessed everyone with. I was certain this would get back to Grace and I silently scolded myself for letting her get to me and for having a reaction that was reportable. I'd hate to give her any modicum of satisfaction on that front. A lesson I'd learned not too long ago from Miranda at good old Camp Reject. I knew I had to do better. Be better.

Reluctantly, I made my way back to the Big Top in search of water. I dreaded it for fear of running into Grace again, but was happy to find it nearly deserted except for a few workers cleaning up and a low din from the kitchen area as lunch preparations were beginning.

I found a bottle of water in a bucket behind the serving table and twisted off the cap, taking down the tepid fluid in three big gulps.

I thought about taking another bottle, but stopped myself, remembering that I was trying to be a better person and being greedy, with or without an audience, would disqualify me from that mission.

I eyed the workers as they bustled about and a wave of jealously briefly washed over my body setting my imperfection ablaze again. They were contributing and I was not. My students had found other things to fill their time, more important things. I held the empty bottle to my cheek, and wished it would help douse the flames of envy that were threatening to singe the birthmark right off my face.

I stood staring for a few minutes, and wished I knew what to do. How could I make a difference that would matter? How could I make my mark?

A hand on my shoulder made me flinch. I whipped around, immediately defensive. I had expected to see Grace, smug and omnipotent. Instead it was Rebecca. I had met her at dinner a few nights ago. She'd been with the group for almost a year. She was soft spoken and seemed nice. *I won't bet money on that fact,* I thought as I managed to force a smile at her. I realized at that moment that I wasn't a great judge of character.

"Sorry, Dawn, did I scare you?" she asked, her face turning crimson, her blue eyes wide and apologetic.

I shook my head. "Not really. I'm just distracted today," I said, knowing that was the partial truth.

Rebecca seemed nervous. Her hands shook and seemed almost on the verge of full tremors. I wondered if she was always like that or if my demeanor was affecting her. I tried to soften my edge that had been sharpened earlier by Grace and her intrusive meddling.

"Do you want to see something I found?" she asked. Her eyes, I noticed, looked everywhere except at my face.

"What is it?"

Rebecca swallowed hard and I thought about offering her one of the bottles of water that lay behind the table. "It's probably better if you see it for yourself," she said and finally mustered enough courage to glance at me.

I shrugged. "I've got nothing else going on, might as well." I followed Rebecca out of the Big Top. She led me to a part of the grounds that I hadn't visited yet. We stopped just outside another red-and-white-striped tent that was much smaller than the main tent. Once we entered through the flap, it was like a whole other world had opened up and swallowed us in one bite.

Costumes of all kinds lined the walls on plastic shelves. I marveled at the hand-sewn sequins and slippery satins. In the corner, I noticed an old coat rack draped with feathery boas and felt hats. Another shelf was covered in fake, plastic faceless heads that were crowned with wigs and hairpieces in various styles. More loose wigs lay discarded on the shelf and looked like a bunch of pelts from animals that were having a much worse day than me.

The color in the room from the multitude of costumes was bright and cheerful and immediately made my mood better. I was grateful that Rebecca had brought me here. Her kindness and this fantastic room were just what I needed.

After pawing over the costumes and trying on a few of the wigs and hats, our giggling faded and Rebecca led me over to a table that had a mirror surrounded by round light bulbs. It was clearly the perfect spot for the performers to get ready. Without power at the camp, the light bulbs were dark, but it was still fun to pretend that I was a star and this was my dressing room and I would come out looking fabulous and feeling fabulous too.

"Would you want to try some of this stuff?" asked Rebecca. Her voice was so soft I almost didn't hear her question.

"What is it?" I asked as I carefully replaced a puffy afro-style wig onto a nearby shelf.

"Makeup," said Rebecca. She waved her hand over the table top and I could see that she had carefully arranged the selection by hue.

I furrowed my brow. "They left all the makeup too? Is it any good?"

"I've used it. It seems okay to me," said Rebecca with a cautious smile and brief eye contact.

I squinted at Rebecca and tried to gauge her objective. Sensing no ill intentions from her, I shrugged and gamely sat in the swiveling chair. "Do you know what to do? I've never used makeup before."

A broad grin spread over Rebecca's face. She seemed happy and grew more relaxed as she pulled my hair back into a pony tail to expose my face in the darkened mirror.

"I love makeup. I wear it whenever I get the chance. I'd love to be a hairdresser or cosmetologist, but I don't think anyone would hire me… could hire me," she lamented as she compared containers of various shades of light beige makeup to the skin on my good cheek.

"Well, you can practice on me. This could be fun," I offered and smiled at her. My stomach bubbled with excitement at the prospect of some pampering and the results of a decent job.

"I'm going to use this type of sponge," said Rebecca as she held up a white sponge that was mottled with makeup from previous use. "Are you okay if this goes on your cheek? Is it sensitive?"

"No, it should be fine," I said and I hoped it would be. I'd never put anything on it other than soap and some lotions.

"Okay, here we go," said Rebecca. She squirted a dot of makeup onto the sponge and gently patted it onto my imperfection.

Like a magician, Rebecca slowly made the purplish blemish disappear. I watched in awe as she dabbed and brushed and contoured it with a variety of liquids and powders. By the time she was done, I had nicely shaped eyebrows, shimmering pink eye shadow on my eye lids, berry colored lips and perfect, flawless skin.

"Holy cow," I said as I leaned toward the mirror and reviewed her work.

"Do you like it?" asked Rebecca, her voice meek and worried.

"I don't know what to say," I responded. "It's…breathtaking."

Rebecca giggled and put a makeup stained hand over her mouth to stifle it.

"I mean, breathtaking is an odd way to explain yourself, I know, but I've never seen myself look like this before. It's as if my birthmark never existed. It's… amazing." I leaned toward the mirror again. I raised a cautious hand to touch it, but not daring to smudge her hard, miraculous work, I let it drop into my lap.

A thump behind us caused us both to flinch. In the mirror, I saw a person approaching us and when I saw who it was, my shoulders instantly slumped.

"Hey, Queenie," said Rebecca, her tone hollow and defeated. With the surprise appearance of Queenie, Rebecca's body language had changed too. She hunched over and seemed to be trying to block the table with her body as if she didn't want our guest to see what she was doing.

"What's all this?" asked Queenie. Her eyes glistened with pleasure as if she'd just busted up a bank robbery and was waiting on a medal from the mayor.

"Just having some fun," said Rebecca, as she shifted her body again to block Queenie's view of the table.

"Wow. Quite the load of makeup," said Queenie. She craned her neck around Rebecca and took a good look at my flawless face in the mirror. She peered at me in the darkened glass and boldly took hold of the chair and spun me around so she could inspect Rebecca's work with her own beady and judgmental eyes.

"Cut it out, Queenie," I said, but I knew I sounded weak and she was going to do what she was going to do with or without my blessing.

"Gee, Dawn, with all this crap on your face you look almost… normal," sneered Queenie, her expression a combination of awe and jealous admiration.

"Um, thanks?" I said and secretly wanted to punch her in her snotty little nose.

"Why are you bothering with all of this?" asked Queenie in an accusatory tone. Clearly, she still thought she caught us doing something wrong.

"It was my idea," offered Rebecca with a sideways glance at me as if looking for my confirmation of her confession.

"What's it to you, Queenie?" I asked, suddenly emboldened by the fact that my improved appearance was a bother to her sensibilities.

Queenie leered at me, and her eyes slanted into thin slices of suspicion. "I guess if you want to look even better for Tommy, that's none of my business now," she sputtered and turned on her heel to leave.

I thought about calling after her and telling her that there was nothing going on with me and Tommy, but I changed my mind and let her leave in a huff. I liked the idea of her seething and thinking about how Tommy would find me even more alluring with my fixed face. Secretly, from the way my stomach did a somersault at the thought of Tommy liking the way I looked, I worried that, in some small way, she might be right.

5

Rebecca and I finished up our makeup session shortly after Queenie's exit and I strolled back to my end of the camp feeling pretty darned good about myself. Not only did I look great, I felt great. I'd chased off Queenie, her mangy little tail between her legs, and now I could show Bert and Tommy how pretty I could be. My stomach flip-flopped again as I neared our bunk houses and it made me second guess my confidence. I suddenly wished I'd washed off Rebecca's work. Drawing attention to myself was a very foreign thing and I didn't know if I would like the consequences.

Before I had a chance to run back to the costume tent and search for makeup remover, I heard a man's voice call out to me. I froze in my tracks as his footsteps approached from behind. "Wait up, Dawn," said Tommy as he hurried to catch me.

I stood unmoving and waited for him to circle around to my front. I half hoped he'd continue walking and I could match his steps or gradually fall behind, unnoticed. No such luck.

"Whoa," said Tommy. He grabbed my wrist to hold me still as I tried to turn away from his inspection. "Let me look," he urged with a little squeeze to my wrist.

"It's no big deal," I started and was silenced by the admiration I saw in his brown eyes. *Were they always so deep and brown?* I wondered as I let him continue his perusal of my improved face.

He nodded approvingly. "You look great, Dawn." Suddenly his grin seemed shyer than before, as if he'd already said too much.

"Thanks," I muttered and pulled my wrist from his grasp.

"Really," he continued, "you're beautiful. Bert's a lucky dude." He swallowed hard as a crimson blush began to creep up his neck and onto his tanned face.

"Super lucky," I agreed with a soft chuckle.

Tommy laughed too and seemed to appreciate my obvious attempt at making our exchange a bit less awkward.

"Seriously, though, what's the makeup for?" he asked without taking his eyes from my face.

"Just goofing off. Rebecca found some old stuff and we were bored so I let her fix me up."

"Well, it looks great. Not that you need it, you look great anyways, but... well, you know what I mean" The blush shot back across his face and this time he looked down at his grubby sneakers.

"Thanks. It's probably a one-time thing so don't go getting used to it."

Tommy nodded and took off his baseball cap to run a hand through his overgrown bangs. I noted his hair was blonder now. Maybe it was from the constant sunshine or maybe it just appeared lighter because he was so tan now. The sun had done other things for him as well. His complexion was much clearer. I hadn't noticed how handsome he had become since we'd been here until now. My stomach did another Olympic caliber vault and I felt a rush of heat wash over my face and I worried I'd sweat my makeup off before Bert got a chance to see it.

Tommy and I walked the rest of the way toward our little homes and found Bert sitting outside in a tattered lawn chair.

"Hey, guys," Bert greeted us.

"Hey, buddy," said Tommy, a hint of guilt in his response.

"Hi," I said and looked into the dirt by his feet, unable to make eye contact with him for some reason.

"Dawn. What'd you do?" Bert asked, his tone bordering on anger instead of awe.

My head snapped up and I looked him square in the face. "What do you mean?" I asked, suddenly defensive.

"Why do you have all that crap on your face?" he demanded.

"I like it," I said and crossed my arms over my chest.

"I think it looks good," offered Tommy. Bert glared at him and Tommy took a few paces backward. "I'll catch you guys later," Tommy said and with a few more hurried steps, he disappeared into his shelter.

Bert didn't acknowledge Tommy's departure. He continued his laser beam analysis of my face. "You don't need all that stuff," he said, his tone a bit softer now.

"I know," I said and let my arms fall to my sides. "Rebecca and I were just playing around. I thought it looked good," I said and fought the tears that were welling up in my eyes.

Bert grabbed my hand and held it to his chest. His hands were hot on mine and I wondered if he was just cranky from a long day of work in the hot sun. "You do look good. Too good," he said and a small smile broke across his handsome face.

"Yeah?" I asked, liking the intense way he was looking at me and the hint of jealousy in his tone.

Bert pulled me a step closer, and from his seat, stretched his back and neck toward me to kiss me. Despite our initial tension, I let him. Suddenly, with his soft lips on mine, the makeup didn't matter and I melted into him, my boost in confidence giving me the permission I had needed to allow myself to get closer to him. Hand in hand, we entered our shelter. That evening, with only his actions, Bert showed me how much he loved me, imperfection or not.

6

The next morning, Bert woke me with cheerful whistling as he got dressed. I stirred and sat up; he stopped mid-tune. "Sorry, Dawn," he whispered and sat down on the bed next to me.

"Chipper today, are we?" I asked and patted his jean clad thigh.

His cheeks flushed and he looked down at my hand. After a moment, he looked into my eyes and grinned. "Best night of my life," he said and the flush returned, darker this time. "Are… are you okay?" He asked and looked at the row of plastic ducks that'd had a bird's eye view of our delightful evening.

"Yes. I'm perfectly fine," I said and I was. Last night had been the first time for both of us and even though we were awkward at times and some things hurt before they felt good… really good… I was happy we'd done it and could now show the rest of the camp that we were serious about each other. At least, I was serious, and I was pretty sure he was serious about me too.

He trained his eyes back on mine and smiled a smile so broad I worried it would crack the skin at the sides of his mouth. "You're amazing, Dawn. I… I love you. You know that I love you, right?"

Heat filled my body and my brain felt light and far away, like it had been removed and was suspended in a jar of preserving fluid to be studied. I'd never been loved before or felt loved before and I wondered if this odd floating sensation was what it felt like.

Bert tapped my shoulder and it brought me back from my love-induced coma. "Dawn. Did you hear me? Are you sure you're okay?"

I smiled apologetically and grabbed his hand before he could pull it away. "Bert. I love you too. Sorry I faded on you for a minute. I just realized that I've never been loved before. Well, at least not like this or… like last night."

Bert laughed loudly and clapped a work worn hand over his mouth to keep his glee from waking our neighbors. "Me either. I hate that I have to leave. I'd like to stay in here with you all day." He leaned in for another, more urgent kiss.

I kissed him back and then pushed on his shoulders to get him to stand up. "Are you kidding? We'd die from heat stroke in here during the day," I said playfully although it was the truth. Our shelter did become somewhat of an oven during the high heat of the day.

"True," said Bert with a sheepish grin. He turned away from me and gathered a few more items he'd need to start his day and stuffed them into his pockets. Before he left, he cocked his head as if a thought had suddenly occurred to him. He turned and knelt in front of the bed. He took both of my hands into his and looked directly into my face. "We'll be okay here, Dawn. We'll take care of each other. I love you." And just like that, he was out of the shelter and birthed into the hot Florida sun.

7

I stayed in the shelter for a bit longer after Bert left and reviewed our evening in my mind. It brought me great pleasure to know that I had made Bert so happy. I hadn't realized how intense a physical connection to a man could feel and I was kicking myself for not allowing it to happen before now. At this precise moment I understood all the commotion that had been coming from Sally's shelter and with a cringe, I realized that the same adult activities had been going on between Tommy and Queenie. In reality I'd figured as much, but my previous man and woman experience was limited to what I'd seen on basic daytime television. Knowing what I now knew, it was almost shocking to think about and it bothered me more than it should. To imagine Tommy doing the same things to Queenie that Bert had done to me last night was almost unbearable. I shook my head and internally scolded myself for a) imagining them doing unspeakable things and b) caring so much that he was doing them to her and not to me.

"Ugh," I groaned, and covered my face with my hands, and imagined that I was going straight to hell for such putrid thoughts.

Realizing my only way to stop these images from dancing in my brain was to get my day started, I figured I'd go find Rebecca and see if she'd be willing to do makeover part two on my face which had mostly smeared onto my pillowcase with my exertions from the night before. I hoped she didn't ask how the makeup had come off so thoroughly. I'd have to tell her the truth. Quite frankly, maybe I wanted to tell her. It felt like a secret too big to keep to myself. And, I was pretty sure she had been assigned a partner so she'd probably understand. Maybe she could tell me if I did everything right.

I grinned at the prospect of talking about me and Bert. I knew other women in the camp thought he was attractive so maybe there would even be a bit of jealousy and even though the notion was petty, it kind of made me happy to think that someone out there in the world would be jealous of little old Dawn. After dressing and wiping my face clean with a towel, I crawled from my shelter and into the sunshine.

As I was lost in thought, I'd made my way back to the tent where all the makeup was stored. To my surprise, Rebecca was there, sitting on a wooden stool that had once been inside the tent. As I got closer, I could see that she was upset. Fresh tears washed down her cheeks and her chest heaved as if she was trying to catch her breath between epic sobs.

"Rebecca? What's going on?" I asked as my eyes checked her over for any obvious injuries.

"Oh, Dawn," she wailed and she gasped as her words were caught in another hitching breath.

"Are you okay?" I asked and sat on the ground next to her to rub her back.

She shook her head and wiped her cheeks with both hands. "No. It's gone. All of its gone," she said and waved one of her wet hands toward the door of the costume tent.

My brow furrowed. "What's gone?"

"Everything. Someone trashed the whole place." She started actively crying again, her sobs drawing curious attention from others as they passed by on their way to work.

"Someone trashed this place?" I asked as I started to realize what that meant. The costumes were one thing but… the makeup. Did they ruin all the makeup?

Unable to speak in coherent sentences, Rebecca nodded her head and finally gave up on communication in general and put her head on her knees in defeat.

I gave her back one last pat and stepped inside the tent to get a look for myself. The room was a mess of shredded fabric, loose sequins, and gobs of hair that had been ripped from the rubber scalps of the wigs. I stepped through the colorful rubble and made my way to the makeup table. Each round light bulb that had been so festive and fun yesterday was now broken into wasted glass shards. Their metal bases were still screwed into the outlets, but the glass had been smashed off and the metal insides reached out crooked and limp, like tentacles from some odd sea creature. The makeup had been crushed and smooshed all over the table and the floor like a toddler had decided to finger paint with it.

But it was clear that this was not done by a toddler. This was cruel and intentional and I had a pretty good idea who'd done it. It had to be Queenie. That spiteful bitch hadn't liked seeing me improve my looks with the makeup and now she'd gone and ruined it all so I wouldn't be able to steal Tommy away from her.

I whirled around with angry fire when footsteps came up from behind me. I half expected it to be Queenie, here to enjoy my reaction to her carnage, to her act of war, but it was Rebecca. She'd calmed herself enough to make her way inside. "I told you it was all gone," She swept her arm dramatically over the remnants of a life that could have been.

I nodded curtly. My seething anger was too intense to speak just yet.

"Who would do this, Dawn? Why would someone do this?"

I couldn't answer her. Not yet. I began to pick through the ruined makeup to see if there was anything I could salvage.

"Don't waste your time, Dawn. It's trashed," said Rebecca, clearly waving her white flag on this whole mess.

I pushed aside a small pile of rubble with my foot and noticed a drawer at the bottom of the makeup table that had still been closed. My heart leapt at the possibility that it had been missed, that maybe after the tabletop items had been destroyed and the light bulbs had been smashed, maybe, just maybe it would have been too messy to see this low drawer.

I took a deep breath and pulled on the wooden knob. The door slid open and I was thrilled to see a few brand new, unopened palates of the same type of makeup that Rebecca had used on me.

I must have gasped at the sight because Rebecca rushed to my side and squealed with delight at the sight of the undamaged packages. "This is a miracle!" she proclaimed and bent to grab the palates from the drawer.

She swept the table clean with her arm and placed the palates on the surface. "Four. There's four!" she said and clapped her hands like a kid watching an exciting magic show.

I nodded and felt a twinge of satisfaction in my belly and a pleasing heat crawled across my imperfection knowing that Queenie hadn't won this round.

"You need to take this, Dawn. Keep it safe in your shelter and don't tell a soul that you have it," she advised while she looked around for a scrap of fabric big enough to wrap and camouflage the palates.

"What about you? Don't you want any?" I asked and suddenly felt stupid for asking when she looked at me incredulously. I'd momentarily forgotten that I was the one with the ugly birthmark over half my face. Rebecca was beautiful without any alterations.

She gave me a thin smile and I instantly felt bad for putting her in an awkward position. "No, you keep it," she said and handed me the bundle. "I can show you again how to apply it if you want," she said without looking at me, her eyes scanning the floor for anything else she could salvage and to avoid my gaze.

"Okay, thanks. That would be great," I said and left it at that. I was glad to have some makeup left. I'd felt super confident with it on and I'd hate for Queenie and her desperate need for vengeance to take that away from me.

"Let's get outta here. This place is giving me the creeps now," said Rebecca, and she was finally able to look me in the face.

I nodded and gingerly stepped through the rubble so I didn't risk my precious bundle.

As we stepped back into the sunlight, Rebecca turned to me and shrugged her shoulders, her defeat evident. "Who would do this?"

Without hesitation or worry about being wrong and accusing the incorrect individual, I said, "Just one person… Queenie."

8

I marched back to our shelter and after safely hiding my salvaged makeup, I went looking for Queenie. Instead, I ran into Tommy. His eyes scanned my face and I sensed a hint of disappointment behind his eyes. I wondered if he'd expected me to start wearing the makeup every day.

I shrugged off his unspoken judgment and focused on my mission at hand. "Tommy, have you seen Queenie anywhere?"

"Me? Nope? She's been avoiding me like the friggin' plague. She hasn't been around since our fight. I'd heard she left camp altogether."

"No way," I said, startled at the notion of a Queenie-free existence. "You really think she left?"

He shrugged and a wave of guilt washed over his tanned face. "I dunno. Maybe she found someone else."

I nodded, although I wondered what masochist would want her. I patted Tommy's slumped shoulder and wondered if the idea of his ex-girlfriend with someone else really bothered him that much or if he was giving me the reaction that he thought I would expect from someone on the heels of a fresh break up.

Tommy's eyes suddenly brightened and his back straightened. "Oh, Dawn, I'm glad you ran into me. There was something I wanted to run by you."

I swallowed hard and worried what it could possibly be. His face was suddenly alive again and full of excited expectation, I worried he was going to ask me out. I cocked my head at him and waited for the other proverbial shoe to drop.

"There's a job opening at the restaurant. A cashier position. At the counter. You don't really have to be a waitress. You'd just ring up the checks and help out the counter staff if a customer needs something and they're tied up at a table or out back."

"You think I'd be able to get a job like that?" I asked and was certain he had me confused with someone else. Anyone else.

Tommy looked down at his grubby sneakers and his face reddened beneath his tan. "Well, when I saw you with the makeup on, I thought you'd be a good fit for it. They hire Imperfects there as long as you don't have anything too obvious going on." He gulped at the air as if he'd been punched in the neck and then cleared his throat and made eye contact with me. "I think you'd be perfect for it."

My brow furrowed at the mere thought of getting a job. I'd love to have some money, maybe start saving for a future with… someone.

"What ya thinking?" Tommy was staring at my face and was clearly trying to read my odd expression and failing miserably at the task.

"Uh, you really think the makeup hides this enough?" I asked and brushed my fingertips across my imperfection and immediately regretted it as it prickled with heat.

"I think so. You looked pretty damn good to me," he said and sucked air in between his lips as if he'd just given away a state secret.

My imperfection blazed as embarrassed heat crawled up my neck and washed over my face. My head even felt a bit dizzy at the idea of looking 'damn good' to anyone. "Thanks," I muttered and looked away.

"Well, think about it," he pressed. "I could take you over tomorrow so you could talk to the owner. He's really nice. You'd like him. Plus, if you got the job, we could hang out more." He squinted at me as he said the last part and I hated myself for giving him a satisfied expression.

"I'd like that," I said without thinking and I instantly scolded myself inside my head for wanting something so stupid. Especially given what I had just done with Bert a few hours before.

"Me too," he said and for a brief second, I thought Tommy was going to grab my hand.

"I'll talk to Bert. See what he thinks. I'll talk to you tomorrow morning."

Tommy's face fell at the mention of Bert. It was as if we'd both gone nutty for a few minutes and forgot that there were other people in the world that mattered.

Tommy nodded, gave me an awkward wave and dipped into his shelter. I took a deep breath of the humid air and looked up at the sky. The roiling clouds in the distance mirrored the emotions that were churning inside my stomach and the guilty thoughts that whizzed through my mind like highway traffic. A job would be amazing. A job at the place where Tommy worked would also be amazing, but I sensed danger would be had if I took it. I looked at the approaching clouds again and before I took shelter, I worried I'd convince myself that danger was just what I needed.

9

Bert thought the job was a fantastic idea. He'd been saving money for us on the sly so we could leave the camp and get our own place and if I was able to add to the pot, it would make his dream happen even sooner. The idea of me and Tommy working together didn't seem to bother him in the slightest bit. Oddly, I'd wished he was a little more jealous of the connection between me and Tommy, but he seemed to not even see it. Maybe it was all in my head after all.

I got up early and found Rebecca so she could help me with the makeup. I didn't dare apply it myself on such an important day. I needed to look perfect in order to have a chance at the job.

After I was ready, I stood outside Tommy's shelter and exhaled between pursed lips. *What happens today might change things*, I thought and knocked on the plywood that covered the window.

After a moment of silence, I knocked again and was greeted with a groan. "Coming. Damn it."

Tommy emerged from his shelter with his shirt in his hand and his pants unbuttoned as if he had just thrown them on.

"Sorry. Did I wake you?" I asked and cringed at how stupid I sounded.

"What? No. I mean, yeah, but I had to get up for work anyway. No worries." He squinted at me as his eyes adjusted to the bright morning light, and then grinned. "I take it you're coming with me?"

I nodded. "I'm going to try to get the job." I hated myself for sounding like such a stupid robot.

He grinned again and pulled his shirt over his muscular torso. "Excellent. You have breakfast yet?" he asked as he pulled his door closed behind him. We started walking together toward the Big Top.

I shook my head. "I'm too nervous to eat," I admitted.

"You'll be fine, Dawn. Just fine." Tommy lifted the flap to the Big Top and strode toward the chow line.

My stomach churned with nervous energy as I watched him spooning lumpy bites of oatmeal into his mouth. From behind the chow line, I could see Grace giving us the hairy eyeball and I turned my body away from her so I didn't have to see her knowing glare. Either I had sighed aloud or Tommy could just sense my disgust.

"What's with that lady?" asked Tommy as he peeled a banana and took a bite. "She's always asking me questions that are none of her business," he added before he took a second piece of banana into his mouth.

I nodded. "Me too! I thought she just harassed me."

"Nope. She's all over me with questions about me and Queenie and shit like that. None of it is her friggin' business," he said and threw the banana peel into his empty bowl.

"Right," I agreed and suddenly wondered if I was supposed to get permission or something like that to get a job outside of the camp. I let the thought go and decided that it was better to ask forgiveness later than to ask for permission in the beginning.

"Let's go get you a job," said Tommy. He stood to throw out his trash and returned the dirty bowl and spoon to a cart by the door.

"Sounds good to me," I said and exited the Big Top with Grace's laser like eyes burning holes into both of our backs.

10

Interviewing for this job was the most nerve-wracking thing I had ever done. It was even scarier than going all the way with Bert. *At least with Bert I knew I'd have one happy customer*, I thought and cringed at my lack of focus during such an important and potentially life changing meeting.

"So, Dawn, no outside work experience?" Mr. Spencer repeated.

I shook my head in the negative and opened my mouth to explain how I'd worked in the office at Riverbend, but then thought better of it when I realized that would be a dead giveaway that I was an Imperfect, a Tester, which would make it harder for Mr. Spencer to play dumb should the matter arise in the future.

Mr. Spencer checked a box on a sheet of paper that sat on the tidy desk in front of him with a nubby pencil. "That's okay. We're pretty good at getting smart kids like you trained up in no time. And, if you're anything like Tommy, you'll be just fine here." After making a few more scribbles on the paper, he looked up from the sheet and gave me a warm smile. "Can you start today?"

"Uh, like right now?" I asked and worried he'd think I was dumb and immediately regret his decision to hire me.

Instead, he chuckled and nodded. "Like right now," he said with an amused twinkle in his gray eyes.

"Yes, sir. Mr. Spencer. I'd love to," I said and worried the nervous blush that was crawling up my neck would melt the makeup off my imperfection and give away my biggest secret.

"Follow me," he said and opened the door to his office.

We were immediately enveloped into the hustle and bustle of a busy kitchen. Tommy was at the sink scrubbing pans and wearing yellow rubber gloves that went up to his elbows. He grinned at me as I gave him a lame thumbs up and continued to follow Mr. Spencer to the front counter.

"Angie, this is Dawn. She's going to be working here at the counter with you," said Mr. Spencer. "Holler if you need anything," he said, and disappeared through the swinging door into the kitchen.

Angie looked me up and down and I could almost hear the groan in her rolling eyeballs. "You ever work a register before, honey?"

"No, Ma'am," I said, embarrassed at how inadequate I was already.

"Ang is just fine. Here, watch," she said and she punched a few keys on the register. "You know how to make change, I assume?" she asked with a furrowed brow that suggested she didn't think I could do it.

"Yes. Ang. Yes, I can do that."

"Okay, Dawn. Here's your first customer. Ring him up," she said. She grabbed a paper check from a man's hand. He had been waiting impatiently in front of the register during our previous exchange.

I copied the instructions from before and was able to ring in the purchase quite easily and then I made him proper change from his twenty-dollar bill. He handed me a five-dollar bill from his change and gave me a wink.

"For the new girl," he said, and then strode out of the diner as if he'd given me a diamond necklace.

I sensed Ang was looking at me so I turned in her direction. "Was that okay? Should I have said no?"

Ang shook her head. "I've waited on that cheapskate for nearly ten years and he's barely left me a dollar that whole time," she marveled. "You must have some sort of charm about you." She almost sounded like she was scolding me.

I shrugged, and was unsure of what to say. An unfamiliar feeling was roiling inside my chest and I wondered what it could be up until this moment. Then I realized: it was pride. I'd gotten hired, done a good job and people seemed to like me. I was so grateful for Tommy getting me this job. I knew I'd have to think of some way to thank him. *Some way that won't get me into much trouble,* I noted before I took the next check from two women and successfully rang them up.

11

A few weeks passed and I enjoyed the routine of getting ready in the morning. After Bert would leave for his construction job, I'd do a full face of makeup, eat breakfast with Tommy, and then walk with him to the restaurant. On most days I'd work the register for a good eight hours before heading home to tell Bert about all the customers I'd helped. At times, I was also given extra responsibilities by Mr. Spencer if someone called in sick or if it was really busy and they needed help. I'd even gotten a paycheck and with Bert's guidance, we cashed it and put the money into a tin box that Bert had found and hidden behind a loose board within the wall of our shelter. It was amazing to be earning money and having a goal. It made me feel important and lucky and… happy. Yes, happy.

Bert and I had become even closer in those weeks. We'd spent more time exploring each other at night and I must admit that he was doing a very good job spelunking. My unexplainable attraction to Tommy had waned as Bert and I continued our evening dalliances. Grace had been leaving me alone too. She seemed to tire of giving me knowing stares when I fought like hell to quell any reaction to them, and she'd moved on to some other relationship within the camp that she felt needed her prying.

Walking to work with Tommy on this gorgeous Friday was ordinary and perfect. He talked about a girl he'd met at the camp that he kind of liked and I was happy that I didn't feel a twinge inside my body one way or another as he talked about the possibilities of asking her out. Things were finally seeming normal, until a few hours into my shift when the whole world came crashing down around me.

****

The lunch hour had just passed and I was busy wiping the counter and straightening the sugar bowls and condiments, my back to the door. The small bell on the doorjamb jangled as another customer entered and I turned to greet them. My heart sank when I was met with the horrid smirk of Queenie. She sat at the counter right next to the register and turned the coffee mug over as if it was some sort of beacon that would force me to come to her.

I glanced at Ang at the other end of the counter and saw that she was busy with a customer who liked to regale her with long winded stories from his trucking route. She leaned on the counter, her heavy breasts inches from his plate and chuckled at all the right moments, even swiping at him with a dish towel once or twice as she laughed. I wondered why she looked like she was enjoying herself so much if he annoyed her, but I figured maybe he was a good tipper or maybe she really liked him and didn't want me to know.

I turned back to the grinning Queenie and inhaled deeply. In my head I warned myself to be careful. I needed to be nice. She was a paying customer and I had to be welcoming and gracious even if she wasn't.

Tucked safely behind the counter, I walked toward Queenie. She sat stick straight, perched on her stool like the pigeon she was. "Hi, Queenie," I said and nodded toward her upturned mug. "Coffee?"

She pushed the mug away and shook her head. "No coffee for me."

My brow furrowed as I tried to read the odd expression plastered on her smug face.

"Something to eat then?" I asked and pulled a menu from below the counter and placed it on the paper placemat in front of her.

"Nope. Not hungry," she stated and kept her eyes trained on my face.

I worried that her unwelcome stare would cause me to sweat which, in turn, might make the makeup run, exposing me to the world, but I fought the uncomfortable tingling feeling that was building in my chest and pressed on. "Do you want anything?"

Queenie smiled and for a moment I was struck by how pretty she was when she wasn't being a lousy shit. Unfortunately, the genuine smile quickly faded back to her regular crooked smirk and I knew something bad was coming.

"Has everyone at camp been missing me?" she asked and for a brief moment, I thought she genuinely wished people did miss her. Too bad it wasn't even close to being true.

I shook my head. "Nobody has talked about you being gone as far as I know." It was the truth. Even Tommy hadn't mentioned her lately. I'd thought about how nice it was to have a break from her, but that was about it, and I had no plans to tell her that little tidbit.

"What about Tommy? He missing me?" She smirked again and she craned her neck as if she was trying to see beyond me and into the kitchen where she obviously knew Tommy was working.

I followed her gaze toward the kitchen and then turned back to face her. "Nope."

Queenie squinted at me and her eyes roved over my face clearly taking in every detail of how well the makeup covered my imperfection. Heat flashed beneath my cover-up and I again worried that her mere presence would ruin the good situation I had going here at the diner.

"You two hooking up, or are you still stringing Bert along?" Her smirk morphed into a look that clearly showed she was quite pleased with herself. Two digs for the price of one.

"Not that it's any of your business, Queenie." I fought to keep my voice even and quiet, "but Bert and I are just fine. And you know that Tommy and I are just friends."

"Right." She looked down at the menu and pretended to be looking for something to order.

My heart raced beneath my apron and I wished she'd be satisfied with her current level of torture and just leave, but the heaviness in my belly told me that she was just getting started.

She put the menu down and pointed to the drinks section. "Chocolate milk please," she said as if she'd chosen the one item on the menu that might be a pain in the ass to make.

"Sure," I said and turned to the cooler behind me and pulled out a small carton of chocolate milk and placed it in front of her. "Straw?" I forced a genuine smile instead of the righteous grin I'd wanted to give her.

"Yes." She looked a bit defeated.

My heart rate slowed a bit. I'd won the first battle no matter how insignificant it was to outside eyes.

Queenie shifted her weight on the stool and leaned closer to the counter. "Guess what?" she whispered.

I didn't lean closer to her, I just couldn't. I didn't want to give in to her whims like that. "What?"

She pushed her feet on the bottom rung of the stool and leaned even further over the counter, almost knocking over her carton of chocolate milk. "I'm pregnant," she whispered. Her eyes never left my face.

I shook my head as thoughts bounced wildly off the inside of my skull. She was only sixteen, maybe seventeen—how on earth could she be pregnant? Tommy was an Imperfect, a Tester. He shouldn't be able to produce offspring. As my muddled thoughts continued to ricochet inside my cranium, I heard myself asking, "What?"

Queenie's smirk was plastered on her face. Clearly, I was giving her the reaction she wanted. "Well, not really, but that's what I've told… people."

My brows knitted together. "What people? What the hell are you talking about, Queenie?" I demanded a bit louder than I'd planned. An old couple at the window turned in our direction so I finally relented and leaned toward her. "What's going on?" I whispered harshly.

Queenie leaned back a bit as if she found being so close to my face distasteful. "Do you like fireworks, Dawn?"

Thoroughly confused, I shook my head again and tried to figure out what pregnancy and fireworks could possibly have to do with one another. "Queenie… what the hell…?"

The bell behind Queenie jangled and she turned to look at who had entered. My eyes followed hers and I saw that two uniformed police officers had just walked in the door. Their presence wasn't unusual. I'd waited on a ton of cops here at the diner. What was unusual was the fact that they nodded at Queenie as if they knew her.

"Enjoy the fireworks, Dawn," she said and hopped from the stool. She approached one of the police officers and pointed toward the kitchen. The other officer had approached Mr. Spencer. He pointed toward the kitchen as well and the crestfallen expression on Mr. Spencer's face spoke volumes.

The officers pushed through the swinging door and after a bit of murmured talking and a loud bang from a pan hitting the bottom of the stainless-steel sink, the officers came back through the doors escorting Tommy from the kitchen. His hands were pulled behind his back in handcuffs, and his wet apron was still tied around his neck and waist.

"Oh my God," I said as I watched them march Tommy toward the front door. One of the cops held a handful of Tommy's t-shirt at the scruff of his neck to firmly guide him toward the exit. "Queenie, what the hell did you do?"

With a wave of her hand and malice in her grin, Queenie pointed in my direction. "Her too," she said as if she were the master of ceremonies and we were mere characters in her little performance.

If you asked me about this later, I would tell you that I swear I could see the devil himself dancing in Queenie's eyes as they placed cold, metal handcuffs around my wrists and escorted me and Tommy outside to an awaiting patrol car.

12

Luckily for us, they placed me and Tommy in the backseat of the same police car. I didn't know exactly what was going on, but I figured I could at least tell Tommy the lies that Queenie told me she'd been spreading.

Whispering, I leaned toward his ear. "Did they tell you why you were arrested?"

Tommy shook his head in the negative and eyed the lone officer in the driver's seat. The second officer had taken Queenie in his car.

Leaning even closer, I whispered, "Queenie told them that she was pregnant."

Tommy's eyes bulged. He shook his head in the negative again.

"I think she's lying," I added and shifted back to my spot when I noticed the police officer was watching us intently in the rear-view mirror.

"Of course she's lying," Tommy hissed with a glance toward the front seat. "I can't have kids. She knows that." His was tone bitter and angry.

I nodded in agreement. "Why do you suppose I'm here?"

Tommy shrugged. "Revenge," he said firmly.

I rolled my eyes. Queenie was many things and vengeful was just one of her lovely qualities. I figured that they would take us to the station and it would all get straightened out. The main person I worried about was Mr. Spencer. I didn't know what the penalty might be for hiring not one, but two Testers to work in his diner. Florida was more easygoing about this rule, but now that the law was involved, it might be hard or impossible for us to go back.

Sadness at the probable loss of a job I loved crept into my consciousness as we made our way through town. Suddenly, like a bolt of lightning, a horrible thought occurred to me. I leaned toward Tommy again. "Do you think she'd expose the camp? All the Riverbend kids are there, they'd know we were connected to the raid."

Tommy's eyes grew wide as the idea of Queenie sinking the whole camp dawned on him. "Shit, I hope not," he whispered, his eyes silently pleading with the universe to make her a little less vindictive.

I leaned my head back on the seat and was overcome with a wave of nausea. Not only was my job gone, but the camp might get broken up and I'd have no idea how to find Bert again. *How on earth can this day get any worse?* I groaned and leaned my head against the window as the police car pulled away from the restaurant.

# 13

I'd heard stories about how badly Imperfects, especially Testers, were treated once picked up by law enforcement, but I had no first-hand knowledge, just campfire tales, and to be quite honest, I thought most of them were grossly exaggerated. I knew when Bert was picked up before the raid, he was treated quite well. They'd fed him and given him a shower and clean clothes, but, I remembered, that was up north. We were in Florida, and although they seemed to let things slide here or there, it was a whole other animal.

After arriving at the station, I was promptly forced to strip so a woman dressed in a khaki uniform could search me and every inch of hiding space a human body could offer. As she squatted in front of me to poke and prod personal places, her uniform stretched tight over her ample thighs and I worried the stitching would burst open and somehow, I'd be blamed.

The worst thing came next. Yes, worse than having a multi-cavity search. She made me take off my makeup so they could photograph me. With a thin, dingy towel that had clearly seen better days, she had me scrub the makeup off without a wisp of remover. Being theater makeup, it was like scrubbing fresh pine tar from the bottoms of your feet. My imperfection screamed at the abuse and I was brought to tears during the whole humiliating ordeal. Removing the makeup was bad enough, but the female officer and a few of her male counterparts made certain that I could hear them snickering as each layer came off revealing more and more of my disgusting face.

"I could tell she was an Imperfect from a mile away," one lout bragged from his desk in the corner. "Not enough makeup in the world could cover that ugly mug," said another as I fought back burning tears and the hatred that crept into my belly in a gnarled bundle of emotions.

After I was thoroughly cleaned up, I was outfitted in a bright orange, boxy jumpsuit. Then, I had to survive the snap of an excruciatingly bright flash as my mugshot was taken. The snarky officers pulled the images from the camera one at a time, taking more photos than necessary so they could each hold a copy in their judgmental hands. Hooting and hollering followed each reveal with my ruined face at the end of every punch line.

As I fought the heavy weight of humiliation that threatened to smother me like a blanket, I thought about Tommy and wondered how he was faring. I hadn't seen him since we'd arrived and were separated. I also wondered where Queenie was and hoped that she wasn't within earshot of the comedy show that was happening at my expense.

When the deputies seemed to have had their fill and run out of "face like hamburger" jokes, I was escorted to a cell and was locked inside. I sat on the concrete slab meant to be a bed and thought about Bert and Camp Big Top. I tried not to imagine them being raided, but my mind flitted between images of scared children being scooped out of the only home they'd ever known and the adults being handcuffed and taken away in prison vans.

Tears started to burn in the corners of my eyes and thick layers of anxiety and stress formed into a ball in the pit of my stomach and sat there, waiting for me to imagine my way out of it or succumb to it and let the tears flow. I didn't want to give the deputies the satisfaction of seeing me cry so I fought the growing sensations of doom with every fiber of my being and pushed them down until they were just an uncomfortable twinge at the edges of my brain. I realized I needed to plot my next move. I needed to get the hell out of here and see if Bert and the others were okay. And, I needed to get Tommy out of here too.

My plotting was interrupted by a sharp "psst" from the cell next to mine. At first, I didn't know what the sound was, maybe a malfunctioning vent or air conditioner, but it came again and this time, it had a voice.

"Psst. Hey. Is that you?" the voice whispered, almost too low to understand.

"Tommy?"

"Yeah, it's me," he said and a hand emerged, twisted awkwardly between the bars.

"Oh, Tommy!" I gasped and grabbed the waving hand almost wanting to kiss it in relief.

"Shhh. Ow, hey, not so hard," he said. I released his hand and it slipped away. "Are you okay, Dawn?" he said, his tone a hushed whisper.

I sniffed and realized that tears had started, despite my hard work in denying them. "I'm okay. You?"

"I'm good." He exhaled and sighed as if he was relieved to have confirmation that I too was okay.

I leaned my head on the cold metal that separated us and whispered between the bars. "What's going to happen to us?"

"I dunno. Did you get your call yet?" he asked, a hint of hope in his voice.

"Call?"

"Your one phone call. Did you call anyone yet?"

My brow furrowed. I'd forgotten that we were allowed one phone call upon being arrested. Momentarily, I mentally flogged myself for forgetting. With my vast knowledge of television shows I should have known about the call. But, I reckoned, that could have been just television rules, not real-life rules.

"Did you?" Tommy asked, this time he sounded impatient, as if he was dealing with someone who was slow on the take.

"No. Did you?"

"Yeah. I called Malcolm to warn them that they might get a visit from the fuzz. They were going to clear out for a bit just to be safe."

"Oh, that's great, Tommy, really great." My entire body relaxed at Tommy's revelation. I had no idea that Malcolm had a phone or that Tommy would know the number. I guess there were a lot of things at Camp Big Top that I wasn't privy too. But it made sense to have a phone line and that Tommy would have it since he's on the outside every day and he might get an early inkling of anything that might be brewing. Especially at the diner since we wait on cops all day long. You never knew what you might overhear in a conversation or on a static filled radio.

"So, who are you going to call?"

I shrugged even though Tommy couldn't see me and my mounting confusion. I didn't have anyone to call. Not one soul. I couldn't even call Bert. He certainly didn't have a phone. I was sure about that.

"Do you want a suggestion?"

"You know who I should call, Tommy?" I said, the surprise at this notion made my voice go higher than I'd planned.

"Shhhh," Tommy scolded me from the cell next door. "Not so loud. You never know where there are ears listening." He grunted with dissatisfaction.

"Sorry. This is my first time in here, you know." I hated how condescending I sounded.

Tommy chuckled. "I know, Dawn. Sorry. Just try to keep it level, okay?"

"Okay." I felt like a fool nodding to the shadows.

"So, the person you should call is a bit out there. You might not agree," said Tommy, his voice hesitant.

"Just say it," I wanted to know what he was thinking before we were interrupted and possibly separated by a cruel guard.

You should call your dad."

"My dad?" My mind buzzed at the mere suggestion. I wouldn't have thought of calling him in a million years. "My dad," I mumbled again as I rolled the idea around in my head.

"What?" asked Tommy. "What'd you say?" he added when I didn't answer right away.

"Uh, nothing. Just thinking." I wanted him to be quiet for a moment so I could gather my thoughts. My dad was a cop up north and I knew he had been looking for me, so he might just be the one person in this unkind world who would give me a fair shake. In the very least, with just the call, he might be able to get me out and maybe Tommy too. It started to make sense. The only problem I faced was that I didn't know his number, but I knew the town he worked in so I felt confident that I could get the operator to connect me to his station. I just needed him to be at work and willing to accept my call.

"Guard," I yelled, my confidence in Tommy's plan growing. "Guard! I want my phone call!"

Heavy, booted footsteps approached from the far end of the cell block and I was greeted by a guard with a permanent smirk plastered on his face. "Who's missing you, beautiful?" he asked, his voice oozing sarcasm and condescension.

"Leave her alone," Tommy growled from next door and the guard recoiled at his volume, as if he was afraid to be overheard by someone who might actually care about the treatment we received in this grim place.

The guard unlocked the gate with a key attached to his pants by a long chain. He slid my door open and pointed for me to step out. I made certain to take a half step backward so I could see Tommy to verify that he was okay. He gave me a quick thumbs up and mouthed 'good luck' and then I was marched down the hall to make my call. *God, I hope he can help,* I thought and instantly my steps felt lighter as I imagined a future with my dad in it.

14

After speaking with an extremely patient telephone operator, I was connected to the correct police station in New Hampshire. My palm was sweaty on the receiver and it slipped a few times from my grip. Worried I'd lose my privilege if the line became disconnected, I squeezed it until my knuckles turned white with exertion. As I listened to it ring on the other end, my stomach twisted uncomfortably as if it had been flattened out and was then being used for an origami project by a person with big, unskilled fingers. I imagined that if I coughed or sneezed hard enough a swan made from my intestines would come floating out of my mouth.

Finally, the ringing stopped and my call was answered by a woman. "Dover Pond Police Department. How may I direct your call?"

I hesitated, suddenly uncertain how to word my question.

"Hello? If this is an emergency please hang up and call 911," she instructed, her tone bordering on irritation.

"Um, sorry, no, it's not an emergency. I'm trying to reach my dad. Um, my father. Officer Baker. Is he available?"

"Oh, hey Abby!" she said, clearly mistaking my voice for my sister's. "I'll get him for you honey, hold for just a second," and with a click she was gone.

"Shit," I said aloud, and worried that he'd already be angry with me for being an imposter. *And,* I thought, *I guess my sister is named Abby.* An officer at the desk nearest to me glanced up at the clock and then over at me and I silently wished for my dad to hurry the hell up. I had no idea if my one phone call included a time limit.

A click brought me back to the task at hand. "Hey, Abs, everything okay?" asked a voice that was warm and caring. My stomach instantly seized at the idea that I'd missed out on eighteen years of someone giving a crap about me.

"Um, sorry, it's not Abby. The lady didn't let me finish before she put me on hold. I'm… uh… your other daughter," I said and squeezed my eyes closed, a silent prayer on my lips.

After a moment of silence and a deep exhale, he responded. "My other daughter? But, how… how did you find me? How do you know about me? Shit. Sorry, I'm a little surprised here. Are you okay? Where are you?"

Tears burned in the corners of my eyes. *He cares about me,* I thought as I fought the lump that was forming in my throat which seriously risked my ability to speak clearly.

"I'm okay," I said and released a whimper that surprised even me.

"Where are you?" he asked again, this time forcefully, clearly the cop inside him was coming out.

"I… I'm in Florida. I'm at a police station. I'm sorry. I didn't know who else to call," I sobbed into the phone.

"Sweetie, it's going to be okay. Tell me what station you're in and I'll contact them directly to get you out. I'll come get you," he offered and my body went weak at the idea of my dad coming to rescue me.

"I'm in Jupiter Hills. I didn't do anything wrong. I just had a job," I said and silently prayed that he believed me.

"Okay, Jupiter Hills. Got it. I don't care what you did, honey, I'm coming to get you. Uh, stupid question, but what do you call yourself?"

I laughed despite the emotions roiling around within my slight frame. "Dawn. My name is Dawn."

My dad chuckled too. "Nice to meet you, Dawn."

His warm voice washed over me and I sensed that he loved me. Not like how Bert loved me of course, but like how a dad would love and take care of his daughter. "You too, uh, dad," I said and cringed, as if I'd said the wrong thing at the wrong moment.

He chuckled softly again. "I am your dad. I'd recognize your voice anywhere. You sound just like your sister. Her name's Abby. She's your twin," he added after a slight hesitation.

Of course I knew I had a twin—I'd been inside their house and seen the pictures from her fabulous life, but I didn't think now was the proper time or place to admit that I had broken into his house with ill intentions so I tried hard to fake surprise at his revelation. "A twin? Wow."

"I can't wait for her to meet you. I can't wait to meet you. Your mother won't believe this," he said more to himself than to me.

"Will my mother be happy?" I asked and my stomach shriveled in anticipation of a negative answer.

"Are you kidding me? Of course she will. She never wanted to give you up, Dawn. She fought like hell to keep you, but you know the rules. It was devastating to let you go."

I took a deep breath and tried to speak, but my words were finally gone. The mere idea of a dad and a mom wanting me, that they were happy to find me, was beyond anything I could ever imagine. And, a sister was in my future too. A sister who looked just like me. *Well, except for one thing*, I thought and felt the heat growing in my imperfection and I suddenly worried they'd regret finding me when they realized how ugly I was compared to my perfect sister.

"Still there, Dawn?" my dad said, his voice soft and comforting.

"Yeah. I'm just overwhelmed. I didn't think you'd want me." I dabbed at the salty tears on my cheeks with my orange sleeve.

"We love you, Dawn. Hang in there, kiddo. I'll get things straightened out and come get you."

"Thank you," I said and then decided to push for more. "Do you think you could help my friend who got arrested with me? He was just working too. His name's Tommy."

"Tommy," he said as if he was writing the information down on a sheet of paper. "Anyone else?"

"No. That's it," I said and wondered if I should mention Bert now or if I should just wait and get out of here first. I'd need to tell him about Bert eventually. I would not go back to New Hampshire without him… that was for certain.

"Hang tight, Dawn. Just behave and do what they ask. I'll try to get you released and then we can meet up in a few days. Do you have a place to stay?"

"Yes. We'll be okay," I said and my heart ached to see Bert so I could tell him all that had happened today.

"Ok, Sweetie, I'm going to hang up now and get on the phone to that station. You good?"

"I'm good," I said and from the comforting warmth of familial love emanating from my chest, I realized it was true. Who would have imagined that I'd get arrested and reunited with my family all in the same day? And, the person I'd need to thank was none other than the salty Miss Queenie, I thought as I replaced the receiver and signaled to the officer that I was finished.

"Queenie," I muttered under my breath as I was escorted back to my cell. I was anxious to get back near Tommy to tell him that the cavalry was coming and it was being led by my dad.

15

"Well, hol-y shit. Lookie who has friends in high places," said the snarky guard as he opened my cell door.

I ignored his comment and stepped out into the hall, curious if Tommy's door would be opened next.

The guard continued his verbal assault with a glint of malice and satisfaction in his dark eyes. "Who the hell would be looking for a purple faced freak like you?"

"You'd better bite your tongue," Tommy hissed from the cell next to us.

With a content smirk at the bait being taken, the guard leaned toward Tommy, the bars inches from his face. "Whatcha gonna do about it, freak?" he snarled at Tommy. He lifted a hand and made a fake punching motion toward the bars. He seemed unsatisfied when Tommy failed to flinch.

"Norton!" a voice bellowed from a door where the hall of cells ended and the office area began. "Just get them out and get them over here. Quit messing around."

"Both of them?" the guard asked. His face turned red, and he was clearly nervous at the prospect of freeing both of the people he had just insulted.

"Did I stutter before? Yes. Both of them," said the voice from beyond the door.

The guard turned toward me and nodded curtly. "You stay right here," he ordered although all the bravado had left his tone.

He turned toward Tommy's cell door and paused with the key inserted into the lock. "No funny business from you," he said and turned the key, opening the door with a metallic creak.

Tommy stepped out of the cell and sidled up next to the guard who I'd noticed had begun shaking. "None from me, Officer," Tommy breathed into his face. A pleased smirk spread over Tommy's face when a bead of sweat dripped down the guard's temple.

The guard pointed a shaking finger toward the door and weakly said, "Get walking."

Tommy looked at me with a grin of contentment and, with a swipe of his hand, let me lead the way out of the cell block.

We exited the echoing hall of concrete into an office area that was very quiet. One officer was perched on a stool near a tall table by the front door. Another greeted us with a brisk nod as he exited a room with vending machines and a microwave. He finished what he was chewing and pointed toward a door marked 'Chief.' He turned the knob for us and pushed the door open. We were waved in by a man in a blue uniform that was creased to perfection. He was on the telephone but indicated that we should sit in the chairs in front of his desk while we waited for him to finish his conversation.

"Yes, sir. Yes. They're right here. Just came in. Yes. I will. You're welcome and thank you for understanding." He returned the telephone to its cradle. He rested his elbows on the desk and leaned toward us. "Hello, Dawn. Tommy." He cocked his head to the side as he reviewed both of our faces.

"Hi," I said and gave him a faint smile.

Tommy nodded a silent greeting and kept his face blank, clearly not wanting to give this person any ammo in case we were in more trouble than we realized.

"Dawn, that was your dad on the phone. He's ordered you to be released. You and Tommy. Normally we don't pay a lick of attention to other stations when it comes to you people, but since your crimes were minor and Tommy's bigger crime is unsubstantiated, we agreed to release you assuming you both leave town and don't come back. And, we'll need your promise that you won't make any noise about how you were treated here. Do we have an understanding?"

I nodded vigorously. I was relieved to have this whole mess over with.

Tommy leaned toward the desk with a questioning expression on his face. "What bigger crime?"

I raised my eyebrows at Tommy. Obviously, he hadn't heard that old statement about not poking the bear. He shrugged back at me; his hands raised. Clearly his curiosity was piqued and the need to know his crime was more important to him than a swift, clean exit.

The chief grunted as if he too was not pleased with the delay. He'd probably expected we'd hightail it out of the station as soon as we were released. He put a pair of reading glasses that were hanging on his chest by a string over his eyes and grabbed a file from the top of a stack of paperwork on the corner of his desk and flipped it open. "Contributing to the delinquency of a minor. Kidnapping. Rape. Need more, son?" He looked over the top of his glasses at Tommy and flipped the file shut. It was clear that he was done playing games.

"Rape?" Tommy muttered. "What the hell?"

"Queenie," I whispered and flashed my eyes wide at him as if he were stupid for not understanding why we were here.

"No. No way," Tommy sputtered and shook his head.

"The female juvenile that initially reported you has recanted. Luckily for you," he said. His droll face was unmoved by Tommy's sudden stroke of judicial fortune.

"Who? Was it Queenie? C'mon, you've got to tell me," urged Tommy, his face turning ashen.

"Sorry, son. File's been closed. And, I don't owe you a damn thing. Take your friend here and get the hell out. Now, since it's so late which is unusual for releases, I took it upon myself to get you two a motel room up the block at Twin Pines. I'd recommend you go and get some rest before you head to wherever you're heading."

"Thank you, sir. That was very kind of you. We'll be leaving," I said and stood. I grabbed Tommy's quaking hand and pulled him to his feet. "Ready, Tommy? Let's go."

Tommy followed me out the door and held fast onto my hand.

The chief followed behind us and watched us with narrow eyes as we neared the exit. "At Twin Pines, tell Beverly that I sent you. She'll take care of you. And, remember, I don't want to see either of you around here after tomorrow."

"You can bet on that," I said and pushed my way out the door, into the dark, toward freedom.

16

On the short walk to the motel, Tommy and I discussed the possibility of skipping the free room and instead heading back to Camp Big Top. However, we reasoned that the camp might have cleared out based on Tommy's warning call. Also, it was entirely possible that we were being followed and we didn't want to risk bringing down the whole camp with our selfish desire to sleep in our own beds with our own people. Also, there was the urgent matter of our bright orange, matching prison wear that we needed to change out of. Our clothes had been shoved into our hands in bags as we'd exited the police station. We didn't even have a chance to check that everything was there in our haste to leave that unwelcoming, awful place.

The air was heavy with heat and humidity and a rumble of thunder told us a storm was close so we scurried into the office of the Twin Pines motel and entered quickly as the first fat raindrops started to fall.

A woman behind the desk looked up from a tabloid magazine and rolled her eyes at us as if she hated being bothered by two imperfect losers who'd had their room paid for by the same people who had arrested us hours before.

Tommy ignored her bored expression and boldly approached the counter. "Are you Beverly?"

She gave him a nod and the bangles on her wrist clanged musically as she flipped the page of her tabloid, and set it on the counter, opened to a page with a story about a celebrity's lush wedding.

Tommy leaned onto the counter and deliberately placed his elbows on top of her magazine. I watched with amusement as he deftly eliminated her ability to turn the page to the next inane article and forced her to deal with us if she wanted to continue her reading. "The chief sent us and said you had a room for us. We'd like our room now," said Tommy, his gaze direct and unmoving.

"Fine," said Beverly with a southern twang that reminded me of a country singer that I'd seen on a television special years before. I squinted at her face and quickly determined that she wasn't any country songstress, just a country bumpkin with a boring job at a lowlife motel.

Beverly snatched a key from a pegboard behind her and turned back toward us with fresh venom in her eyes. "You two married? I don't like letting rooms to couples who ain't married. It ain't Christian," she said and continued to give us the once over, her bloodshot eyes roving over our bare hands clearly looking for wedding rings.

Tommy chuckled. "Of course we're married." He threw his orange clad arm around my matching shoulders. "My little woman and I would like our room now," he said, his voice strong, making it quite clear that he didn't want any more shit from a woman who had probably been married several times to several un-Christian men.

She grunted at his overture and led us out of the office and back into the rain. The overhang of the roof kept us dry as we made our way past curtain covered windows and closed doors from behind which came muffled sounds of televisions playing or voices chattering. We finally stopped at the last door at the end of the building and Beverly inserted the key into the lock and pushed the door open. "Check out is at ten. Try not to make a mess; I don't have any help with maid service this week and I don't like having to clean up messes. And, bring your suits to the office tomorrow. I gotta return them to the station."

I nodded my agreement to her rules. Tommy smirked at her. She grunted her disapproval at us again before she turned away and scurried back to the main office, her bracelets jangling the whole way.

Tommy stepped inside and then turned back toward me. "Shall I carry you over the threshold, wife?" he asked, his smile broad and charming.

"Don't be stupid," I scolded and walked into the room.

Tommy shut the door, tossed his bag of clothes onto the floor and started flipping switches here and there to see what turned on what. He found an air conditioner in the window next to the bed and turned a dial to start it up. The ribbons tied to the grill sprung to life and the coolest air I'd ever felt came whizzing out in a stream of modern magic. I was suddenly quite pleased with our decision to stay the night here instead of going directly home. A humid night like tonight would have been a tough one to sleep through in our camp.

After standing in front of the cool air for a few moments, I noticed Tommy sitting on the edge of the king-sized bed. He'd been watching me with an amused expression on his lips, his eyes showing admiration that made me a bit uncomfortable in this room, all alone.

"One bed," Tommy said and patted the quilted top of the blanket.

"I noticed," I said, my eyes scanning the room for other options for sleeping. Unfortunately, Twin Pines was short on décor. There was a small bistro table with two wrought iron chairs, one nightstand with a blinking clock and a lamp, and one king-sized bed. I walked to a small closet, closed my eyes, and said a silent prayer for a cot to be hidden behind the door, but my eyes were met with a small ironing table and an iron on a shelf above the rung. The room didn't even have any extra blankets or pillows.

"You can have it, Dawn. I can sleep on the floor. I'll just take the comforter for padding, maybe I can get some towels too," he said as he got up and walked toward the bathroom to inspect what was available. He held up two towels. "Just two. Cheap bastards." He tossed the towels unceremoniously onto the bathroom floor.

"We can share, Tommy. It's fine. I'm not going to have you spend the night on the floor like some animal. We've already been treated badly enough today. I'm not going to continue it."

"You sure?" he asked. A boyish grin crawled across his lips although I could clearly see he was trying desperately to fight it from completing its trek across his face.

I pointed at him and shook my head. "No funny business. Promise?"

"Cross my imperfect heart," he agreed. He traced his index finger across his chest in an invisible X.

"Alright then. You want to watch some T.V. or do you just want to get some sleep?"

"I'd be up for television. It's been a few years since I'd been able to watch anything."

"Wow, really?" I asked as I pulled back the quilt and crawled under the sheet which was amazingly cool on my hot legs. I grabbed the remote from the bed side table and set it on the comforter.

"Yes, really. No power at either camp. I'd only catch stuff occasionally at places I'd worked, but not enough to follow any programs or know what was really going on in the world."

"I'm used to cartoons from Riverbend. That's about all they'd let us watch."

Tommy nodded. "I remember," he said and lay on the bed next to me, careful to remain on the top of the covers. He folded a pillow in half and stuck it behind his neck to prop it up. He grabbed the remote, pushed a few buttons and the television snapped to life.

"I'm not even sure how to use this thing. Guess I'll just go up or down the channels until we find something interesting." He started hitting the up arrow.

"Sounds good." I rested my head on a pillow, sensing that I wasn't going to be watching for long as a wave of exhaustion passed through me.

A sharp rap on the outer door of our room made both of our bodies jerk. I sat stick straight and Tommy climbed off the bed and ran to the door. He peered through the peephole and muttered under his breath.

"Who is it? Beverly?" I asked as I watched him pace back and forth in front of the door for a few seconds. He mumbled to himself again as if he were mentally calculating the hardest math problem in the world.

Finally, he stopped and turned toward me. "It's not Beverly," he growled.

"Then who the hell is it?" I asked and my question was quickly answered when he grabbed the knob and threw open the door. Standing there, dripping wet and crying was Queenie.

"Hi, Tommy. Can I come in?" she whimpered. From my spot on the bed, I saw her peer over Tommy's shoulder and her eyes grew wide when she saw me. I immediately felt uncomfortable so I threw the comforter back and stood so she could see that I was fully dressed in my lovely orange suit.

Tommy moved to block her view into the room and crossed his arms across his chest. "What do you want?"

"I… I'm sorry. Can I come in? Please?"

Tommy shook his head and I wondered what on earth he could be thinking. I hoped he could be strong and would send her on her merry way. She'd made our life hell today and probably cost us our jobs and home. He couldn't forgive her. Could he?

Tommy turned to me and shrugged his shoulders. I shrugged mine back. I desperately hoped he understood that my shrug meant to send the bitch packing, but I thought I sensed weakness in his posture and eyes.

He turned back to Queenie. "Please, Tommy. I've got nowhere else to go," she begged.

Tommy stood to the side and waved his arm toward the center of the room. Queenie grinned and stepped over the threshold. "Thank you, baby," she said and hurried inside before he could change his mind.

I sat back down on the bed and felt angry heat crawl up my neck setting my imperfection on fire. I couldn't believe he let her in after everything she had done to us.

Tommy shut the door and leaned against it; his shoulders slumped in defeat. Queenie looked at Tommy and then back at me. "Got a towel," she asked and smirked at me like she'd won the grand prize at a pissing contest.

I shook my head and bit my lip to keep from laying into her. I worried Beverly would be nearby and ready to call the police on us at the slightest increase in our volume. I pointed Queenie toward the bathroom and crawled back into the bed and slapped at the quilt as I laid it over my legs. I glanced at Tommy still leaning on the door and I shook my head at him. He mouthed that he was sorry and I glared at him. I threw my head back on my pillow, claiming my territory before Queenie could come steal if from me. My last thought as Queenie emerged from the bathroom drying her hair with one of our two towels was that tonight was going to be bad.

17

Tcmmy stared at me, his mouth agape. I wondered what he was thinking. Did he want me to say something to Queenie on his behalf? I worried my language would be too rough for her prim sensibilities and she'd scurry out of here to report us to the police again. *Maybe that wouldn't be the worst thing*, I thought as I saw Tommy's expression change and he seemed to be getting over his shock at seeing her here, in our room.

Queenie finished using the towel and tossed it toward the bathroom door, missing it by at least two feet. She shrugged at the discarded fabric and flopped down on the corner of the bed… my bed.

Heat filled my chest and crawled up my neck setting my imperfection ablaze for the second time since her arrival. I wanted to scoot forward and kick her in the ass from under the comforter, sprawling her smug face all over the hideous vomit colored carpet.

My neck snapped toward Tommy and he held up a shaking hand as if he was trying to stop me from spewing with his half-assed attempt at using 'The Force.'

My eyes bulged at his dismissal. Someone had to set this bimbo right and if he wasn't going to do it, I knew it had to be me. I saw Tommy's Adam's apple move up and down as he swallowed hard and opened his mouth to speak. Queenie beat him to it.

"Kinda cozy in here, don't ya think?" she asked as her eyes roamed around the small room.

"What the fuck, Queenie?" said Tommy, his tone harsh despite his weak posture. It made me smile from one corner of my mouth as Queenie let his words soak into her stupid brain.

"You don't want me here," she whined, her fake sniffles ready to go.

"Why the hell would I want you here? Why would Dawn want you here? You sold us out," he said, shaking his head at her.

"But, but…" Queenie muttered, her lip quivering faster than a hummingbird's wings.

"No buts. You sold us out. Plain and simple," he stated, his tone becoming softer as she continued with her act. I hoped he wasn't buying it. It was blatantly pathetic and uber fake.

Queenie sniffed one more time for good measure and then tipped over onto the bed, quickly rolling onto her stomach so she could cry some loud crocodile tears into the spare pillow.

I rolled my eyes at Tommy hoping he'd see my disbelief in her actions. His face showed another story. He was breaking and believing her. The angry heat from before simmered in my stomach and I worried I'd be sick. How could he be so dumb? I fought the urge to spout everything I was feeling. Not wanting to cause extra drama that Queenie might enjoy, I vowed to bite my tongue, at least for now.

Tommy took a step toward the bed and put his hand on the middle of Queenie's lurching back. She immediately stopped crying and turned her face toward him. "I'm sorry, baby," she whined.

"I know," said Tommy as he continued to rub the center of her back.

I shook my head at him and he shrugged his shoulders apologetically at me as if he had already known he was going to cave. He loved this stupid little girl and there was nothing I could do about it.

After a few more minutes of watching Queenie trying to calm down her performance, she finally sat up and turned so that she was sitting on the top of the bed, leaning on the pillow, her knees up to her neck. She rested her dry face on her knees and looked lovingly at Tommy. She then turned to me and gave me a weak half smile that made my insides boil.

"I really am sorry," she said to the air between us. "I never thought they'd take me seriously. I didn't have anywhere to go so I figured they'd find me a house or something to stay in. Maybe a room like this," she said, waving her hand toward our room as if it was the Ritz

Carlton. "But they wanted to send me home. They called my parents. I couldn't bear to go back there," she whimpered and this time, I could tell it was real.

Tommy sat on the end of the bed so he was facing both of us. "Why didn't you just come back to the Big Top?"

"I didn't think you'd want me," she said and eyed him carefully.

"Even if we weren't together as a couple, I'd still want you around," he said and reached out to run a hand along her shin.

I fought the urge to gag. Seeing them together like this was worse than I'd imagined. I'd never met a girl who needed so much reassurance. It was almost like the perfect child was more damaged than the imperfect one.

"You do?" she said and for the first time, real tears flowed from her eyes.

"Of course, Queenie. You're my girl," he added and I had to get up. I couldn't stand seeing him being so weak and vulnerable to a girl who had him arrested for rape. I threw back the blankets and started pacing beside the bed, trapped in our box-like room with two nut jobs who clearly deserved each other.

"Can we go home then?" she asked, her tone hopeful.

"No. We can't go home. Thanks to you," I blurted out. The heat that had been simmering in my belly had to escape somehow and throwing angry words at her was working just fine.

"What does she mean, Tommy?" Queenie's eyes bored into Tommy's as if she wanted him to tell me that I was wrong and everything was fine.

"I… I used my one phone call to call Malcolm. They've probably all cleared out expecting the cops to come. We don't know where everyone is or if it's even safe to go home." He hung his head as the full consequence of Queenie's selfish actions became woefully apparent.

"I might never see Bert again," I seethed. The little jab momentarily made me feel better until that statement sunk in and I realized it could be true.

"No," said Queenie, her tears flowing freely now. "I never meant for any of this. I just needed a place to stay," she sobbed into her knees.

"I had to call my dad, too," I added, hoping to bury her a bit more. I sensed we'd be letting her off the hook soon since, in reality, we would probably need her help getting all of this straightened out.

Queenie's brow furrowed and she turned her tear streaked face toward me. "Your dad? What dad? I didn't think you people had dads."

I shook my head at her not wanting to answer. Somehow, my family seemed like it should be off limits to her and her manipulations. I still didn't trust her, no matter how much she cried and felt sorry. I probably never would.

"Dawn's dad is a cop from up north. He's coming down to get her," said Tommy, his eyes glistening with tears of his own.

"You're leaving?" asked Queenie, the question ending in an odd squeak.

I nodded. "Probably. We don't have anywhere to go. At least, we don't think so, anyway."

Queenie buried her face into her knees again. "I'm sorry," she whispered into her knee caps. Her body began to lurch again as she started to cry. This time, it was for real.

18

After Queenie had finished her crying jag the night before, I'd softened a bit, not something I was particularly proud of, and allowed her to stay. We'd fit ourselves into the bed, me on one side, Tommy on the other and Queenie smack dab in the middle. I drifted off to sleep to the sounds of zippers being unzipped and movement from snuggly neighbors with roaming hands. I'd never tried so hard to fall asleep in my young life.

A sharp rap on the door the next morning roused us all from an uneasy sleep. The urgency of the knock stirred us all quickly and we exchanged glances of concern. The last knock we'd received on the very same door had brought the lovely surprise of Queenie. God himself only knew what the second one would bring.

Tommy extricated himself from twisted sheets and, hiking up his boxer shorts, hurried toward the door. Another insistent bang on the wood caused me to exit the bed and stand next to it, guilt smeared across my face, my imperfection thumping with my raised heartbeat, although I had no reason for it.

Queenie remained on the bed, a dopey expression of satisfaction and unconcern was spread on her face and it made me shiver to think about what actions had happened mere inches from me as I tried to doze off the night before in our odd communal bed.

Tommy opened the door and we both exhaled in unison when we saw it was Beverly from the front office.

"Morning," Tommy greeted her, crossing his arms over his naked chest, the sun illuminating his discolored scar from his childhood heart surgery.

Beverly peered around Tommy into the room and her eyes grew wide as she took in the view of two half dressed women beyond the threshold.

"What's going on?" said Tommy, interrupting her perusal of the interior.

She shook her head as if startled. "Oh, sorry to bother you so early. There's a police officer here and he's looking for your wife," she said and glanced into the room again. Her eyes darted from me in my underclothes, standing by the bed, my crumpled orange jumpsuit discarded onto the floor during the night, and down at Queenie who had now raised herself up on one elbow, no doubt the word 'wife' catching her ear.

"Ok, thanks. We'll be right down," said Tommy and he started to close the door.

"He's in my office," Beverly yelled into the crack before it closed on her prying, judgmental face.

Tommy leaned on the door and gazed at us. A wry smile spread across his face. "She must think I'm a total stud," he mused as he walked back toward the bed and plopped down in his spot that was still warm from a few moments before.

Queenie squinted suspiciously at Tommy and pushed herself toward him with her elbow. "What's this wife business? What's that weird lady talking about?" she demanded.

I rolled my eyes behind her and threw my head back. *Of course she'd focus on that remark,* I thought. I was more worried about yet another cop looking for me. I hoped it was my dad, but he would have had to have broken the sound barrier to get here so fast.

"Did she say who the cop was?" I interrupted.

Tommy shook his head. "No. Do you think your dad's here already?" Clearly, he was thinking the same thing I was.

I shrugged. "I guess it could be. But if it's not, what are we going to do with her?" I said, and jerked my thumb toward Queenie who was starting to pout because her question had so far been ignored.

"Well, I guess our plans have changed," said Tommy. Before we'd gone to bed last night, we had discussed our next move. We thought we should go back to the diner to see if anyone from camp had come looking for us or given them an inkling of where they'd go, assuming they'd left camp in anticipation of a visit from the po po. If nothing had been reported at the diner, we'd very carefully make our way to the camp and see for ourselves if anyone was still there. If not, we'd search for any sign that might indicate where they'd gone to hide out.

I nodded. "I guess so," I agreed. "We should get dressed and see who's in Beverly's office."

"What about me?" Queenie whined as she fingered the scar on Tommy's chest. "You aren't going to leave me behind, are you?"

Tommy put his lips on the top of her head and gave her a kiss. "No baby, we'd never leave you. Never again," he promised.

I rolled my eyes for the second time this morning and walked toward the bathroom to splash some water on my face to try to calm the heat that was crawling into my imperfection at the spectacle I had just witnessed. *She's good*, I thought as I reviewed my appearance in the mirror. *Damn good*, I corrected my reflection. I left the bathroom to find my bag of street clothes and to discuss exactly what our plans were for the mystery cop the office.

19

The three of us decided that it would probably be best if I went to the office alone to see who was there and what they wanted. Queenie was a problem we had yet to discover a solution for if it was the local police. And, Beverly had said the officer was looking for me. Not Tommy and me. I also assumed that Tommy and Queenie would make the most of the time that I was away and the mere idea of them connecting on that level made heat rise into my imperfection again and it throbbed in the humid Florida air as I made my way down the row of doors and windows and into Beverly's office.

Beverly's tight face eased when I walked in the door and it made my stomach lurch with nervous energy. If the officer was stressing her out, what on earth does he want with me?

"He's in the back," Beverly said and pointed an arthritic finger toward a door with a bright red sign that read, 'Employees Only.'

I pushed my way through the door and found a man with his back turned toward me. He was reading a wall that was covered in aging newspaper articles. I cleared my throat and looked down at the floor. "Excuse me. Are you looking for me?" I asked. My imperfection thumped uncomfortably on my cheek as a fresh wave of anticipation and fear ran through my body.

The man spun on his heel and his eyes fell right on my face. Instantly, I bent my neck down making me look deeper into the threadbare carpet. The sharp movement caused my hair to fall across my cheek as if in a desperate effort to cover up the one thing that made me stand out in this world.

"Oh my God," murmured the man. He slowly covered his open mouth with a quivering hand.

Here it comes, I thought, waiting for the initial wave of shock to ease and then the barrage of insults to spew from this stranger witnessing my hideous appearance for the first time. I'd experienced it many times in my life. What was one more?

"You… you look just like her," he stammered and took a hesitant step closer to me.

My brow furrowed. "Who?"

"Abby. Your sister, Abby. Holy shit, you look just like her."

My chest burned as my heart exploded into a thousand pieces inside my chest. I'd expected a local cop here looking for me to maybe answer some more questions about camp or Tommy, but instead I was greeted by… my dad. "My sister?"

I repeated and instantly worried he'd think I was mentally compromised in addition to having the ugly welt on my face.

"Yes, sorry. I'm Charles Baker. Uh, Chip. I'm your dad," he added with a grin that told me he was happy to call himself that.

Tears began welling up in my eyes rendering me momentarily blind. I tried to squeeze them away, but they came faster and I let them flow. "Hi, dad," I squeaked. I wanted to run to him and hug him, to feel love oozing from him, the very love that I'd needed and dreamed about my whole life, but my feet were suddenly frozen blocks of ice turning me into a motionless crying statue.

My dad moved closer to me and reached a shaking hand toward me. He stopped and a wave of concern washed over his face as if he didn't want to scare me by loving on me too much too fast, but it passed in an instant as his fatherly instincts clearly took hold. He closed the gap between us and scooped me up in a bear hug that would stay with me for the rest of my life.

20

Awkward silence filled the air between us after my dad finally released me from his strong embrace. His face was a mix of guilt, relief, and happiness. I hoped he sensed that I was happy too. The seething anger that I'd felt after I'd left Riverbend had subsided long ago and my family up north had become a fun fantasy for me to imagine myself becoming enmeshed in if we were ever reunited.

My dad finally broke the silence, his manner becoming less fatherly and more cop-like. "Are you alone or are you here with someone?"

"My friend Tommy is back in the room. Thank you for helping him too." I thought about mentioning Queenie, but hated the idea of subjecting him to her even if it was only by name.

"Is he… uh… your boyfriend?" My dad's face turned crimson and for a fleeting moment, he resembled me.

Heat blossomed across my imperfection and I placed a clammy hand over it to calm it down. "No. He's not my boyfriend." The blaze won out and I let my hand fall to my side. "But I do have one," I added, wanting him to know that I was loved by someone in this shithole of a world.

Dad nodded. "What do you want to do now? Do you want to come home with me? You could meet your mother and your sister. They wanted to come, but we could only afford one ticket to fly down here so quickly."

My brow furrowed. I couldn't believe that he'd fly all the way down here on short notice and spend a small fortune to find me.

"Something wrong?" Dad asked as his puzzled eyes searched my face.

I shook my head. "No. I'm okay," I said and realized that it was true. For the first time since I'd left Riverbend, I felt safe. Like I had a future. Not that I didn't feel that way when I was with Bert, but we were always on the run or at a camp that could be infiltrated at any moment, so here, in Beverly's crappy office in nowhere Florida, I felt… special.

"So, what do you think? Do you want to come home with me?"

I nodded. "Home. Home sounds good," I added and hugged my dad again.

21

I couldn't bear to leave with my dad without at least trying to find Bert. I'd ask B to come with me and if he said no, well, I guess that would be that. Long distance relationships with a man that lived in a nomadic group that could pull up stakes at any moment probably wouldn't be the best choice to entertain if I intended on starting a new life up north. It would kill me to leave him, but I had to put every ounce of effort into making things work with my family. I sensed that so deep in my bones that they actually ached at the idea of things not working out.

My father agreed to take Tommy, Queenie, and I back to Camp Big Top after swearing that he wouldn't turn them in should they still be there. He promised easily and I believed him although Tommy kept giving him sideways glances on the way as if my dad was secretly transmitting our location to the local cops.

As we arrived, my heart sank. From the lack of human noises emanating from beyond the chain link fence, I sensed from the car that the camp was deserted. My dad waited outside while we entered the gate and went in to investigate. "Remember," said Tommy, "Look for anything that might tell us where they went. A note, a sign, anything," he instructed as we spread out across the fairgrounds searching for clues.

I helped Tommy search Malcolm's office and saw the telephone on his bookshelf that had started the mass exodus.

We turned over every paper and folder searching for information on their next location, but came up empty. Tommy and Queenie went off together to search more spots and I went off alone to search my shelter that I had shared with Bert.

Stepping inside the shelter, my aching heart broke into more unsalvageable pieces. It was thoroughly torn up, as if things were packed quickly. It looked like a good amount of my personal items were missing. I assumed Bert had taken them for me in the hopes that we'd be reunited after my release from jail. My heart was instantly warm with a deep love for him. He'd been thinking about me in a moment when he should have been thinking about himself and getting the hell out of Dodge before he too was picked up by the law.

The neat little row of plastic ducks that I had used as decoration was the only thing that remained in place. Their squat little faces stared blankly at me as if it were up to me to save them from forever being forgotten on the shelf.

I picked up the blue duck on the end and gave it a squeeze. It didn't squeak. The plastic indented under my grip and then slowly popped back into place. I thought about taking him as a memory of my time here with Bert. A nice memory of our first place together, our first kiss, our first sexual encounter, all of it happened right here with these little voyeurs watching it all go down.

Heat crawled up my neck and into my imperfection, setting it ablaze at the notion that these little dudes, although plastic, had seen me at my most vulnerable. Suddenly, the idea of leaving any of them behind was overwhelmingly sad and I knew I had to take them all with me no matter how stupid it might seem to someone on the outside.

I found an empty grocery sack balled up in the corner of the small shelter and I stuffed each duck inside after smiling at each one like a proud mama. After the shelf was cleared of ducks, a deep sadness hit me at how bland and bare it seemed. I was glad to be bringing these little guys along with me to start a new life together.

I took one last glance around and turned to leave the shelter when something caught my eye. Behind one of the ducks, a small word was carved into the wood. The carving seemed fresh. There were still sprinklings of wood dust on the tiny lip of the shelf. I brushed my fingers over the carving and knew that it was a sign from Bert. I committed the unfamiliar word to memory and ran from my shelter to find Tommy and Queenie to tell them that I knew where they'd gone.

22

Tommy, Queenie and I met back at the Big Top. Tommy, still suspicious of my father and not afraid to tell me so, didn't want me to tell them what I'd found in front of him so we had a quick tete-a-tete before going back outside to his idling vehicle.

"Did you guys find anything?" I asked, eager to hear if they'd found any clues that would confirm what I had seen.

"No," said Tommy, shaking his head.

"Just the regular dump," added Queenie with a smirk on her face that told me that she probably wouldn't have come back here to live with Tommy no matter how much she tried to whine him back into her life. She needed more and that was okay, she just needed to leave him alone in her search for it.

"What about you, Dawn? Did you find something?" asked Tommy. His face was eager but the stress of being left behind weighed down his usual youthful exuberance which made him appear years older than he was.

I nodded, eyes wide and held up my sack full of ducks.

"What's in there?" asked Queenie though the outline of the ducks inside the bag was apparent in the hot Florida sunshine.

"Not in here. I found something behind them. There was a fresh carving in the wood behind one of the ducks. It had to be from Bert."

Tommy shook his head. "I don't know, Dawn. How can you be so sure? Other people were probably in there before you and Bert. It could be old."

"It's not," I objected. "There were wood shavings on the shelf. Those were not there before, I'm sure of it."

"How could you be sure of anything in that dirty, dilapidated shack?" asked Queenie, a malicious sneer on her pretty lips.

My face grew hot and my imperfection throbbed at her rudeness. "My place was clean, Queenie. Some of us were raised to take care of ourselves better than others," I sneered and turned away from her before she could retaliate.

"Cut it out, you two," ordered Tommy. "We don't have time for you to argue like children." He turned to me. "I believe you, Dawn. What did it say?"

I squeezed my eyes closed and imagined I was looking at the wall to see the letters again. It was going to be hard for me to pronounce it since I'd never heard the word before. I wondered if it was a Native American word. "It said, 'Immokalee.'"

"Em ok olee? What the hell does that mean? It's not even English," snorted Queenie from my left.

I refused to look at her or give her any indication that she was annoying me to the core.

Tommy was nodding as if he understood. "I know where that is. There's a casino there, I think."

"Really?" I asked, relieved that I was probably right about the carving.

"One of the busboys at the diner was from around that area. Brad or Gordon, one of them. I didn't work with them too much except when we were busy and needed two of us on the Saturday shift, but I'm pretty sure one of them was from there. The high school had the same weird name."

"So, what do you want to do?" I asked, hoping somehow all of this would work out.

"Are you going home with your dad?" Tommy asked, his face turning ashen despite the humid air.

I nodded. "I think so. At least for a while."

I caught a glance of Queenie in my peripheral vision and I could see a smug grin spread across her face. "What about your lover boy? Just going to ditch him?" she sang, clearly enthralled at the idea of me leaving and crushing someone's heart in the process.

"Shut it, Queenie," Tommy ordered and she immediately started to pout, her bottom lip puffed out like it'd been stung by a bumble bee.

Tears formed at the corners of my eyes as the gravity of my decision started to become apparent thanks to the insensitivity of one little brat, namely Queenie.

"What about Bert, Dawn?" Tommy asked softly as if he understood he'd be the one to break it to him.

"Will you tell him where I am, Tommy? Tell him to come north and find me. He knows where my family lives. He'd be welcome there; I just know it. Promise me, Tommy. Promise me that you'll tell him to come find me," I urged. Tears crested over my lower eyelids and dripped down my cheeks in wet trails, and burned over my imperfection as if I'd been sliced across the face by a laser.

Tommy nodded. "I promise. I'll tell him."

"Thank you," I wept and fell into Tommy's arms. His body lurched a bit during our hug and I knew he was crying just as hard as I was.

The honk of a horn from beyond the fence split us up. "Your daddy's getting impatient," noted Queenie as she eyed me and Tommy, still locked in our embrace, with fresh suspicion.

Tommy took a step back from me and gave Queenie a dirty look. She scowled and turned her head away from us as if she'd had enough of being told what to do today.

"You should go," Tommy said and nodded toward the car idling behind the fence. "We'll be okay. We'll find the group and tell Bert that you're safe, and that you went home with your dad."

I nodded and sniffed and dabbed at my cheeks with my sleeve.

Tommy put a hand on my arm and gave it a reassuring squeeze. "B will understand," he promised, "I'll make sure he does," he added and reluctantly released my arm.

"Okay," I said and turned to leave through the small entrance in the fence. "Good luck, Tommy," I said and slipped through the rusted metal and into my new life.

Leaving Tommy behind the fence had been one of the hardest things I'd had to do in my young life, but it didn't compare to the despair that I felt leaving Bert behind, especially since he had no idea where I was or if I was ever coming back. I had to count on Tommy and the evil Queenie to tell him where I'd gone and with whom, which didn't make me feel much better. Tommy, I trusted, but I worried Queenie could easily manipulate him into a lie that would make Bert believe I'd left him for good.

My heart ached at the notion and fresh tears welled in my eyes and rolled down my cheeks in messy rivers. My imperfection burned with each passing drop, which made me feel even worse about my decision. My dad was sympathetic to my plight and even offered to turn around and look for my group, but I shook my head. I had it in my mind to go home and meet my twin and my mother and I knew in my soul that Bert would understand, assuming he was given the correct information. I hoped he'd come find me, like in the movies when the handsome prince shows up for his princess. Not that I was remotely anything like a princess—more like the hideous ogre that was forced to live in exile because he was too ugly to live among the pretty people. At least, that was the way I felt at times, my imperfection the first thing a person would see when they met me. Tommy's scars were hidden; mine were evident to even the smallest child. I remembered my encounter with the little boy on the bus who had compared me to a singing dinosaur. I smiled despite the hurtful memory. "Stupid kid," I muttered under my breath.

"What's that?" my dad asked leaning toward me and turning down the radio as if whatever I'd been mumbling was the most important thing in his world.

I shook my head. "Just remembering something from a while ago."

My dad reached across the console and patted my knee. "You can trust me, you know, Dawn. I'm here for you with whatever you want to share. When you're ready," he added as he withdrew his hand and placed it back on the steering wheel.

I nodded. "I know."

"Good. So, are you excited to meet your mom and sister?" Dad's grin was broad across his face and his happiness was evident by the smile inducing crinkles surrounding his twinkling eyes.

I shrugged. "Do they know I'm coming?" I asked, and was suddenly worried that I'd be an unwelcome surprise on a Tuesday morning.

"Of course," he reassured me. "I called your mother yesterday. She can't wait. This will be good for her, you know. She'd never stopped worrying about you. Not for one single second. And, with Abby being your twin, we had an everyday reminder that there was another sweet angel out there who was a part of us. No matter what the government had to say about it," he grumbled.

"What's Abby like?"

Dad grinned. "Hmm. She's a lot like you, I suppose. Although she's a bit more immature than you, I'll admit. We sheltered her quite a bit. I assume your upbringing and the time after you left Riverbend forced you to grow up a lot quicker. She's a good kid though, you'll like her, I'm sure." I wondered for a moment if he was reassuring me or himself.

"Did she know about me? Abby?"

Dad shook his head. "We didn't tell her. We worried she'd have guilt over being the one that we kept, so we didn't. I'm sorry about that. I hope you don't think we were hiding you from her. It was just a fact of life we didn't feel like we were ready to share just yet."

"I'm sure it would've been hard for her," I agreed, a painful twinge in my chest at his statement about her being the one they chose to keep. Clearly, I was damaged goods. That fact seemed to be the furthest one from his mind, I noted as I listened to him telling me all about Abby and how she was a good athlete with lots of friends.

"Sounds like she had a lovely childhood," I said with more acid in my tone than I'd anticipated when he finally stopped talking to take a sip of water from a bottle he'd ordered at our last fast food stop.

"Gee, Dawn, I'm sorry. I'm blathering on like an idiot. I assume your childhood wasn't that great. We'd tried to keep tabs on Riverbend, but they were very secretive. Even being in law enforcement didn't allow me any exclusive access. I'd been there once or twice on calls when there was trouble with a resident, but they made sure to keep the kids who weren't involved away from outsiders."

I nodded. I'd remembered a few lockdowns when the police had been called and someone was hauled away, never to be seen again. It was usually an older resident, one who was close to release, so I always figured they just dumped them early from the system. *Fend for yourself, you ungrateful brat,* I thought with a wry smile.

"So, was it okay? You were okay in there?"

I sat silent for a moment. I sensed that my hesitation in responding to his question was a bother to his guilty conscience, but I really needed to think about it. Finally, I said, "Riverbend was… adequate."

"That good, huh," Dad mused and took another swig from his water bottle. "They didn't, uh, hurt you?"

I shook my head. "No. But there wasn't a lot of love there, at least not from the staff. I had friends, though." I smiled and remembered Mindy from my childhood, my pseudo mother. Until she disappeared. And then there was Wendy. My lips pursed at the memory of her. She'd died in my arms after the power had been cut and her oxygen pump had shut off during the raid. The raid that I had participated in.

"That's great," my dad said, his excitement clearly as forced as his smile, the missing crinkles around his eyes a dead giveaway.

"I think I'm going to try to sleep," I said as the memories of my missing and dead friends began to overwhelm me.

Dad nodded. "Go ahead. I'll wake you when we get close. I'm going to try to get there in one trip instead of stopping. Your mother is going to be anxious to get ahold of you."

I balled up a blanket from the floor and propped my head against the window. My last thought before I fell into a deep sleep was about Wendy and how my actions had ended her life.

24

"Dawn. Dawn, wake up, we're here," a voice called, rousing me from a sleep so deep I didn't even have a single dream.

"What?" I asked, still groggy. I turned my head for more information and the muscles felt strained, as if they'd been locked in the same position for way too long.

"We're here. We drove through the night. We're home."

"Home?" I asked, still dumb from my epic slumber.

"See, Mom's in the window," Dad said and pointed toward the front door.

I followed his finger and saw a woman waving from the screen door. She let it slam behind her and she took the three steps all at once, and almost did a face plant on her way to the passenger side of the door.

"Shit, jeez," Dad said and opened his door. "Slow down, don't break your ankle," he shouted at the woman.

She slowed her pace and stopped just short of my door. I could see her face now and it surprised me at how much she looked like an older version of me. Minus the massive blemish on her cheek, of course.

I put my hand on the handle and started to pull it. My dad had slid back into the car and stopped me with a firm hand on my arm. "You ready for this, Dawn?" he asked, true concern in his warm eyes. "Don't worry if there isn't an immediate connection. This will take time," he added with a half-smile that made me wonder if he was soothing himself with the same bit of advice.

I nodded and pushed the door open. The woman beyond it had clasped her hands together under her chin and I could see her body was jittery with nerves. I stepped from the safe confines of the car and let her approach me with wide arms, ready for an enveloping hug. "My baby," she murmured into my hair. "You're home, baby," she said and squeezed me with a second hug before she released me and grabbed both of my hands in hers. "Wow, you look just like Abby. It's amazing," she marveled.

Dad made his way around the car and stood proudly next to her side. "I told you, Rita. Just like Abby, right?"

I smiled. My dad was named Charles and my mother was named Rita. I'd known that from my file, but I'd never imagined in a million years that those names on paper actually translated into real living, breathing human beings.

"You hungry, Sweetie?" my mother asked as she put an arm around me and steered me toward the front door. "I made a bunch of things, hopefully you'll like something," she fretted.

"Where's Abby?" Dad asked, clearly anxious for the twin sisters to reunite.

My mother's brow knitted together and she shook her head to shush him.

"Oh, is she with Jake?" he asked, his tone suddenly fatherly and stern.

My mother nodded. "It's okay. We'll get to know Dawn here and Abby will be by later. We don't want to overwhelm her anyway," she added as if trying to make a solid excuse for Abby's absence at such an important time.

"True," my dad agreed, and I wondered who they were worried about overwhelming: me or Abby.

"Let's get you settled inside and get you some food," my mother said and led me into the house. I took a glance around and it looked the same as the day I'd broken in. Warm and inviting. I suddenly hoped she'd made macaroni and cheese like the kind I'd eaten when I came here stalking them all those months ago.

"Why don't you go wash up and come eat?" my mother instructed, pointing me toward the bathroom down the hall.

I nodded obediently and locked the door behind me. The half bath was decorated nicely in an ocean theme. It reminded me of everyone I'd left behind in Florida. I sat on the toilet lid and closed my eyes, inhaling deep breaths of the sea breeze air freshener that was plugged into the outlet. Somehow, without knowing much about either of these people or this place, it felt like home, and, despite missing my friends, I was happy.

25

My mother had not been kidding when she said she'd prepared food for me. It was like a Las Vegas buffet in the dining room. Roasted chicken, salad, mashed potatoes, rolls, and my favorite, macaroni and cheese were laid out on the table in gleaming dishes. I wondered if she'd stayed up all night to have this ready for us. For me.

I sat down at the table and let them serve me. A slice of white meat, a dollop of frothy potatoes and a healthy mound of cheesy noodles were plopped onto my plate in front of me. My mouth watered in anticipation of enjoying the bounty.

I had just finished my second plate of food when the front door clicked and my father's body instantly went rigid. My mother stopped in mid-sentence and craned her neck toward the entrance. "Was that the door?" she asked my dad although I sensed she already knew it was.

"Abby?" my dad called.

"What?" The irritated tone of the visitor's response was not promising.

"Excuse me," said Dad. He quickly got up from his seat and left the room.

My mother seemed nervous. She tried to distract herself by mixing the salad with wooden spoons and offering me some. I shook my head no and listened.

"Hi Dad," came the voice again from the living room. Oddly, it sounded just like me.

My stomach turned over despite being weighed down with a pound of food and my mother's nervous energy started rubbing off on me.

"Come meet her." I heard my dad urge from the living room.

"No," said my voice from afar.

"Come on, Abs, you knew I was bringing her home," he reasoned.

"Fine. But just for a minute," my voice twin huffed. Stomping feet started making their way toward the dining room.

I swallowed hard and looked toward my mother. A thin film of sweat had appeared on her forehead and upper lip. She smiled at me despite her obvious concern about the contentious meeting that would take place in mere seconds.

Abby bustled into the room. She scowled at her mother and then trained her eyes, my eyes, on me. "You're in my seat." She moved a step closer to me, her eyes slanted suspiciously at the girl who was clearly trying to take her place, one meal at a time.

"Oh, sorry," I muttered and stood up to move.

"Abigail!" our mother scolded. "Be polite. This is your sister. Dawn, this is Abby," she added and wiped at her forehead with her napkin.

"Right. Hey, Dawn," she said and plopped down in the seat that I had once occupied. She pushed my plate away from her and grabbed a new one. She slapped a big scoop of macaroni and cheese on it. "Are there any unused forks out here?" she asked, her eyes trained on her mother's stressed face.

"Uh, I'll get you one," our mother relented and disappeared into the kitchen.

I thought I heard a gasping sob from the direction of the kitchen, but I was so entranced by Abby that my ears buzzed and had lost all function.

"Abby, please be on your best behavior," my dad said through gritted teeth as he sat back down in his own seat. "Just sit over here, Dawn," he said with a tired smile and pointed to the empty the chair across from Abby.

"Thank you," I muttered and sat down, my body jittery with an energy that I couldn't quite explain. It was as if Abby had sucked all the breathable air from the room with her arrival and now everyone was afraid to exhale and give up the little oxygen they had left.

"How long are you staying?" Abby asked me through a mouthful of bread.

I blinked my eyes. I felt stunned, unsure of how to answer such a direct question. "Uh, I don't know," I finally said after processing this odd situation for another moment.

Abby turned toward our dad. "Is she slow, too?"

"Abby!" he scolded.

She shrugged. "What? She took forever to answer. I didn't know if she was given away for just that thing on her face or if she was retarded too?" She said feigning innocence with an exaggerated shrug and a flap of her eyelashes.

Embarrassed heat scorched across my face setting my imperfection ablaze. I put my hand on it to cool it down, but to no avail. My mind reeled with anger and confusion. I couldn't believe that my own sister, my twin sister, could be so heartless toward me. I closed my eyes to prevent the tears from rolling down my cheeks and further irritating my blemish, but it was too late. The little bitch had been awful and got to see her reward. I lost the battle and was reduced to a quivering mass of tears and mucus. I instantly hated her with every fiber of my being. How could I have been so stupid to come this far and assume they'd all want me? My parents clearly did want to be a part of my life, but this twin of mine certainly didn't. She didn't even bother hide her disdain for me. She reminded me of the worst person I knew in this world. She reminded me of an even more disgusting and rude version of the jerk I'd left behind in Florida. She reminded me of Queenie.

26

Dad got up and stormed from the room. He'd headed toward the kitchen, no doubt looking for our mother who was taking an enormous amount of time to find a simple fork.

His leaving left Abby and I alone in the dining room surrounded by luscious food that I wouldn't be able to eat any more of. Not with her here. Not with her watching. I was suddenly grateful for being pretty full already.

"Looks like they rolled out the red carpet for you," she said, and waved her hand over the table at the spread our mother had clearly toiled over.

I dabbed at my face with my napkin and sucked back the snot in my nose. I was pulling myself together and was getting ready for combat. My momentary weakness at her rude words was passing. "Guess they were happy to see me," I said and blew my nose on the napkin, not caring if it was rude to do so at the dinner table.

"Lovely," Abby noted and rolled her eyes at me as if I was the most putrid thing she'd ever seen.

"Right back at you," I said and squinted at her to indicate that I was ready for more.

"What are you after?" Abby asked, her eyes just as slanted in suspicion as mine. "We don't have money," she added and watched my face closely.

I shook my head. "I don't want your money." I threw my napkin on the table.

"Then why are you here?" she pushed.

"Your dad… our dad, he came and got me. I was down in Florida."

"Yeah, in some cult or something. You Imperfects are all the same. Trash," said Abby, her disgust evident.

"It was at a camp. We're as normal as anyone else. We just don't get a fair shake," I said with conviction.

She grunted and looked at me with wide eyes. "Normal? I think not. Have you looked in a mirror lately?"

I shook my head. "You were this close to being just like me," I said, holding my fingers an inch apart. "One chromosome the other way and you'd be saddled with this instead of me," I added and pointed at my throbbing cheek.

She gave me a sly grin. "The Lord works in mysterious ways, what else can I say?" she said and scooped noodles into her mouth with her fingers.

"What's your problem with me?" I asked and realized I really did want to know. Her hate toward me was unexpected and I needed to know what I had done to deserve it.

"Not just you. All of you," she sneered.

"All of us?"

"Yes. Imperfects are a scourge on society. Don't you read the papers? Maybe you can't read." She grinned at her dig. "You're the lowest of the low. Thieves, rapists, prostitutes, and murderers… trash, all of you."

I wondered if growing up with a father who was in the police force had a big part to do with her language and bad feelings toward Imperfects. It made sense. But it was not an excuse.

"I'm a good person. My friends are good people," I said and swallowed hard. In the back of my mind, an image of Wendy taking her last breath popped into my head. She was dead and it was my fault. Maybe Abby wasn't so far off in her image of what kind of people we were after all.

Abby dropped her hands onto the table hard enough to shake the dishes of food. "I don't want you here. And I always get my way." She pushed herself up, her hands squeezing and wrinkling the table cloth on both sides of her plate. "You'll see, Dawn the Imperfect, you'll see." She stomped dramatically all the way down the hall and slammed the door to her bedroom, the very bedroom where I'd smelled the sweet vanilla scent on her pillow not too long ago.

I sat boiling in my chair and glared at her empty seat. I wondered why they'd bother to bring me here if this was how I was going to be treated. I knew I'd made a huge mistake coming all the way back to New Hampshire and I decided right then and there that, come hell or high water, I needed to leave.

27

With Abby safely ensconced in her bedroom, my parents came back into the dining room and I finally understood the walking on eggshells analogy. I momentarily felt bad that they were being cautious around me, but that quickly abated when I saw in their apologetic eyes that they'd set me up. They knew Abby was a vicious shit and they still let her come at me like a pit bull in a dogfight and I was the pathetic bait dog that wasn't meant to survive.

"Are you okay?" my mother asked hesitantly. She cowered before I answered as if she was ready for me to verbally pummel her just like Abby had done to me. I was certain that they'd been on the receiving end of many of her rants.

"What the hell was that?" I sputtered, hating the nasty tone in my voice that mirrored Abby's.

"We're so sorry, Dawn," said my dad, his usually warm eyes glassy as if he were in shock. "I hoped she'd have learned to deal with this situation better before we got home."

"I knew she was having trouble with us finding you, but I had no idea she could be so awful to someone in her own family," said my mother although, based on her forlorn expression, I had a tough time believing it wasn't a regular occurrence in this farce of a happy home.

"Awful is an understatement," I said as a fresh wave of heat set my imperfection to throbbing again. I worried the pulsing would be visually noticeable in my current state of upset so I put my hand over it hoping to calm it.

My mother walked over and took my hand from my cheek. "Don't cover yourself up, Sweetie. You're beautiful and perfect just the way you are." The honesty in her voice made my eyes well up. I blinked back fresh tears before they could sneak down my cheeks.

"Perfect, hmpf," I grumbled. "Perfect is clearly overrated," I joked, hoping to ease the tension in the room.

My dad grinned at my lame attempt at a joke. "Nice one," he complimented and chuckled hollowly.

"Dawn, please don't let Abby's initial rejection, uh, attitude toward you make you feel uncomfortable here. We really want you to stay," my mother urged as she continued to hold my hand, giving it a reassuring squeeze.

Dad nodded vigorously. "Yes, please stay. You complete our family, whether Abby wants to admit it or not."

My mother's eyes flashed toward my father as if she wanted him to stop talking. He opened his mouth to speak and after catching her drift, he closed his mouth and remained silent.

"C'mon Dawn, tomorrow is another day. Let's get you set up in the guest room and things will seem better after a good sleep."

I nodded in agreement and let her lead me down the hall, past Abby's room which was vibrating with loud, pounding music, and into a nicely decorated spare bedroom. I looked around and realized that this probably would have been my room had I been allowed to be raised with my family all those years ago.

"Is this okay?" my mother asked after she fluffed the pillow on the tightly made bed and smoothed an errant wrinkle out of the beige satin comforter.

"Yes. It's great." I sat on the bed and gave it a little bounce. I felt like a little kid exploring a playground for the first time. "Comfy," I added and smiled at my mother.

She grinned at me. "Sorry I didn't know your favorite color, but I figured you could add stuff later on… if you stay, that is." Her tone was wistful.

I nodded again, not wanting to promise too much so soon. I still missed Bert desperately and I wondered what it would be like to share such a nice room with him. My heart ached at how lonely I was, despite being surrounded by people who loved me.

"Get some sleep," my mother said. She stepped toward me and kissed me on the top of the head. She opened her mouth to say something else, thought better of it and left, closing the door behind her with a soft click of the knob.

In my room, alone, I listened to the hammering music from next door that belonged to my angry sister. I threw myself on the bed and despite not feeling tired when I walked in, I fell into a deep sleep and this time, I dreamed of Bert and my other friends, even Wendy. For the first time in a long time, my heart, despite its constant ache, was full.

28

The next thirteen days passed at a speed that should only be reserved for glaciers. I was basically a prisoner in my parent's home. I don't think it was on purpose. I sensed they felt uncomfortable with the stares that I received on the few outings we'd taken to the local grocery store and restaurants in the first few days of my visit. The outings slowly dropped off as the weeks went on and curiosity about me grew.

Don't get me wrong, I really enjoyed spending time with my dad, but, unfortunately, he was the bread winner of the family and had already used his accrued vacation time to come get me, so he had to work nearly every day and his hours were incredibly long. My mother was okay. I could tell she wanted to please me, but didn't quite know how. She tried very hard to buy my affections with little gifts she'd bring home for me. One morning, she'd brought me a whole shopping bag full of different colored concealers from the drug store. She'd apologized profusely at the underlying indication of such a purchase, as if I'd worry she'd think I was hideously ugly and needed to cover my imperfection to function in the outside world. When I'd kindly refused to try any of them, a bit of rebellion on my part since I truly did like to wear it, she stopped taking me places.

And then there was Abby. She seemed to enjoy torturing me with snide comments when her parents were out of earshot, but it wasn't like their presence would stop her either. She'd refused to sit next to me on movie night. Apparently, I had yet again taken her special spot and she'd throw an epic fit. That was fun. Luckily, she spent a good majority of her time with the mysterious Jake who our parents seemed to know very little about despite their helicopter nature.

On day thirteen, mom and dad had dared leave us alone to go to church. Abby was still getting her beauty sleep, which I strongly recommended and would never disturb with the hopes it would somehow improve her rotten personality, and I was staring at the television although the inane reality show that was on had failed to keep my interest beyond the opening credits.

I was startled from my introspection of my boring life by movement in the kitchen. My stomach dropped immediately as I peered over the couch and saw Abby rooting around in the cabinets for dishes and food for her breakfast.

She must have sensed my spying or finally heard the television because she whipped around and gave me that slanted suspicious stare that I had become accustomed to. "Take a picture, it lasts longer, Dawn," she huffed and then grinned as if she was quite pleased with her fifth-grade dis.

I turned my attention back to the T.V. and was surprised that she plopped down in her usual spot on the end of the couch instead of retreating to the safety of her room for her mid-morning chow.

"This show is so lame," she muttered as she swirled bits of cereal within the milk in her bowl.

"Flip it. I don't care," I said and tossed the remote control toward her.

"Watch it, Dawn," she seethed.

"It wasn't even close to hitting you, Abby," I said with a fair amount of piss and vinegar in my tone. I was feeling cranky and didn't want to allow her to verbally assault me again.

She scowled at me and grabbed the remote off the couch cushion and began flipping through the channels at a dizzying speed. "This sucks. There's nothing good on," she lamented and ended up back on the same show I had been watching.

A knock on the front door startled us both and Abby got up to answer it. As she approached the door, I heard her mumble, "This had better not be Jake. He still needs to apologize for being a dick last night."

Abby stood on her tiptoes and peered through the peephole and grunted her disapproval. "There's some dude at the door," she stated.

"Who is it?" I asked, almost certain I wouldn't know whomever was on the other side.

"I dunno," she answered and peered through the peephole again. "But he's kinda hot," she added with a shrug that was almost playful.

"A hot guy that you don't know?" I verified. My heart skipped like a rock on a lake within the walls of my chest. Could it be someone for me? Maybe Tommy? Or, better yet, my Bert?

"I just said I don't know him," she sneered at me from the door. "I probably shouldn't answer it. Dad doesn't like me to open the door for strangers," she added, using our poor father as an excuse for allowing the stranger to leave.

"Let me see," I said and bounded from the couch to the door just in time to hear a second, more urgent knock on the wood. I peered into the peephole and my heart climbed up my throat and tried to push itself through the tiny hole. "Oh my God! Thank you, Lord!" I yelled and grabbed at the doorknob.

Abby pushed her body between me and the knob preventing me from opening it. "Wait just a second. Who is that?"

"That's B! My boyfriend. Oh my God, oh my God. Move, Abby," I said and made another move toward the knob.

Abby scowled at me. "Your boyfriend. You have a boyfriend. Stop lying, Dawn."

My brow furrowed and I shoved her away from the door with both hands. "Yes! Move, you bitch!" I yelled, my arms shaking with frustration and a surge of adrenaline.

"What the hell, Dawn?" moaned Abby from her new position a few feet away. "Relax, I was kidding you. Gosh," she muttered and slunk away toward her room.

I didn't have time to care if I'd really hurt her, God knew she'd hurt me enough with her words over the last few weeks. Desperate to get to Bert before he gave up and walked away, I grabbed the knob and pulled on it. The door creaked open and Bert's once stressed face broke into a handsome smile when he saw me.

"There's my Dawny-girl," Bert said with a twinkle in his eye. He took a half step toward me and opened his arms.

I closed the gap between us in a nanosecond and launched myself onto him. I smothered his cheeks with kisses and whispered, half crying, into his ear, "You found me. Thank God, you found me."

29

I hustled Bert inside almost afraid to share him with the outside world for a moment longer. I ushered him toward the living room and grabbed his hand to pull him down next to me on the couch.

"Glad you missed me too," he mused as he sat down and gently kissed my marred cheek. His stubble scraped against my face and although it was a tad painful, it was heavenly.

"You have no idea how much," I replied and kissed his lips. *He tastes the same,* I noted and tried to ignore the delicious heat crawling across my imperfection.

"Wow, nice digs," he said after I'd released him from my smooch and he had a moment to look around the living room.

"It's okay," I agreed half-heartedly.

"Uh oh. It's not okay?" Bert asked.

I marveled at his ability to read between the lines of my comment despite the fact that we'd been apart for what seemed like a solid year. "There are some things that aren't so great." I hoped Abby wasn't around the corner eavesdropping.

"What could be the matter? You've got a bed, a living room, a television. You've got air conditioning! What's wrong with that? Except for my not being here, of course," he joked and grinned at me, his eyes bright, boyish and charming.

"It's not the place," I whispered. "It's the people." I added and rolled my eyes toward the darkened hallway.

Bert nodded. "Not all they're cracked up to be, huh?"

"My parents are fine," I offered. "It's my sister. She's just awful," I added with a well-timed shiver.

"Your sister? Really? I would've thought she'd be thrilled to meet you."

"Shhhh," I scolded and again eyed the hallway that led to the devil's den. "She's down there," I whispered, and jerked my thumb toward her room. "She's moping or plotting my demise. Something horrible, I'm sure of it."

"Huh. Go figure," said Bert, clearly still surprised that someone who looked like me and shared a good portion of our DNA could act like a puke.

"She's like Queenie on steroids," I said, my eyes wide.

"Ugh. I'm sorry Dawn. That's terrible," he agreed.

Just hearing those words from him made my eyes tear up. It had been a long time since I'd had someone to tell my secrets to and someone to be completely honest with. Faking happiness was much harder than I would've thought. I sighed and leaned into his muscular arm and closed my eyes, thoroughly enjoying this brief moment of peace.

"So, why stay then?" Bert asked, breaking the quiet moment I craved much soon than I'd wished.

I looked away from his confused stare. A wave of guilt washed over me that set my imperfection to thumping. "I dunno. I guess some of the perks you mentioned earlier sort of outweigh the crap I put up with." I shrugged. "I guess creature comforts beat out psycho sisters in the right circumstances."

Bert nodded. "The air conditioning is nice. We definitely don't have that in Florida," he lamented and I'd worried I hurt him by picking cold, manufactured air over being with him.

I squeezed his hand. "It's not just that. My parents are pretty good. My dad, I really love. My mother, she tries hard, but I can see that I disappoint her with… this." I brushed my hand across my cheek and immediately wished I hadn't because the guilty thumping got stronger at the inadvertent touch.

Really? What makes you think that? I'm sure she thinks you're beautiful. You're her daughter for crying out loud."

Bert's ire made me smile. *At least he thinks I'm beautiful,* I thought and sighed again at my good luck. "She bought out the concealer section at the drug store and she kind of pushes me to wear it if I want to go anywhere. When I refused, she stopped taking me places. I've been stuck inside these boring walls for four days now."

"That's not right. I won't let you settle for that. By the way, where are Mom and Dad?" Bert asked, his eyes roving around the room and into the adjoining kitchen.

"Church. Actually, they should be home any minute. I hope they're okay with me having a visitor."

"This isn't a prison ward, is it?" Bert huffed. "And it's not Riverbend. You're a grown woman. You shouldn't have to ask permission."

Bert sounded confident in his argument, but I wondered if he was worried about seeing my dad again. The last time they'd met, he'd been arrested and in jail. But he was my initial link to my dad and I was exceedingly grateful for it. I had a feeling my dad would be too.

A key jangling in the lock on the front door caused us both to stand as if we were teenagers getting caught necking on the couch in some Fifties sitcom. The door opened wide and my mother stepped in wearing her flowered purple dress that was reserved for Sundays. Then my dad strode inside. He looked quite fresh in a white shirt and tie, which was a big difference from his usual khaki police uniform.

"Hi, Dawn," my mother croaked as if she was shocked that her ugliest daughter would be in the presence of a man. And a really good looking one at that.

"Hi, Rita," I answered, still not comfortable calling her mom, although she really hadn't asked me to either. "Hi, Dad," I added with a shy smile.

My dad stepped forward with his hand extended. "Hello, Bert. Nice to see you under better circumstances," he said, his eyes twinkling with delight.

Bert shook his hand. "Yes, sir. I wasn't sure if you'd remember me."

"Remember him from where?" my mother asked. Clearly Dad didn't share every detail of his Dawn investigation with her. He probably worried about getting her excited about a lead and having it turn out to be a dead end.

My dad grinned at us, obviously amused that he had a secret to share with us. "Never mind, Dear. Let's make Bert feel at home."

My mother glared at dad as if she would speak to him about this secret later. Then she turned to us with a pleasant smile. "Of course. Where are my manners? Can I get you a beverage, Bert? A soda perhaps?"

"If it's cold, I'll take it," said Bert with a grateful smile. Dad joined us in the living room and we sat down to talk. My nerves calmed and after a few minutes it all felt really normal. From the outside, we looked like a regular family welcoming a boyfriend into the house. From the inside, the story couldn't be further from the truth.

30

After we'd talked for a while and the conversation started to dry up, my parents finally realized that Abby wasn't among us. "Did Abby go out?" Dad asked me, his brow furrowed.

I shook my head. "No. She went to her room after Bert arrived."

My mother patted my leg. "I bet she was just trying to give you two privacy," she said, her eyebrows raised in hopeful possibility.

I nodded once and let her have the fantasy. Things were going too well right now to risk throwing my dear sister under the proverbial bus, although I'd bet she'd look just fine with a tire tread running the length of her trim body.

My dad stood and clapped his hands together. "Well, I'm starving. Anyone else up for some lunch? Maybe we could go out. The diner sound good?"

"I'll ask Abby if she'd like to go," offered my mother, the hopeful glimmer still present in her eyes. "You want to come, Dawn? I could help you get ready."

I squeezed Bert's hand and he squeezed mine right back. I couldn't believe she was pushing me to cover up my imperfection in front of him. A fresh wave of hot humiliation rushed across my face making it throb uncomfortably. "I'm ready to go," I said firmly and watched her disappear down the hall, the glimmer finally gone.

We stood by the front door and waited for my mother and Abby to return. After some shouting from down the hall, my mother returned alone, her face almost as red and enflamed as mine. "Abby's not coming. She's got plans with Jake," she said although I sensed she was lying through her perfect white teeth.

Dad clapped his hands together again. "Just the four of us then. Sounds good to me."

31

The diner was busy, but we were able to find a booth in the back corner. Ironically, it was the same spot where I was sitting when I met Tommy. I wondered if the mirror was still cracked and would show me what could have been had I been the perfect twin. I shrugged away the thought when the waitress came over to take our order. She eyed me with a smidge of disdain. I wrote it off as the end of a long shift and maybe it was in my head, but it was hard to ignore her kind recognition of my father and mother and her flirtatiousness with the handsome Bert.

Our food came quickly and we were approached several times by people from town that knew my father and who probably wondered if I was Abby and had had some terrible accident. He was proud to introduce me as his daughter which warmed my heart immeasurably. It made me love him even more to hear him claiming me over and over again. My mother nodded politely, but remained mum at the curious questions, allowing my dad and his friendly nature to take over. I wondered if she was embarrassed to claim me as her own with my imperfection plastered like a mask over my face, but I fought the negative thoughts and basked in the continuing approval from my dad and the people who clearly respected him.

When we finished our food and returned home, the house was dark. Abby was gone and I felt a little guilty for thinking my mother had lied about her having plans with Jake.

Guess he apologized for being a dick, I thought when I remembered that they'd had a fight the night before. Even if he hadn't apologized, I was certain she'd be gone when we got home. It would be hard for her to see her father fawning over me and my unexpectedly good-looking boyfriend. She certainly wasn't one who enjoyed sharing the limelight.

We decided to play cards and chat about life in the camps. I worried Bert would give away too much information, but he was very careful with what he shared and I wondered why he didn't have more responsibility at camp. He was very diplomatic with his responses. He'd give away just enough to seem like he was sharing, but not enough to get into any trouble. It was amazing to see him weave his way through the conversation, considering my father was a cop and was doing his best at interrogating him without seeming like that was what he was doing.

The phone ringing interrupted our game and my mother rushed to answer it as if she was expecting a call. I immediately felt sorry for her. I sensed she hoped that it was Abby, maybe calling to apologize for being a beast and wanting this whole family thing to work out, but I could tell by the sadness in her eyes when she returned that it wasn't her perfect daughter on the other end of the line.

"It's for you, Chip. Someone from the station," she said, her tone tired and dull.

"Excuse me, folks," said my dad cheerfully, their yin and yang personalities balancing them perfectly.

My mother smiled awkwardly at Bert and me as we waited for my father to return. She'd barely talked all night, playing second fiddle to my dad, who clearly had the gift of gab and wasn't afraid to use it. "So, Bert, how long do you plan on staying?"

Bert swallowed the soda that was in his mouth and I watched his Adam's apple bob up and down as he cleared his throat. "I'm not sure. As long as I'm welcome, I guess."

"I'm sorry, Rita, I haven't even asked if it's okay if Bert stays here," I chimed in, my face blushing at my rude supposition, my imperfection ablaze for the one hundredth time this evening.

"Of course he can stay. Whatever makes you happy, Dawn," she said and acted surprised at my implied thoughtlessness. "Separate rooms, of course," she added, her own cheeks flushing crimson.

I nodded and saw an uncomfortable red heat crawling up Bert's neck too. "Yes, ma'am. Of course. Thank you so much," he said and squeezed my thigh under the table.

"I just hope Abby's okay with it," she mumbled as she stood to clear some empty dishes from the table.

Bert and I made eyes at each other at the mention of Abby's name. He'd yet to see her wrath and I almost hoped she'd put on a good show for us tonight. Somehow, I wanted him to see the misery that I'd had to bear while living here.

Dad returned to the table and plunked down. His face was ashen and he grabbed his beer bottle and finished it in one large gulp. My mother, reading his face, sat back down with the stack of dishes in front of her. "What is it, Chip? Is it Abby? Is Abby okay?"

My father nodded. He briefly looked at Bert and then he looked me square in the eyes. "Someone from the diner recognized you two. They said you were with the truck that pulled the raid on Riverbend. You were last seen in a rest area on the highway, but the couple that called was certain it was you two."

"How can they be so certain? That was months ago," my mother asked, her face becoming pale too.

"Dawn's face. They remembered seeing her imperfection," he said and twisted off the cap of a second beer and made the brown liquid disappear.

32

"So, let me get this straight. You two were involved with the raid?" my father confirmed, his eyes hollow and the life that had once been beaming out of them was gone, disappeared with the cold hard truth. He cleared his throat. "Participated in it?"

Bert and I nodded sullenly. The tears that streaked my face had stopped stinging an hour ago as we explained some of the details from that horrible night.

"We didn't want to, sir," said Bert. "The leader, Miranda, had us over a barrel. She threatened Dawn that if we didn't go and help, she'd make sure that you were set up for it. She'd done it before. Dawn wouldn't let that happen to you. She knew you had a family."

My dad shook his head. "Kids died." His voice lowered to almost a whisper. "Lots of them."

"We know, sir," said Bert. "Dawn lost her best friend that night. She died in her arms when they cut the power."

I openly wept now, and a gasping moan escaped through my quivering lips.

"Oh, Dawn. Come here, sweetie," said my mother. She sat next to me and wrapped her arms around my hunched shoulders and hugged me from our confessional spot on the couch.

"Her… name was… Wendy," I said between sucking breaths. "She was… only… six-teen."

"That's awful. Shhhh," soothed my mother.

"I had to help clear them out. All those bodies. I can't believe this," muttered my dad, more to himself than to the rest of us.

"Chip…" my mother started, clearly urging him to let it go, at least for now.

"One little boy had tape across his mouth and his hands were tied. He choked on his own vomit because he couldn't pull the tape off. He suffered, Rita," my dad's eyes were wet from the memory.

I leaned away from my mother's embrace and leaned hard into Bert's strong arm. I wondered if that was the boy I had personally taped and zip tied. This was awful. I had pushed any notion of suffering out of my head, except for Wendy's, and that was only because I had witnessed hers. And, hers had been quick. That little boy's suffering might have lasted quite a while. I hated having to remember what we'd done and now having to confess our misdeeds to my parents. Maybe Abby was right; we were thieves and murderers. We were the horrible people, the imperfect nobodies that everyone loathed and feared.

My mother must have sensed that I was in need of Bert's consoling instead of hers so she released me and stood to pace the room, wringing her hands and mumbling incoherently to herself. Finally, she stopped and looked to my dad. "What do we do, Chip? Are they coming for them? Do they know they're staying with us? Should they turn themselves in?"

My dad turned to my mother and stared her dead in the eyes. "There's only one thing they need to do."

"What?" my mother breathed into the tension filled air, her eyes brimming with a fresh round of tears.

"Run."

33

"Run?" my mother gasped from behind her shaking hand. "Oh, Chip, do you think that's the only option?"

My dad grimaced. "Unfortunately, yes," he replied, his face bleak and impossibly pale.

"Can't they just turn themselves in? Face the music. Don't you usually offer leniency for things like this?" my mother mused. Her pacing was becoming more frantic with every step.

"Rita. They didn't lift a pack of gum here. Kids died. Lots of kids died. There are severe consequences for this. And, it's not up to me. This is the government we're talking about not the local police. They'd be happy to hang them in the public square to prove their point about Imperfects and reinforce the rules we have against them. It won't work," he lamented and put his face in his hands.

"What if we offered them a bigger target?" asked Bert, his voice strong and clear despite our predicament.

"You could," my dad nodded, "but it wouldn't be enough. You were there too. You'd go down with the ship. I've seen it happen before."

"What if we gave them the whole camp?" I asked. My voice was meek and terribly weak in my own ears, like a mouse offering up the lions.

"Still not enough, Dawn," said my dad, his shoulders hunched in defeat.

Bert eyed me from the side, his face a mix of surprise and pride as if he couldn't believe I'd be willing to give up everyone to save our own asses.

"Do they just leave then?" my mother squeaked, her voice high, and her eyes darting to each of our faces. "Just like that? Gone with the breeze?"

Suddenly, my father stood with fresh purpose and a glimmer of hope on his face. "Rita, pull everything out of the cabinets that they can eat. Don't forget a can opener. You two, gather all your stuff. I'll be right back."

My father disappeared down the hall and returned before any of us had begun our tasks. He had a pile of twenty-dollar bills and slipped them into my hand. "Take this. It'll get you pretty far."

I shook my head. "I can't take all your money, dad," I protested but he pushed the wad further into my palm.

"I'd been saving for a rainy day, and girl, it's pouring," he said and smiled wryly.

I smiled back, despite the heavy guilt that felt like a thousand-pound weight inside my chest.

My mother paced her way into the kitchen and began filling reusable grocery sacks with everything she could find that was in a box or can. I went to my room and pulled together the meager amount of clothes and toiletries that I had acquired since my arrival.

When I came back to the living room with my backpack, I witnessed my father handing Bert a set of car keys. "She's old but sturdy," he said and dropped the silver duo into Bert's hand.

"Thank you, sir," said Bert. He leaned in and gave my dad and awkward half hug.

"It's Chip. Call me Chip," my dad murmured into Bert's ear.

A click at the front door caused us all to freeze where we stood. My father gulped and looked at the clock as if he'd known we were on borrowed time and it had just run out. The door swung open and to our relief, Abby sauntered into the living room, her eyes already slanted with suspicion.

"What's this?" she demanded after her eyes had searched each of our faces and lingered on the bags on the floor.

"Uh, Dawn and Bert are leaving, honey," offered my dad.

"Good riddance," she muttered and started to walk around the piles to head toward her room. "Uh, what the hell is that?" she asked and pointed at the keys dangling from Bert's hand.

"Keys?" asked Bert holding them up for her perusal.

"Dad's keys? To the Jeep?" she sputtered.

Bert shrugged.

"They're just borrowing it, sweetie," said my mother, stepping forward to put a calming hand on Abby's shoulder.

"You're letting these freaks drive your Jeep! You don't even let me drive it!" shouted Abby, sounding like a crazy teenager instead of a perfect young lady.

"Abby, c'mon," said dad.

"You people make me sick," she said sourly. "I hope I never see your ugly face again, Dawn," she said and pushed through us and went to her room and slammed the door shut.

All eyes turned toward me and I put my hand up. "I'm fine. I'm used to it. Can we just go?" I bent to pick up my bag.

My dad nodded. "Take the car as far as you can. I'll report it stolen in a few days. That should give you enough time to get ahead of them and to cover us. If they come sooner, I'll have to report it earlier. They won't believe me if I let it go too long. I'm a cop and a stolen vehicle is something I'd probably notice, especially if it was mine." He chuckled softly to himself.

"Okay," agreed Bert. "Warn us if you hear from them so we have an idea of how deep we need to hide."

My dad shook his head. "I can't do that."

"Chip, why?" asked my mother, her brow knitted together in confusion and worry.

"No contact. Zero. We can't. It's too risky. They'll probably tap our phones, the phones at the station. It's bigger than us. I'm sorry. You guys are on your own. It's like witness protection. You need to forget everyone you knew before. And, don't tell us where you're going. I don't want to know anything and please be damn sure that you don't leave any clues in the car. No ticket stubs or toll receipts… nothing. Leave the car at an airport or bus station. From here on out you need to be ghosts."

My eyes filled with tears. I'd just found them and now I had to forget I knew them and they had to forget about me. My heart ached at the mere idea of it. "No, Dad. Can't we keep in touch, like, maybe a few months from now?" I whined and hated how much I sounded like Abby having a fit.

My dad put his hands on both of my shoulders. "I'm sorry, Dawn. This is the end for us. I love you. You'll always be in my heart. You and Bert. But we can't. I'm sorry." He pulled me in for the best hug I'd ever received.

After a good minute, he finally released me, his eyes red-rimmed and tearing up. "Say goodbye to your mother, Dawn."

I turned toward my mother. She openly wept and her body shook involuntarily. I walked up to her and put my arms around her neck. I buried my face in her hair. "Goodbye, Mom," I whispered and kissed her on the cheek.

"Goodbye, my love," she said and reluctantly released me.

Bert and I gathered the items from the floor and brought them to the Jeep that was parked on the side of the house. We put the bags into the backseat and climbed inside. As we pulled out of the driveway, the last thing I saw through the glass of the front window was my parents in a tight embrace. They clung to each other like a couple mourning an unwanted daughter who was never meant to be. My parents, bless their souls, had just lost their baby… again.

34

I think I cried through four solid states. Bert was quiet and let me do it, as if it would cleanse me somehow and make me not so sad when I was finished, if I ever finished. When the tears did finally dry up, I sat zombie-like and stared out the window as the trees whizzed by. Even a close call with a police cruiser tailing us wasn't enough to snap me out of my trance. Poor Bert had to deal with that stress on his own. He drove as carefully as possible and prayed out loud that my dad hadn't been forced to call his car in as stolen just yet.

A few days later, I was feeling a bit more like myself and was able to converse easily with Bert again. I think a small part of me blamed him for us having to leave when it was clearly me and my easily recognizable face that had given us away. That stupid old couple from the rest area who had recognized us received most of my evil thoughts when I'd start to feel dark again.

We ditched my dad's Jeep in Virginia and used a handful of our borrowed money to rent a motel room and discuss our next moves.

"Do you want to go to Florida?" Bert asked.

His question was a surprise to me. "Don't you?"

He shrugged. "We don't have to. We could go somewhere else and try to make it on our own. Just the two of us," he added softly.

My eyes fluttered at the idea of me and Bert taking on the world all alone. It was very tempting, but we weren't guaranteed to get jobs wherever we ended up. I didn't know much about the country and was worried the laws wouldn't be as loose as they had been in Florida.

His eyes were trained on my face as I mentally calculated the odds of our solo survival. "Not feeling it, huh?" he finally asked when the silence was clearly too much for him to take.

"Well, what about jobs? Do you know any other states where we might easily get jobs?"

Bert shook his head. "No. I know about as much as you. We could try though," he said although the glimmer that had been in his eyes at his first suggestion of it had diminished greatly and was replaced with doubt.

I was sorry to douse his excitement, but we had to be realistic. We were screwed if we couldn't get work. Being hungry and homeless was not something I wanted to experience. "I love the idea of it, I really do, but I think we need to go back with the others and get work. We could start saving again. I loved having our secret stash of cash and a plan. We could work toward that. Maybe, like, a year from now we could manage to leave and strike out on our own.

Plus, we could try to learn more about other places, like California, and see if there are any opportunities for us out there before we just go. Does that make sense, B?"

He nodded and grinned at me. "Smart and beautiful," he said and his boyish smirk made my heart skitter inside my chest.

"You stinker," I said and pulled on his shirt to bring him in for a kiss.

After I released his shirt, he pulled away and gazed at me. The admiration in his eyes made my imperfection thump under my cheek. "To Florida," he said held up an invisible glass.

"To Florida," I agreed and gamely held up my fake glass to silently clink into his. I pretended to gulp down champagne and hoped it would quell the gnawing nerves in my belly that had instantly started ramping up when our final decision had been made.

35

We spent most of the money my dad had given us on bus tickets and food. It took a few days to finally make it to Immokalee to try to find the others. A truck driver we met near the bus station was kind enough to bring us closer to the camp to save us from overheating on a trek in the hot Florida sun. We had him drop us near the end of a huge orange grove that Bert knew was close to camp, but not close enough to give away the location should the truck driver prove to be a rat in a plaid shirt. Sadly, we knew we couldn't trust anyone. Not anymore.

We walked about a mile, our brows dripping sweat when Bert nodded toward a path in a field off the side of the road.

"That's it?" I asked, my tone of disbelief more evident than I'd intended.

"I'm pretty sure. But, wow, it is so overgrown. It almost looks like it hasn't been used in a while."

"That's not good."

"No. It's not good. They might be gone already."

"You think so?"

Bert nodded. "I was worried about this. I hope they left us a clue if they did leave. Otherwise, we might be on our own anyway."

I gulped at the humid air and lamented the money we had spent to get here. *What a waste,* I thought, as I mentally flogged myself for not taking Bert up on his offer to go it alone days ago when we were still flush with cash and hope.

"Let's go see," urged Bert. He turned onto the path and pushed branches out of the way for me.

We walked for about ten minutes, our clothes damp from brushing against the overgrown foliage and sweat. "It's not too deep in here. I'd think we'd be able to hear some noise by now," lamented Bert as we neared the edge of the makeshift camp.

I saw a pile of trash near a tree and I knew we were close. I strained my ears for the sound of voices or the clatter of work being done, but I was only met with the incessant buzzing of eager mosquitoes and a family of birds squawking their distaste of our intrusion on their forest.

We passed the last rim of trees and came to an opening in the forest that had clearly been lived in. The forest floor had been matted down by many feet, although new life had already begun to spring up between the squished pine needles and stumps of saplings. There weren't any living structures, but there were a few rings of stones from old campfires filled with soggy remnants of burned wood and ash.

"This is bad." Bert's eyes roved over the deserted campground.

"Really bad," I agreed and looked to Bert for guidance.

Bert shook his head. "I guess we should put our stuff down and spread out. We can look for clues and meet back here in a few minutes."

"Okay," I agreed and happily placed my backpack on the pine needles under our feet.

"Check everything. I mean every scrap of paper, markings on trees, anything," Bert said with wide eyes, as if trying to implore the importance of my careful review of the camp with his baby greens.

"I will," I said and went to the right. Bert went left. I didn't find much—a few scraps of paper here or there, but they didn't have anything useful on them. I checked every tree trunk for carvings or a note tacked to them and also came up empty. I found a discarded shirt and picked it up, hoping it would have the name of a town or state in someone's handwriting, but it was just a picture of a running horse and I dropped it back onto the ground, worried the potato bug who had called it home would start crawling up my arm if I held it for a second longer.

After circling my side of the camp for thirty minutes, I walked back to our stuff and sat on my backpack to wait for Bert. A few minutes later, he walked back over toward me. "Did you find anything?" he called from a few paces away, his shoulders hunched.

I shook my head. "Nada. How about you? You find anything."

"No. Just another pile of trash and I think I found the latrine which was disgusting."

"Gross," I said, holding my nose between two fingers.

"You have no idea." He grinned. "Lots of flies," he added and made a fake gagging noise.

We both chuckled and Bert flopped down in the pine needles to join me on the ground. Exhaustion etched into his face made him appear older than he was.

After taking a few moments to rest and catch our breath, I reached over and grabbed his hand. He dropped the handful of dried pine needles that he'd been picking up and dropping into a small pile in front of him and trained his eyes on mine. "So? What do we do now?"

He shrugged. "I guess we're on our own. I was sure Tommy would leave us a clue. From how clean this camp is, he would've had plenty of time to do so."

"How do you know that?"

"If they'd had to clear out of here quickly, there'd still be structures, old food, and people's belongings… that sort of stuff. It looks like they made a decision to move on and packed up carefully, taking everything that was important."

I nodded. I hadn't thought that far ahead, but the Big Top had lots of stuff left over when they'd taken off after Tommy's warning call. This place was clean. Too clean. "Do you think they had help?"

Bert cocked his head toward me. "Help? What do you mean? Help from another camp?"

I shrugged. "Maybe. Or maybe help from the police."

Bert cringed and looked around suspiciously. "I hadn't thought of that. It is really clean. Maybe they got busted up and the local police cleaned everything out," he agreed, his face solemn.

"Except for the latrine," I added, hoping to lighten the moment.

Bert grinned. "Right. Except for the piss and shit." His eyes had a playful spark in them for the first time in a long time.

I pushed myself off my backpack and stood. "Well, sir, where to?"

Bert stood and brushed a few pine needles from the legs of his pants. "Wanna check out California?"

I frowned. "Do we have enough money to get there?" I mentally calculated how much two bus tickets from Florida to California would cost.

"We'll figure it out," said Bert, his tone clear and strong and confident.

I smiled. "California? Let's do it," I agreed. I grabbed my backpack and placed it on my back. My damp shirt instantly stuck to my hot, sweaty skin.

Bert picked up his pack and slung it over his shoulder. "Our future awaits," he said and waved his hand toward the overgrown path.

I smiled as we made our way past the bushes that greedily grabbed at our clothes, the tree branches that slapped at our shoulders and faces, and even at the irritated, squawking birds who yelled at us from afar. From here on out it was going to be just me and Bert. We'd work hard to get a place to stay, then jobs and then, who knew, maybe the stars. We could create our own future. Even though I was sad to lose our friends and I fully understood that we'd probably never see them again, I was, for the first time in forever, excited to start over in a new place with a loving, trustworthy partner by my side. B and I would do our very best to find our way in a world that didn't want us. And, it would be awesome.

About the Author – Stefanie Jolicoeur

In 2008, Stefanie left the world of finance to raise her four children and to write books. *The Imperfects* is her debut Young Adult novel. Stefanie has also published a novel for adults called *Devil's Chair* and a novel for middle school children called *Gabby Michaelson Has Fleas.* She has also published five children's books *(Mousamus – A Gladiator's Tail, Sir Mousalot – A Knight's Tail, Sola's Wish, Rat-a-Claus,* and *Colorful Critters)* and had short stories in two anthologies, *Dark Waters* and *In the Shadow of Monsters.*

When Stefanie isn't busy writing, she enjoys reading, creating art in many forms and spending time with her family. She also enjoys visiting schools to share her books and her love for reading and writing.

Stefanie's books and much of her artwork are available for sale on her Etsy.com store – HappyHeartStudios.

More information can also be found on her website or on social media:

www.thehappyheartstudio.net

Etsy.com (search HappyHeartStudios)

https://www.facebook.com/thehappyheartstudio/

Twitter: @tsjolicoeur

Instagram: stefaniejolicoeur